FALLEN FIVE : THE LIGHKEEPERS, BOOK 3

Published by

Front cover design by Hoffman/Miller Advertising
Printed in the USA.

Back Cover and Interior Format
©THE KILLION GROUP, INC.

ERICA SPINDLER

FALLEN FIVE

DOUBLESHOT PRESS

DEDICATION

For all those who shine a light in the darkness

CHAPTER ONE

New Orleans, Louisiana

Friday, February 9
4:00 P.M.

THE SUSPECT MADE HER SKIN crawl.

He sat at the small, scarred wooden table, the picture of self-confidence and calm. Keith Gerard. Twenty-eight. A graphic designer with the largest ad agency in New Orleans, he was ridiculously handsome and unabashedly hip—from his trendy fade haircut to his perfectly stubbled jaw.

Too confident. Too calm. His direct gaze seemed soulless as he sized her up the way one would a lab specimen.

The lack of emotion, that's what really got her. As if nothing remotely human lived inside that handsome facade.

NOPD Detective Micki Dee Dare returned the favor, holding that dark gaze, letting the silence swell uncomfortably. Not uncomfortable for her. Not for her partner Zach Harris, either, who was leaning casually against the interrogation room door.

For him. That was part of the game—making him wonder why he had been called in for questioning, what they might have to link him to his girlfriend's death, and why the hell they weren't getting on with it?

She started to sweat. She had literally cranked up the heat before entering the room.

Gerard shifted restlessly, glanced over his shoulder at Zach, then back at her. He let out his breath in a frustrated-sounding puff. "How can I help you, Detectives?"

"You tell us, Mr. Gerard. You're the one who found your girlfriend, Sarah Stevens, in a pool of blood."

"That I did." He folded his hands in front of him. "I found her *and* called you. The experience was quite traumatic."

He said the words without the slightest quaver, without the slightest flicker of emotion crossing his face.

Micki didn't blink. "I'm sure it was."

"You doubt that's true?"

"Did I suggest that?" She looked over at Zach as if for confirmation, then back at Gerard. "I certainly didn't mean to. All that blood, someone you supposedly cared about—"

"I did care about her. Very much."

Micki glanced at her notes. "How did you happen to just 'stop by' this morning?"

"She and I spoke last night. She was upset and I—"

"Why was she upset?"

"She suffered from bouts of depression." He opened his hands in a sort of what's-a-guy-supposed-to-do gesture. "So it wasn't unusual to find her upset."

"When she got that way, what did you typically do?"

"Talk her off the ledge, so to speak."

"You didn't think to go to her place to comfort her?"

"I used to, when we first started dating. That got old."

"You mean boring."

"Yes. You can't blame me for that, can you? It was her same fears and my same reassurances, over and over. Nothing ever changed."

"But you kept dating her?"

He couldn't have missed the censure in her voice, but seemed oblivious to it anyway. He unfolded his hands and began to absently thrum the fingers of his right on the tabletop. "I enjoyed her company the rest of the time."

Micki narrowed her eyes. "You're a real peach of a guy, aren't you?"

"Actually, yes, I am." His fingers stilled. "I have things to do today. Are we finished?"

"No, Mr. Gerard, we are not." She glanced at the notes again. "Why did you pay Sarah Stevens a visit this morning?"

"She wasn't answering her phone, and I wanted to make sure she was okay."

"Suddenly you cared about her well-being?"

"You really have the wrong idea about me, Detective Dare. I'm a good guy. I really am."

Then why was every fiber of her being recoiling from him? "A good guy," Micki repeated. "And, no doubt, a great catch? I mean, look at you. Handsome. Successful. Charming."

"Thank you." He smiled slightly. "But I assure you, I don't think of myself that way. Especially at a time like this."

Of course he did. It was as obvious as his Cole Haan loafers. "Let's cut to the chase, shall we, Mr. Gerard? We have reason to believe you were complicit in Sarah's death."

"She slit her wrists, Detective. After months of threatening to do it, she followed through. I don't see where that has anything to do with me."

"So, you're saying you didn't encourage her to go through with it?"

"What kind of monster would that make me?"

"You tell us, Mr. Gerard."

"This is about her crazy sister, isn't it? What did she say?"

"That instead of talking Sarah off the ledge, as you put it, you encouraged her to follow through with it. To just do it."

"Encourage her to kill herself? That's ridiculous."

"Is it?" Micki held his gaze. "Her sister claims Sarah's bouts of depression didn't begin until after you two started dating."

He shrugged. "That's her opinion."

"Not just her opinion. Sarah talked to her about it. Several times."

His lips curved up ever-so-slightly. "The ravings of a woman on the brink."

Micki leaned forward. "When someone's on the brink, the right nudge from a loved one can send them over the edge, don't you think?"

"Is that personal experience talking?" He leaned toward her, stopping so close she felt his breath against her face. "You know what this sounds like to me? A guilty conscience. Blame Sarah's suicide on the boyfriend instead of accepting responsibility herself. I knew Sarah six months, Teresa knew her all her life. Who do you think would have more culpability in her death?"

"Have any of your other girlfriends committed suicide?"

"Pathetic, Detective." He stood. "I believe we're done here."

"Sit down, Mr. Gerard. We're most certainly not *done* here."

He smiled and shrugged into his coat. "The wild ramblings of a grief-stricken family member. You've got nothing. If you need anything further from me, go through my personal attorney."

He retrieved a card from his inside lapel pocket and dropped it on the table, then started for the door.

Zach blocked his exit. He held out his hand. "Thank you for coming in today, Mr. Gerard. We appreciate your time and are very sorry for your loss."

Gerard hesitated before taking his outstretched hand. Zach held it—and his gaze—a few moments longer than was comfortable, and Micki saw Gerard squirm.

Despite the squirm, Micki figured Gerard had no idea he was being mind-fucked—her description for Zach's ability to reach into somebody's head and see and feel their thoughts.

Zach was part of a secret FBI initiative called Sixers. Individuals with psychic abilities had been recruited, trained, then sent to local police departments to help combat crime. Even within the force only a handful of folks knew about the program; she'd drawn one of the "lucky" insider straws and been partnered with the NOPD's recruit.

It was a damn slick trick, one that often irritated the hell out of her, but had proved unbelievably useful. Especially at times like this.

"Elevator is right across the hall," Zach said, releasing Gerard's hand. "First floor's your stop."

The man jerked his hand back, two spots of angry color blooming in his cheeks. "I've used an elevator before."

Micki joined Zach, and they watched as the elevator doors slid shut behind Gerard. "I can't tell you how much I hate letting that one walk away."

"Don't have to, partner."

He grinned down at her, those amazing blue eyes crinkling at the corners. She cocked an eyebrow. "You reading my mind, Hollywood?"

"You know better than that, Mick."

She'd caught him doing that shit once, and had warned him if he did it again, the partnership was over. He'd promised her he wouldn't, and so far, had kept his word.

"I didn't need to. You made it pretty clear what you thought of Mr. Slick. No super-mojo-power necessary."

"You get anything when you picked his brain?"

"No confession, but a startling lack of response. No grief or shock, no guilt or regret. Nothing but this flat . . . curiosity."

"Curiosity?" she repeated. "In what way?"

"I saw him standing there by the bathtub, just studying her. He was fascinated by the blood, the way it pooled. And by how pale and cold her skin was."

Goosebumps raced up her arms. "Did he touch her?"

"Stroked her hand. Once. Lightly. Then got out his cell phone and called it in. All business."

"You're describing the thoughts and reactions of someone with an antisocial personality disorder. My bet's on psychopath. No empathy or remorse. No sense of personal responsibility."

Zach nodded. "I could definitely see this guy pulling the wings off butterflies. Or worse. A lot worse."

"The question is, did he encourage her to kill herself? If he did and we find proof, we've got something to take to the DA."

They started toward the Detective Investigative Unit squad room. The NOPD Eighth District was housed in a nearly two-hundred-year-old building, one badly in need of renovations. As with most of historic New Orleans, folks either loved or hated the derelict charm. Micki fell squarely into the "loved it" category.

"Hold on, I need to check on my baby," she said and crossed to the window that looked out at Bienville Street. A fat pigeon sat on the ledge, eyeing her as she rolled up the big old window.

"Shoo," Micki said when it held its ground. "Go on." She clapped her hands, and it finally flew off. She peered down at the street. There it was, her midnight blue, 1971 Nova with a 396V under the hood. Three months ago, a perp had taken it for a joyride that ended with him crashing it into Bayou St. John; she'd just gotten it back, restored to its original glory.

Unfortunately, it seemed to have attracted the attention of an unsavory-looking dude in a leather jacket and dark shades.

"Oh, hell no," she muttered, as he sidled up close to the driver's side door. Micki leaned out. "Hey, you!" she shouted, "asshole in the shades!"

The guy's head jerked up.

"Yeah you!" She leaned farther out the window. "Move away from the vehicle or I'm gonna have to come down there and kick your ass!"

He jumped back so fast, he lost his balance. As she watched him right himself and scurry off, another man caught her eye. Walking quickly by in the opposite direction. He was tall and broad-shouldered, with a long, easy stride and a head of thick silver hair.

Her heart seemed to stop a moment, then began banging against her chest. Hank. The man was Hank.

Micki leaned out the window and shouted his name. He didn't hear her and she leaned farther out. A piece of the stuccoed brick crumbled under her weight, and she pitched forward.

"Whoa, partner!" Zach grabbed her arm and hauled her away from the window. "You have a death wish or something?"

Micki looked at him, startled back to her senses. She realized she was shaking and worked to steady herself. How could she have thought that was Hank? Her friend and mentor had been dead six years now.

Zach's expression grew concerned. "You okay?" he asked. "You look like you saw a ghost."

"Yeah, I'm good. Thanks."

He frowned and lowered the window. "You called Hank's name. Not *the* Hank?"

Micki glanced back at the window. The pigeon, she saw, had returned. She felt as if it was laughing at her.

She was losing her freaking mind.

"Yeah." She shook her head. "Someone, on the street . . . he looked like Hank and for a moment, I guess I forgot he was . . . gone."

"Don't worry about it." He grinned. "I used to think I saw my mother and I'd never even met her."

She laughed. "Why is that so *not* reassuring?"

"Angel told me you sometimes call out his name in the middle of the night."

"Young people," she muttered. "They're like frickin' vampires, up all night."

"When are you going to trust me, Mick?"

"I do trust you."

A lie. They both knew it. She trusted him with her life—but not with the deep stuff. The stuff she held close.

They fell into step. "What do you want to do about Gerard?"

"Mr. Slick? I say we see if we can get a subpoena for his phone and electronic records."

CHAPTER TWO

Saturday, February 10
10:35 P.M.

MICKI SPRANG AWAKE, AND THE battered old recliner she'd fallen asleep in snapped upright. Disoriented, she needed a moment to realize where she was and that her cell phone was ringing.

Micki fumbled for the phone and brought it to her ear.

"This is Dare."

"Mick. It's me."

"Zach?" She gave her head a quick shake to clear it. "What time is it?"

"Around ten-thirty. You were asleep?"

Micki pushed her hair away from her face. *Hank.* She'd been dreaming about having seen him on the street. But in the dream, it really *had* been him, though no matter how loudly she yelled his name, he didn't look back.

"Yeah. If you want to call it that." She climbed off the recliner—Hank's recliner—her muscles complaining as she uncurled her legs. "What's up?"

"Turn on your TV. The local news. Any network."

She found the remote and clicked the device on. NBC, channel six. Some sort of commotion downtown, she saw. At the grand opening of 2 River Tower and Hotel. People everywhere, many in formal attire, some crying, others open-mouthed and staring. Sirens. Flashing lights.

"What the hell—" She bit the words off as a news crawl at the bottom of the screen spelled it out for her.

Real Estate Developer Thomas King Plunges to His Death

"Holy shit," she muttered. "What happened?"

"Middle of the celebration, King goes up to his twenty-first-floor apartment to retrieve something he left behind. Next thing anyone knows, it's pancake time on the back terrace."

Just this morning King had been on the morning show, boasting about the food at Thirty-Three, the restaurant at the top of the tower. Even the pancakes were going to be the best anyone ever tasted, he'd crowed. Trust me, he'd said. The best. Fantastic.

Micki's stomach lurched at the thought, and she refocused on the facts. "So what're they thinking—that he took a swan dive on his own? Or that he was helped over the side?"

"No clue," he answered. "Frankly, my guess is they're waiting for us to tell *them*."

Meaning they were waiting for Zach to tell them. He was the super hero. She was his gun-wielding, often cranky sidekick.

"We're getting pulled in," he went on. "Your call should be coming in any moment."

As if on cue, another call beeped through. "There it is," she said. "Wait, how'd you hear before me?"

"P."

Parker. Figured, she thought. Parker was Zach's FBI point man—and his uncle. But that was a whole other can of worms.

"I'll be there in twenty minutes," she said and clicked through to the other call.

CHAPTER THREE

11:20 P.M.

MICKI SPOTTED ZACH IMMEDIATELY. TALL, blond and a dis-concerting cross between Chris Pratt and a young Matthew McConaughey, he looked out of place in the chaos of a crime scene, more a beach-and-surfboard than gun-and-badge kind of guy.

He saw her, lifted a hand in greeting and pointed to the parking spot he'd saved her between two piece-of-shit unmarked cruisers. Then came the smile that had melted hearts from coast-to-coast. It did a pretty good job on hers, but no way in hell she was ever going to let him know that.

A Mardi Gras parade-sized crowd had gathered around the scene's outer perimeter. And like a parade-going throng, the atmosphere was one of revelry and anticipation.

Micki wedged the Nova into the within-spitting-distance-of-a-bunch-of-drunken-idiots spot. She frowned as she cut the engine. It deserved better. But that's what happened when you were last to the party—you scored the crappy parking spot.

She climbed out of the car; the crowd roared. Like she was a freak-ing celebrity on the red carpet. Typical Big Easy—every event was the opportunity for a party.

Laissez les bon temps rouler, baby.

"Yo," she called to one of the cops policing the line. He looked her way and she pointed to the Nova. "That's my baby. So much as a spilled drink touches her, I freakin' lose it. Got that?"

He looked appropriately concerned, and Zach chuckled as he fell into step with her. "Poor guy had no idea what was coming for him."

She angled him a questioning glance. "What?"

"Classic Mad Dog Dare, take no prisoners."

"Whatever it takes, Hollywood. Bet nobody messes with my car."

He didn't argue. Lifting her gaze, Micki took in Thomas King's 2 River Tower. King's redesign of the original New Orleans Trade Mart incorporated current design sensibilities with the post-modern style of the original, and the result was spectacular.

Thirty-three floors of pure luxury, revolving restaurant and bar at the top; two floors down, an observation deck; on the main floor, another restaurant, coffee shop and jazz club.

Zach leaned toward her. "I hear the apartments start at a million and a half bucks."

They reached the inner perimeter. The still-wet-behind-the-ears scene officer checked their credentials, then held out the log.

"Where's the vic?" Micki asked, signing it.

The officer grimaced. "Where *isn't* he?"

The image of Wile E. Coyote running afoul of one of his own plans filled her head.

Ker . . . splat!

In real life, not funny. And not something anyone should have to see. Unfortunately, ugly came with the job. And this was going to be real ugly.

The officer glanced at the log, then back up at Zach. "You're Hollywood Harris, aren't you?"

Here we go, she thought. The obligatory "fan boy" moment.

"The one-and-only," Zach answered, pretending he didn't see her eye roll. He held out his hand and flashed the kid one of his thousand-watt knee-bucklers. "Good to meet you—"

"Ray," the officer offered, taking Zach's hand and pumping it enthusiastically. "I'm a big fan, Detective. It's an honor, really. The way you called that home invasion was nothing short of—"

"Miraculous?" Micki offered.

Her sarcasm rolled right past him. He beamed, pumped Zach's hand some more. "Yeah, that's it. Miraculous."

"Appreciate the love," Zach said. "But I couldn't do it without Dare here."

Trusty, skull-crushing, often cranky sidekick. She sort of wanted to puke. Instead she re-directed the rookie. "The vic? Which way?"

"Right," Jones said, looking sheepish. "Grab some booties and gloves, follow the lighted path around back."

"Nice guy," Zach said. "Great judge of talent."

Micki snorted and tucked the gloves in one pocket, booties in the other. "You're beginning to like that a little too much."

"Sour grapes?"

"Not at all, partner. Just keeping it real."

They followed the path around to the back side of the building, which faced the river. The noise level dropped dramatically as they made the turn and ducked under the barrier. On the river, a tug boat pushed a barge silently past. The entire area had been cordoned off, but only a small cluster of official personnel remained—one of them New Orleans Chief of Police Howard, another Major Nichols.

Micki swept her gaze over the area. Terraced verandas, graceful and welcoming. Landscape lighting and strands of tiny, white lights, twinkling like stars, creating a little piece of heaven on earth.

The scene lights had not yet been set up, so she couldn't be certain, but she suspected that the odd, dark shape on the lowest terrace might be what was left of the unfortunate Mr. King.

So much for heaven on earth.

Micki glanced at Zach. He stood intently still, head tipped back, attempting, she knew, to absorb the moments of King's fall. No, not the moments of the fall, the psychic energy surrounding them. And with the energy, maybe answers.

Another of his gifts. In comparison, her good, old-fashioned police work seemed kind of boring.

She touched Zach's arm; he didn't break concentration to look at her, but then, she hadn't expected him to. "Make the magic happen, partner. I'll keep Major Nichols and the Chief away."

She headed toward her superior officers, aware of Zach heading in the opposite direction.

The two men met her half way. The chief spoke first.

"Thank God you and Harris are here. We've got ourselves a big mess."

He must have realized how that sounded, considering what awaited on the lowest terrace, because he made a face before motioning toward Zach. "I assume he's—" he paused, searching for the right description, before settling on, "—doing his thing?"

His thing. An appropriate euphemism for something the Chief had absolutely no clue how to describe but was convinced he understood.

So "his thing" pretty much covered it.

And didn't cover it at all.

Because what the Chief didn't know, or even the FBI, was that Zach was much more than a Sixer. He was part Lightkeeper, an ancient race sent to earth to battle the forces of darkness.

It had taken her a long time to wrap her head around that one. But she believed now, and God help her, she had agreed to join them.

And ironically, in the process she'd learned she had a teeny bit of Lightkeeper in her, too. Unfortunately, not enough to give her any cool, superhero abilities.

"Yes, sir," she answered. "Bring me up to speed on what we know so far."

Major Nichols stepped in. "At this point it appears to be a suicide."

Micki pictured the perpetually tanned, semi-celebrity braggart she knew from the media, and shook her head. "That would not have been my first guess."

Howard ran a hand through his thinning hair, a rare move from the tightly controlled chief of police. "Before the incident, he was in the ballroom, mingling with guests."

"His mood?" she asked.

"Jovial. Upbeat. I talked to him myself." Chief motioned toward the building. "How could it not have been?"

Exactly. "So what happened?"

"His wife said he needed something from upstairs. She offered to get it for him, but he insisted on doing it himself."

"What was it?"

"She didn't know. He didn't say."

Micki frowned. She looked from one man to the other. "The middle of a party, an important gathering, the host tells his wife he forgot *something* and has to retrieve it, and she doesn't ask what?"

"Maybe she was having a good time and didn't care? Maybe this was something he did?" He shrugged. "Who knows?"

"What about a suicide note?"

Chief Howard shook his head. "Not that the first officers saw."

She looked at him, surprised. "You haven't personally inspected the scene?"

"No. I thought I should help maintain calm in the ballroom."

"And we're sure he was alone?"

"We're not sure of anything yet. When the officers arrived, the apartment was locked, but the door has an automatic lock system."

"What about his wife?"

"Downstairs the whole time. She was one of" —he cleared his throat— "the witnesses."

"Witnesses?"

"To the fall. My wife . . . she—" He stopped, helplessness in his voice. "She was there, too."

Micki glanced up at the building. The ballroom would have a wall of windows to exploit that million-dollar view. "Are you saying that your wife and Mrs. King actually saw—"

"Along with about two dozen others, yes."

That explained the helplessness, the uncharacteristic show of emotion. "Thank you for your confidence in us, Chief. We won't let you down."

His expression cleared, and he nodded, all traces of emotionalism gone. He shifted his gaze from her to Major Nichols. "I want you here overseeing everything. Whatever Harris needs, give it to him. The press is going to want something sooner than later. Hourly reports. Understood?"

"Yes, sir," they answered in unison.

He walked away. Micki turned back to her superior officer. "No one else enters King's apartment until after Harris has gone through it."

"I'll see to it."

She started for the lower terrace, now illuminated by six-hundred-watt scene lights, then stopped and looked back. "We'll need to talk to housekeeping and security, make certain they don't leave before we do. Both would have had access to King's apartment."

He agreed, and she went on, "Do you know, did the Kings have any children?"

"I don't," Nichols said. "I'll find out and if they do, make certain they—and any other family members on the property tonight—are available to you and Harris."

"Perfect." Micki started off, then stopped and looked back once more. "Oh, and I want security footage, from both the elevators and the twenty-first floor."

When he nodded, she went to get a look at what was left of Thomas King.

CHAPTER FOUR

11:55 P.M.

Z ACH STOOD JUST OUTSIDE THE glare of the scene lights. He turned toward the tower, lifted his face and closed his eyes. Bracing himself, he opened his senses to the energy. Pinpricks of electricity rippled over him, up and down his arms, legs and torso. He twitched and jerked, the pinpricks becoming strikes, battering him with the force of an electrical storm.

Zach fought to control his breathing and heart rate. Deep, even. Keep the ship righted. The storm slowed, becoming gusts and bursts, with moments of intensity followed by vacuum-like voids that felt as if they could strip the flesh from his bones.

He struggled to decipher and dissect the chaos—colors, flashes of light, voices and music, spinning like a runaway carousel. Faster and faster, creating a brilliant blur. Then, a face. A woman's. Beautiful, with mysterious, amber eyes. She seemed to be beckoning. Not to King, Zach realized. *Him.* She was beckoning him.

And then . . . nothing. So suddenly, Zach's eyes popped open and his legs buckled. He dropped to his knees.

"Zach!"

Mick. Rushing toward him.

He held up a hand to stop her and focused on his breathing—deeply in, slowly out. Again and again. His tilt-a-whirl world slowed, then stopped. He shuddered, the last ripple of energy like a wave retreating from the shore to the ocean, then gone.

He looked at her, taking in her concerned expression, then forced a tight smile. "Well, that was fun."

"Are you all right?"

He cautiously stood, then shot her a rueful glance. "I'm standing, aren't I?"

"You get anything?"

"Depends on your point of view. I think I got everything." He realized his hands were trembling and balled them into fists. "And nothing."

She frowned slightly, in that way she did. More a furrowing of her brow, always the serious technician, analyzing. "Meaning?"

"There's too much here. I couldn't single any one thing out, but . . ."

Her frown deepened. "But what?"

"A woman's face. At the last moment. Then it all stopped with a . . . crash."

"The moment he hit the ground?"

"That makes sense . . . It's how it felt, but I don't know for sure."

"Did you recognize her?"

He pictured the woman. A sultry kind of beauty. Those amazing eyes. High cheekbones. Somehow familiar but . . . not. Who was she? And what did she want with him?

"Zach? Did you? Recognize her?"

He shook his head slightly. "No. But . . ." He turned and looked Mick in the eyes. "She did seem familiar, though I have no idea where from."

"The media maybe?"

"Maybe. But it was more like . . . she recognized me."

"Recognized you? How so?"

"Like she motioned me to follow her. Like she was aware of my presence." Zach turned his gaze to what remained of the developer, which was nothing recognizable. Even his clothing had burst with the force of impact.

"Is it always like this?" he asked, the taste in his mouth turning metallic.

"When somebody jumps?" He nodded, and she shook her head. "It's different every time. I've seen jumpers who look hardly the worse for wear after impact. This one's particularly bad. Twenty-one floors is a long way down."

Something in the muck caught Zach's eye. He picked his way to it and bent to get a closer look. King's gold Rolex, completely intact, diamond bezel winking up at him.

Mick followed him, peered over his shoulder. "Un-fucking-believable," she said.

Zach cocked his head, focusing on the dial. "What time is it now?"

"Eleven-fifty-six."

"It's still keeping time."

Micki made a choked sound. "Hell of a product testimonial. Rolex, it keeps time even if yours runs out. You need to examine it?"

He thought a moment, then shook his head. "I think I've gotten everything I can get, at least from down here. I need to get inside King's apartment."

The crime scene techs stood at the edge of the terrace, waiting for him and Mick to finish. They were outfitted in head-to-toe hazmat. Zach didn't have to touch them to read their thoughts—this was *not* their lucky night. He sent them a sympathetic glance.

"It's all yours," Mick said as they reached them. "Let me know if you find anything that might indicate this wasn't a suicide."

"Any ideas on that, Detective?"

The tech sounded incredulous. She stopped, looked back. "Other than a bullet or two, your guess is as good as mine. His phone's here somewhere. Watch is on the right, near one of his shoes. Have a ball with that, fellas."

"Screw you, Detective." He said it good-naturedly. "Look for my report in the morning."

They turned back and started toward the building's entrance.

"What did she look like?" Mick asked suddenly.

"Who?"

"The woman you saw."

"Dark hair, mysterious-looking. Beautiful."

"Rich guy, beautiful woman. Figures. You think she helped him over the edge?"

"Maybe. But I don't think so."

"Why?"

"I don't know. I got the feeling that like me, she was just a bystander."

CHAPTER FIVE

12:25 A.M.

ZACH STOOD IN THE APARTMENT doorway. King had lived like, well, a king. The entry opened to an expansive, luxuriously modern interior. The opposite wall, composed of floor-to-ceiling windows, faced the Mississippi River. Beyond the windows, a balcony. The doors to the balcony stood open, the filmy, white drapes billowing in the cold, damp breeze.

Mick had learned a few details about the evening, but at his request, hadn't yet shared them. He didn't want his reading of the scene to be influenced by any so-called facts.

The only thoughts he was interested in were King's.

Zach took a step into the apartment. He felt the familiar tingle at his wrists and inside of his elbows. He breathed deeply, relaxed and let it flow over him. Every human action left a trail of psychic energy, imperceptible to nearly everyone.

But not to him. He had been sensitive to it all his life, but since being recruited by the Sixers, he had learned to exploit that sensitivity and use it to solve crimes.

The stronger the emotion surrounding the event, the stronger the energy—and the easier to read. However, he'd learned that every crime scene read differently—even homicide to homicide, burglary to burglary. Because whenever humans were involved, emotions were involved. And no two humans reacted in exactly the same way to a situation.

Even those not wholly human—like him.

Sometimes it was the victim's energy that roared the loudest, sometimes the perpetrator's, and other times—like on the gore-soaked terrace twenty floors below—everyone's had been clamoring for attention—the party guests, the raucous street crowd, even the media and assembled law enforcement officers.

Zach entered the apartment fully and stopped, frowning slightly. But here, oddly, he got almost nothing at all.

Mick had gone ahead of him; he was aware of her studying the apartment's interior, using her amazing observational skills and sharp mind to piece together the story of what had happened here tonight.

She sought tangible evidence. He sought the intangible. Together, they made an unbeatable team. So unbeatable, they had drawn unwanted attention—like that of young Ray tonight. With a one hundred percent close rate, combined with several very high-profile investigations, they were hard to miss.

This case could test that record.

Zach took two more steps in, moving his own gaze carefully over the room. It landed on the wet bar. An open decanter. Amber liquid in an expensive-looking glass.

He felt a sort of tug. Like gentle fingers urging him in that direction. Interesting, he thought, and let himself be led.

When he reached the wet bar, Zach floated his gloved hand over the drink. Thomas King. Purposeful. Relaxed and confident. Zach leaned in, studying the glass, the liquid inside. Breathing it in.

King, pouring the drink, then setting it down untouched. Why?

Zach turned in a slow circle, working to isolate and follow the subtle shifts in energy.

The tug at his sleeve again. Ever-so-gentle. Beckoning him. The way the woman with the mysterious eyes had.

The tug led him to the bedroom. Oversized bed. Luxurious bedding. Turned down and waiting. He shifted his gaze. A framed photo on a nightstand. A wedding photo. King the groom. The woman at his side not the woman the energy had briefly conjured. This one blond and beautiful. Young. Too young for the sixty-something developer.

Zach slid open the nightstand drawer. A vial of prescription medication. He nudged it with his fingertip, read the label. Viagra.

Not a big surprise there.

The handgun was. A Beretta Px4, small but efficient. Zach didn't pick it up, floating his hand over it instead.

No reverberations. It hadn't been fired tonight.

Zach moved on, nearly tripping over a pair of woman's shoes. Impossibly high heels. A glittery shade of nude. They lay halfway between the bed and the bureau.

Odd, the way they were positioned. Zach squatted beside them. He cautiously reached out, let his hand hover above one, then the other. His palm tingled, then burned.

Raised voices. A man's and a woman's. The burning sensation cooled; the tingling became like pin-pricks, then evaporated.

King and his wife, most likely. Arguing over something. But what?

He made a mental note to ask Mrs. King if the shoes were hers, then turned to the highboy. On its top sat a small tray with some change, a couple of business cards, and a pair of cufflinks. On the dresser top, a watch. Gold case, leather band. Elegant and obviously expensive. He checked out the brand. Cartier.

He picked it up, curled his fingers around it. Images, like the tumbling colors of a kaleidoscope. King, in the ballroom. Whispering into the ear of his beautiful young wife.

King, unfastening the watch, laying it on the bureau top. Reaching for another. The Rolex, Zach thought. Of course.

Suddenly, King began whistling a tune. The notes seemed to dart close, then move away, staying just beyond Zach's reach. What was it? Zach squeezed his eyes tighter shut. He knew the song, but couldn't put his finger on it.

Zach laid the Cartier down and slid open the top bureau drawer. A black leather case. A dozen turning timepieces. One empty space.

Zach frowned. King had left his celebration to change his watch? Odd as it seemed, that's what he had done.

"I know what he was after," Zach called to Mick. "He came up for the Rolex." She didn't respond so he went to the bedroom doorway. He saw her through the billowing drapes, standing on the balcony, inches from the rail but not touching it.

The light from the living room behind her illuminated the graceful curve of her neck—and the determined set of her jaw. Contrasts, he thought. Hard on the outside with a soft, chewy center. Both delicious but so very different.

A man couldn't help wanting to crack open the one to get a taste of the other.

Another man, he thought. Not him. They were meant to be friends and colleagues, not lovers.

It didn't mean they wouldn't be, just that they shouldn't.

He left the bedroom, stopping in the opening to the balcony. "He came up to switch watches," he said.

She looked over her shoulder at him and frowned. "To change watches? That's a little odd, don't you think? Leave a big celebration that way, just to change your timepiece?"

He shrugged. "There isn't much to go on here; the trail is extremely subtle. What's that you're holding?"

"This?" She held it up to the light. A feather, he saw. A black one. "It was on the rail here. I didn't know birds flew this high."

She released it over the side, watched it float a moment, then turned back to Zach. "You get anything besides the watch?"

"You saw the gun, right?" She nodded. "It wasn't fired tonight."

She nodded again. "It's loaded. I checked. Anything else?"

"Two things. The shoes. The ones on the floor. There was strong energy attached to them. I picked up an argument between a man and woman."

"King and his wife?"

"That's my thinking. By the way, King was whistling. I wasn't able to make out the tune—I didn't get enough. But it was upbeat."

"That's how the chief described King's mood as well. So, why'd he do it?"

Zach stepped through the door and a sudden burst of wind caught the drape and blew it across his line of vision. He went to sweep it away, and froze, a sensation like popping firecrackers racing up his arm.

"I don't want you here. . ."

King's voice sounded so clearly in his head, Zach instinctively looked over his shoulder. The drape billowed again, this time catching at his neck, clinging like an octopus's tentacle, stroking like a lover's caress.

"Get out! Leave me—"

King backing away, toward the rail. Gooseflesh zipped down Zach's spine. Desperation. The sensation of being suffocated.

"—alone . . ."

Zach tore the clinging drape from his neck. He looked at Mick in shock. "King wasn't alone. Someone else was here. I heard King. He told the person to get out."

"A man or woman?" she asked.

He shook his head. "I don't know."

Zach crossed to the other drapery panels, ran his hands over them.

Nothing.   Aware of Mick's steady gaze, he stepped onto the deck, crossed to the railing.

"Here," he said. "This is where he went over."

"What are you picking up?"

"Just . . . King. No one else."

The Rolex was the key. Of course. It's why King had come upstairs. It had been on his wrist when he confronted the other person, then when he went over.

Maybe the timepiece had absorbed the moments leading up to King going over the rail.

"I need that Rolex."

"But you said earlier—"

"I was wrong. And I need to read it before it gets handled by anyone else."

CHAPTER SIX

2:10 A.M.

THEY WERE TOO LATE. BY the time Micki reached the crime scene techs, the Rolex had been bagged and tagged and was already on its way to evidence.

Zach made a sound of frustration. "I messed up."

"You're human," Micki said, watching the floor numbers illuminate as the elevator made its way up from the ground level. "We all make mistakes."

"Half human," he countered. "You'd think my Lightkeeper part could do better."

She snorted. "Last I checked, you Lightkeepers were doing a pretty good job fucking things up without any help from us humans. Besides, you may still be able to get something from it."

"Maybe. But doubtful."

The car whooshed to a stop and the doors slid open. Mrs. King was waiting for them in the Grand Ballroom. Alighting the elevator, they crossed to the man standing sentinel outside the ballroom's closed doors. Private security, Micki thought, judging by his dark suit, earpiece, and wary posture.

"Detectives Dare and Harris," Micki said, holding out her shield. Zach did the same, and after examining them both, the man led them inside.

Micki took in the scene. Everyone was gone yet, oddly, the buffet tables were still laden with food, the bars still stocked and set up, and the cake—a stunning replica of 2 River Tower and Hotel—was prominently displayed and waiting to be cut. Balloons bobbled, streamers fluttered, and the unnatural quiet scurried along her nerve endings like a spider.

Natalie King was seated at one of the tables at the back of the ballroom, her back to the wall of windows. Another dark-suited man waited with her, his gaze unflinchingly on them.

As they neared the woman, Micki acknowledged that Natalie King was the most luminously beautiful woman she'd ever seen. Like a DaVinci Madonna in a low-cut, sequined dress.

"Mrs. King, the detectives you were expecting."

"Thank you, Jordan." She didn't stand, but held out a hand. "I'm Natalie King. Please, sit down."

Micki narrowed her eyes slightly. She'd never met the woman, but there was something familiar about her. Plucking at her memory. Maybe it was her voice? She spoke in a soft, southern drawl. The kind that brought to mind hot days and deep porches, and blankets on soft grass in the shade of a big, old oak tree.

And something else. Something that made her twitch.

Micki indicated the two men. "Bodyguards?"

"Yes." She fiddled with her diamond ring while she spoke. "Thom was fanatical about our personal safety. Ironic considering . . ."

She let the last trail off, but what she had been about to say seemed to float in the air between them anyway.

". . . that he took his own life . . ."

Zach stepped in. "Mrs. King, we need to ask you some questions about your husband."

"Of course, Detective. Anything you need." She motioned the chair beside her. Zach took it, but Micki selected the seat across from the widow. She wanted a clear view of her face during the interview.

"You're very calm, Mrs. King," Micki said.

"Only on the outside, I assure you, Detective Dare. Inside, I'm falling apart."

Somehow, Micki doubted that. "I understand from Chief Howard that you witnessed your husband's fall."

"Yes. I was standing right over there. Admiring the view with some of our guests."

"How awful for you," Zach murmured.

"He passed right in front of my eyes."

No tremor to her voice, no hesitation or horror. Was it shock? Micki wondered. Or disinterest?

She looked at Micki. "I know what you're thinking."

Micki cocked an eyebrow. "Do you?"

"Yes. Because of the difference in Thom's age and mine, you think I didn't love him. That I married him for his money."

"It's none of my business if you loved him or not, or why you married him, for that matter. The only thing that's of concern to me is whether you killed him."

"But you already know I didn't. Because I was here in the ballroom the whole time. Standing next to your boss's wife."

The sly edge in King's voice caused the hair on the back of Micki's neck to stand up. "How many years were there between you two? Forty?"

"Thirty-six. But what does age matter? He was my knight in shining armor, my lover and best friend. He was my everything, Detective Dare."

Bullshit. Judging by the way she was sizing Zach up, if he offered her a tumble right now, she'd jump at it.

"The heart wants what the heart wants, Detective. No matter the logic or cost."

Zach looked rapt. He laid his hand on Natalie King's. "I'm so very sorry for your loss."

"You're so sweet." She curled her fingers around his. "Thank you."

Micki mustered every ounce of professionalism to keep from rolling her eyes. "How long were you and Mr. King married?"

"A year. I can't believe he was taken from me so soon." She teared up, looking at Zach. "It seems as if we'd only just found each other."

"How did you meet?" Zach asked.

"In New York. It was Christmastime and I was coming out of Saks, loaded down with purchases. I slipped on a patch of ice, and there he was. He caught me before I went down." She looked at Micki. "So, you see, he really was my knight in shining armor."

The hairs at the nape of her neck stood up. What was it about the woman she found so distasteful? That she was too perfect? That the relationship she described read too much like a cheap romance? Or the fact that Zach was still holding her hand?

She shook that last one off as ridiculous. "Tell us about your husband. How was his mood of late?"

She paused a fraction of a second. "Thom was a very positive person."

"You hesitated a moment before answering."

"Yes . . . It's just that recently, he's been a little down."

"How recently?"

"The last few weeks."

"Do you know why?"

"He has grown children. They refused to accept me. It bothered him. I told him it didn't matter, that I understood. After all, I'm younger than both of them. But he wanted us to all to be happy together. A big, happy family."

"Surely he didn't expect them to call you Mom?" Micki said.

"Of course not. But he expected them to be at least cordial."

"And they weren't?"

"No. In fact, they refused to be in the same room with me. Porsche, his younger daughter, punished him by not allowing him time with his granddaughter. It was cruel."

"Would you say your husband was distraught over their behavior?"

"Distraught?" She cocked her head, her silky blond hair cascaded over her shoulder. "As in thoughts of suicide?"

"Yes."

"Before tonight, I would have said no. And I would have said it vehemently. I guess I would have been wrong."

Micki looked down at her notes. Something wasn't right. Natalie King said all the right things, but they felt all wrong.

Zach stepped in. "Do you own a pair of high-heel, nude-colored shoes?"

"Several pairs. Why?"

"There was a pair on the floor of your bedroom, between the bed and the bureau? Were they yours?"

"Of course. I planned to wear them tonight, but changed my mind at the last minute." She frowned. "Why are you interested in my shoes? Surely not a fetish, Detective Harris?" Her voice turned husky. "Although you wouldn't be the first man with that weakness."

Micki bit back what she wanted to say and let Zach respond.

"We have reason to believe someone else was with your husband when he went over the rail."

"A woman," Micki added, acknowledging the small untruth. "The shoes were on the floor, so we wanted to make certain they were yours."

"That's ridiculous. He was alone. Everyone else was in the ballroom."

The way she would have arranged it, if she had planned to have him

killed. Micki made note of it in her spiral, then looked up at the woman.
"Surely not *everyone*? The whole city of New Orleans?"

"A *euphemism*, Detective. Clearly."

Zach took over again. "Did you and your husband argue about the
shoes? Did he not want you to wear them?"

"Of course not."

"Did you argue about something else tonight?"

"No. We didn't fight. Ever."

"All couples argue sometimes," he said.

"Not us."

"It sounds like you had the perfect marriage," Micki said. "And
oftentimes, a perfect marriage such as yours begins with a pre-nuptial
agreement. Did your husband ask you to sign one?"

She laughed. "I wondered when you'd get to that. No, Detective, he
did not. The pre-nup was my idea."

Micki couldn't hide her surprise. "*Your* idea?"

"I wanted *him*, Detective Dare. Not his empire." She smiled slightly,
as if pleased by some small secret. "I know that's hard for someone like
you to understand, but it's true."

Micki cocked an eyebrow. "Someone like me, Mrs. King?"

King's mouth curved briefly; something flickered in her eyes. Something that caused chill bumps to race up Micki's arms.

"Yes, Detective. Someone who expects the worst of people."

"Speaking of that, Mrs. King, is there any chance your husband was
having an affair?"

CHAPTER SEVEN

2:50 A.M.

"I DIDN'T BUY IT," MICKI SAID as the elevator doors shut. She pushed the button for the tenth floor. Both King's daughters—Mercedes and Porsche—had residences on the Tower's tenth. They had agreed to talk to them and were waiting. Micki prayed they had brewed a pot of coffee—or offered her a Red Bull.

"What part?" Zach asked.

"Any of it. He was her everything? Bullshit."

"You're wrong about that, Mick. He was."

"Don't tell me you bought that load of crap?"

"I didn't have to." Zach met her eyes. "She told me."

"You read her?"

"Of course. That's why I was holding her hand."

"You sure it wasn't because she was knock-down gorgeous?"

"She was that. But yes, I'm sure."

Micki thought of her childhood home, of the girls she had grown up with, raised to put appearance above substance. "No surprise she had a southern accent. I should have asked if she's from Mobile."

"They all like that there?"

"Pretty much."

"Then what am I doing in New Orleans?"

He was teasing her, she knew. But she wasn't in the mood. "You can go anytime, partner. It'd make my life simpler."

"You mean boring. Think back on your life before me—"

"Sane."

"Boring," he said again.

"Okay, I admit, you've grown on me." She lifted her gaze to the illuminated floor numbers. "Like a fungus."

He laughed. "It's a start."

She glanced at him. "So, you're telling me she really loved him?"

"Yup."

"Then why so cool? I didn't pick up as much as a tremor in her voice."

"Maybe she was in shock?"

"Maybe. But that feels too easy with this one."

"Another thing you don't buy?"

"I guess so."

The elevator car stopped, the doors slid open and they stepped off. "Did you have to hold her hand through the whole interview?"

"She was holding mine. What could I do?"

"Let it go."

He grinned. "Jealous?"

She was, God help her. "Of course not. It was just kind of creepy, that's all. This way."

They turned right and headed to the end of the hallway. The King sisters each had corner units at the end, directly across the hall from each other. They'd been instructed to go to the one on the left, which belonged to Mercedes.

"By the way, that last question, about her beloved having an affair, it really pissed her off. She definitely didn't like you."

Micki smiled. "Good, because the feeling was mutual. Big time."

"Interesting."

"What?"

"You've been taking instant dislikes to folks lately."

"More than usual?"

He laughed. "I guess not. Here we are."

They stopped in front of a Chinese red door. Micki rang the call button.

A moment later, the door opened. The woman who greeted them wore a very rumpled, royal blue ball gown. Her dark hair had come partly loose from her up-do, her face was pale and her eye make-up had run, giving her a night-of-the-living-dead sort of vibe.

Micki held up her shield. "I'm Detective Dare and this is my partner, Detective Harris. Are you Mercedes King?"

"I am."

Zach held out his hand. She looked startled by the gesture, but took it. "I'm so sorry for your loss." He looked her directly in the eyes. "I know what a shock this must have been for you."

"Actually, it's not, Detective. We saw this coming."

"Mercedes!"

Mercedes extricated her hand and looked over her shoulder. "It's true, Porsche, and you know it. We've been expecting something like this since that *child* got her claws into him."

"What child is that?" Micki asked.

"Don't play dumb, Detective." Two spots of angry color bloomed in Mercedes' cheeks. "I'm talking about his wife, of course."

Porsche came over and introduced herself. Unlike her sister, she had changed into yoga pants and a long, knit shirt. Her hair was pulled back into a ponytail and her face had been scrubbed free of make-up. Judging by the ring on her fourth finger, she was married.

They followed the pair into the luxurious living room. The sisters sat side-by-side on the teal-colored, leather couch; Micki and Zach took the chairs across from them.

"Again," Micki said, "we're very sorry for your loss. We hate to intrude at a time like this, but it's important to interview those involved while memories are fresh."

Not waiting for a reply, Micki went on, "Where were you two at the time of the accident?"

"I was in the ballroom," Mercedes said. "Mingling."

"And you have witnesses to back you up?"

Her eyes narrowed slightly. "Absolutely."

"Did you see your father fall?"

"I did not."

Micki turned her gaze to Porsche. "And how about you?"

"I was up here, checking on my daughter."

"Your husband's with her now?"

"The nanny. Cherie. David's downstairs. Making calls, reassuring investors." At their obvious confusion, she added, "He's a senior vice-president for King Enterprises."

"Your apartment's across the hall from this one?"

"That's right."

"Was anyone with you?"

She hesitated. "I came up alone."

"That's not what I meant. Is there anyone who can corroborate your whereabouts at that time?"

"She means a witness," Mercedes interjected impatiently. "Her daughter and the nanny, of course. Isn't that right, Porsche?"

"Yes, that's right."

The agreement sounded hollow to her and Micki glanced at Zach. His speculative gaze told her he was thinking along similar lines.

"Late for your daughter to have still been awake."

Porsche clasped her hands together. "It was an exciting day. She tends to get wound up."

"Because you allow her too much sugar," Mercedes snapped. "Why are we discussing my niece's sleeping habits, Detective? I was under the impression you were here to talk about my father. He's dead, if you haven't heard."

Somebody had a temper, Micki noted. And, obviously, was accustomed to having things her way.

"Of course," Micki said easily. "Tell us about your father. What was he—"

"Dammit!" Mercedes swatted the air around her head. "Stupid moth. How does it keep getting in here?"

"Calm down," Porsche said. "It's just a moth. Here," —she snapped off the lamp closest her sister— "it's attracted to the light."

It did seem like an over-reaction to a bug, but the woman was obviously in distress, and Micki had seen the smallest things cause people to snap.

Mercedes let out a tight-sounding breath. "I apologize. It's been a long and traumatic night. What were you asking?"

"About your father," Micki answered. "What was he like?"

"He was a son-of-bitch," Mercedes said. "But I respected him for it. He played to win."

"Very tough," Porsche added. "A smart, shrewd businessman."

"Was he a good father?"

"Define good," Mercedes shot back. "He didn't coddle us. He expected us to pull our own weight."

The tough father had obviously taught his daughters to be the same way.

"He had one weakness," Porsche said.

"Women," Mercedes said. "Young, beautiful ones. Like *her*."

"You obviously don't like your father's wife. May I ask why?"

"You can't guess?"

"In my line of work, guessing's frowned upon."

"Because she's a gold-digger, Detective Dare."

Zach jumped in. "You think she married him for his money?"

Mercedes snorted. "There's nearly forty years difference in their ages. What else would she have married him for?"

"He was a powerful, robust man." Zach cocked his head. "I hear that's an aphrodisiac to some women."

"With the emphasis on powerful." Mercedes made air quotes. "Which goes hand in hand with cash. A lot of it."

"Natalie told us she signed a prenup agreement." Micki glanced at her notes, although just for show. "And that it was her idea."

"I don't believe that for a minute."

"Dad said that, too, Mercedes."

Mercedes sent an annoyed glance her sister's way. "I didn't believe it coming from him either. He was trying to get us to like her."

"Have you seen the agreement?"

"No." Mercedes' gaze sharpened. "But we're meeting with dad's attorneys tomorrow."

Micki decided she was glad she wasn't the one on the receiving end of the woman's ire. She would be a tough opponent. Like a pit bull with a rabbit. "I'd like to know the conditions. It could be helpful."

"I'll see that you get a copy."

"When we arrived, you said you had expected something like this to happen." Micki moved her gaze between the sisters. "You expected him to kill himself?"

"No—"

"God, no!"

They answered in unison, and Zach looked at Mercedes. "Then what, exactly?"

"We expected her to kill him," Mercedes said. "And now she has."

"Whoa," Zach said, "back up. Your father's wife was in the ballroom when your father fell, surrounded by a hundred witnesses."

"It doesn't matter. She killed him."

"I'm game," Micki said. "How'd she do it?"

"He'd changed," Porsche offered. "His mood had turned dark recently. He'd never been like that."

"Depressed? Even with all this?" Micki made a sweeping gesture with her hand. "And not just his business empire, but a beautiful young wife, a grandchild, and two accomplished daughters?"

"Exactly!" Mercedes exclaimed. "She was doing something to him."

"Like what?" Zach asked. "Drugging him?"

Porsche lifted her chin defiantly. "Maybe."

"Do you have any proof of that?"

"No. But the autopsy—"

Micki stepped in. "The autopsy will be complicated by the circumstances. They're not—" She paused, searching for the kindest way to lower their expectations. "It was a devastating fall. The pathologist will do the best he can with what he has to work with."

Mercedes jumped to her feet, hands clenched by her side. "You can investigate her." Her voice turned shrill, with what sounded like a combination of hysteria and exhaustion. "There are ways—I know there are!"

Micki's heart went out to her. "Ms. King," she said softly, "we're limited by the law as to what we can and cannot do. If we uncover any tangible evidence that Natalie King was somehow involved in your father's death—"

Mercedes cut her off. "We don't need 'tangible evidence,' Detective. She killed our father. We don't know how, but we know she did. And I'm going to prove it, even if it takes every dollar of my inheritance!"

CHAPTER EIGHT

5:35 A.M.

THE VIDEO FOOTAGE BLURRED BEFORE Zach's tired eyes. He blinked and poured himself another cup of coffee. The dregs of the pot, he saw, tipping it for the last drop.

Tower security had set them up with all the tapes from the previous evening. He and Mick were tag teaming—he'd pulled elevators, she hallways. So far, after watching King and his wife ride a car from the twenty-first floor to the ballroom level, he'd seen a couple having sex between floors, a husband manhandle his wife, and a host of various hotel personnel coming and going.

Zach sipped the coffee, grimacing at its bitterness. He was exhausted, mentally, physically, and emotionally. Absorbing the feelings of others was like experiencing them himself—for more than six hours he'd been riding an emotional roller coaster.

His vision blurred again and his thoughts wandered. King's death felt like a suicide to him. Or it would, if not for one thing—the amber-eyed woman. He frowned. She could have been one of dozens of people near the scene. After all, he'd been on the lower terrace, being pummeled by energy, surrounded by the mess that had once been the mogul.

But she'd been attached to the watch, he reminded himself. And she had been beckoning *him*. How had that been possible?

The grainy image caught his attention once more. King, stepping into the elevator car, pressing a floor number.

"King's in the elevator," he said. "He's alone."

The doors closed; the car began its ascent. Then it stopped. A young woman with a short, spiky haircut stepped on. Dressed in denims and a hooded sweatshirt, she looked neither hotel guest nor employee.

Curiously, she didn't glance at King, and he didn't acknowledge her, even with a nod. The car reached twenty-one, the doors slid open. As King moved around the young woman, she handed him something.

"Did you see that?" he asked, looking at Mick.

"Hell, yes." She leaned forward. "Rewind."

Zach did and they watched again. It was obvious from the way she surreptitiously slid the item to him that they were both aware of the security video.

"What is it?" Mick asked.

"Key card?"

"Maybe. Let's follow King. We can come back to her."

They switched to the recording of King's hallway, picking up where he stepped off the elevator and proceeded down the hall. Oddly, he stopped once and gave his head a shake, as if to clear it, before moving on. He reached his apartment and disappeared inside.

"Well, that was a bust," Mick said. "Whatever she gave him, he didn't even look at it."

Zach agreed. "And check it out, he left his door partly open. He didn't plan to be in there long."

She looked at him. "First responders said his door was closed and locked."

"So, somebody either followed him in or was there waiting for him."

Mick turned back to the monitor and sucked in a sharp breath. "The former," she said. "And now we know who."

The young woman from the elevator. Walking towards King's apartment, pausing at the door. Looking left, then right, then disappearing into the apartment.

Zach frowned. He hadn't picked up her presence in the apartment. Why?

"What goes in must come out," Micki murmured, leaning forward, gaze riveted on the video image. The seconds ticked past. Ninety-two, to be exact. Then the young woman reappeared, backing out of the apartment. Easing the door shut behind her, she turned and hurried to the elevator.

Zach's heart beat wildly as they followed her, switching from one camera to the next. She exited on the tenth floor, turning right. She was alternately wringing her hands and hugging herself as she made her way down the hall.

And stopped in front of a door at the end of the hallway. She retrieved a key card from her pocket, opened the door and slipped into the apartment.

Not just any apartment. Porsche King's.

CHAPTER NINE

7:10 A.M.

IT TOOK LESS THAN FIVE minutes for them to discover the young woman's name; the head of the Tower's security team recognized her right off. She was Cherie Smith, Porsche King's nanny.

Micki arranged for two cruisers to pick her up and bring her to the Eighth for questioning. Smith had not only been the last to see King alive, she'd been with him literally moments before he plunged to his death. Micki wasn't about to take any chances with this interview—she wanted it logged and recorded.

Micki took a long swallow of water and wiped her mouth with a paper napkin. She and Zach had grabbed a couple breakfast burritos on their way in. She'd wolfed hers down, but was still hungry.

She opened her bottom right desk drawer. It's where she kept emergency supplies—in this case a package of peanut butter crackers and a deodorant stick. Yeah, not only was she exhausted and hungry, she stank, too. Working a case all night did that to you.

She shoved a cracker in her mouth and turned to face the wall. Untucking her shirt, she applied deodorant to one pit, then the other. She glanced over her shoulder and saw Zach was doing the same— minus the cracker.

Micki re-tucked her shirt, then reached for another cracker. "You ready to do this, partner?"

"As I'll ever be."

They didn't speak again until they reached the interrogation room. Cherie Smith sat staring blankly at the wall. Micki crossed to the recording device and turned it on.

"Ms. Smith," Micki said, "I'm Detective Dare and this is Detective Harris."

"I don't know why I'm here."

"Don't you?"

She shook her head, eyes wide.

"You're here because someone close to you died unexpectedly and violently, and you were the last person to see him alive."

"That's not true." She shook her head. "I didn't."

"Didn't what?" Micki asked.

"I mean, I wasn't the last person to see him alive."

"Who?"

"Mr. King."

Zach crossed to the table, squatted down beside her so she would look him directly in the eyes. "May I call you Cherie?" She nodded, and he held out his hand. "I'm Zach. And everything's going to be all right. All you have to do is answer our questions completely and honestly. Do you think you can do that?"

"Yes." She nodded again.

"Good. Believe me, we want you out of here as soon as possible so we can get on with the investigation. Do you have any questions so far?"

She pointed at the video camera. "Are you recording this?"

"We are." He smiled reassuringly and released her hand. "For your protection and ours."

Micki took over, deciding to go straight for the jugular. "Why were you in Thomas King's apartment last night?"

"Why do you think I was?"

"We have it on security footage."

She went from looking uneasy to terrified. Her lips began to tremble and her eyes teared up.

"I didn't do anything wrong."

"So, you don't deny it?"

She shook her head. "No."

"We saw you two in the elevator. What did you hand him when he got off on twenty-one?"

"A name. On a piece of paper."

"A name?" Micki repeated. "Whose name?"

"A woman who works for his company. Brianna Heron."

"What was the significance of that name?"

A tear rolled down her cheek. "I'm so ashamed."

"Ms. Smith, I asked you a question. What was the significance of that name?"

The nanny looked at Zach, then back at Micki. "She's having an affair with his son-in-law. He was paying me to spy on Porsche's husband."

Micki wasn't certain what she expected her to say, but that wasn't it.

Cherie wrung her hands. "He told me to let him know the minute I found out, no matter what the time of day."

"How did you find out?" Zach asked quietly.

"He had flowers sent to her room. I made friends with the bellman; he told me."

"And then?"

"I texted him that the information he'd been waiting for had arrived. He arranged for me to meet him right away."

"Tell us about that," Zach said.

"Mr. King texted that I should go to the elevator. He would text when he was getting on and I was to hit the call button. His car would stop at my floor, I'd get on and hand him the name as he got off. I did that."

"But that's not the end of the story, is it?" She went white and Micki pushed harder. "You went back, didn't you? Instead of returning to the tenth floor, you rode up to thirty-two, then back down to twenty-one. Why?"

She squeezed her eyes shut and shook her head.

"You got off on twenty-one and went to King's apartment. The door was open and you went inside. What did you do in there, Cherie? What did you see?"

"He was on the porch. The sliding doors were open and the cold wind was blowing the drapes. And he was . . . flailing his arms. Around his head. Like he was, I don't know, batting at something."

She paused, visibly struggling to collect herself enough to continue. "I called his name and rushed forward to help, but he told me to get out. That he didn't want me there. His face was . . . twisted. With rage or . . . I don't know. I was afraid, so I left."

She brought her hands to her face and began to sob. "I'm sorry. I never thought he was going to kill himself! I wouldn't have left. I promise I wouldn't have!"

Micki looked at Zach. He inclined his head slightly, indicating that her words matched what he'd picked up from her when he held her hand.

"I have to ask you one more question, Ms. Smith. Why didn't you go home and to bed? Why go back to his apartment?"

"I wanted to tell him something."

"What?" Zach asked.

"That I quit. That I wouldn't be his spy anymore."

CHAPTER TEN

8:55 A.M.

ZACH WATCHED CHERIE SMITH WALK away. "By the way, Smith was telling the truth about all of it. Everything she said jibed with what I picked up."

Micki nodded. "Nichols is waiting for our update. No time like the present." They started toward the major's office. "Are we in agreement on our assessment of what happened?"

"That King killed himself?" He frowned. "We don't have anything else. Even if I hadn't screwed up by not handling the watch, Smith was there, she saw him and saw that he was alone."

"Behaving bizarrely, according to Smith's description." Micki paused in thought. "What's still bugging me is the why. Why then? That moment? He was the superstar that night. It doesn't make sense." Micki looked at him, held his gaze. "I have to ask. Could we be dealing with a Dark Bearer?"

Zach had wondered the same thing. But tracking Dark Bearer energy was his most outstanding ability, and he'd picked up none. Nada. "I would have felt its energy. Hell, it probably would have knocked me on my ass."

His phone went off. He saw it was his mother. He motioned to Mick to hold a second, and answered. "Arianna, hey. What's up?"

"I was hoping we could get together. There's something I wanted to discuss with you."

He frowned slightly and glanced at Mick. "Can I call you back on that? Mick and I are on our way in to see the Major. We're working the King investigation. I'm not sure when I'll have a break."

"Sure," she said. "No problem. I'll talk to you then."

Zach ended the call, and Mick shot him a questioning look. "What?" he asked.

"Still can't call her mom, huh?"

He couldn't. He'd tried. He wanted to feel a mother-son connection between them, and he'd always thought he would, should he ever find her. It bothered him that he didn't. "Nope."

"You want to talk about it?"

Talk about his mother showing back up in his life after giving him up for adoption almost thirty years ago, and how that did or did not make him feel? Hell, no.

"Nope." He shrugged. "I already have someone I call mom."

"Right."

The single word was her way of calling him on his bullshit. He decided to let her have it, and refocused on the investigation. "King's daughters are not going to take this well. Especially Mercedes. She comes off as tough as nails, but was a total Daddy's girl. She's devastated."

"What about Porsche?"

"Not nearly as close to Daddy. Not that close to her sister either, finds her too harsh. And she's worried her husband's having an affair."

"With good reason, it turns out."

"Here's something both sisters agree on. They believed Natalie killed their father. And not just metaphorically."

"Both of them?"

"Yeah. One hundred percent."

"They know that's impossible, right?" Her brow furrowed. "At the moment King leapt from the rail, his wife was twenty floors below, mingling with a ballroom full of witnesses."

"They're convinced she pulled it off somehow."

"She'd have to have been in two places at the same time. Or be two different people—and invisible to video cameras."

"And an eye witness." He thought a moment. "People see what they want to see, don't they? They believe what they want to believe, no matter the facts. Like what the widow King said, the heart wants what the heart wants."

"Or in the case of the King sisters, what the heart hates."

"You got that right." He fell silent a moment, recalling what he'd picked up from the sisters. "They *really* despise her. Almost on a cellular level. The way one might respond to a snake or spider."

"She makes their skin crawl? That's it, isn't it?"

"Yeah, that's what I picked up." He glanced at her, taking in her pensive expression. "You ever had someone affect you that way, Mick?"

For a long moment, she said nothing. Then she inclined her head. "My Uncle Beau. There have been others, including the suspect yesterday, but he springs to my mind first."

"Why's that, Mick?"

Her expression didn't change. He longed to know the rest of the story. He could cheat, position himself to read her mind. Duck in, duck out, she wouldn't even know. But he'd know. And he'd promised he'd never cross that line again.

"He was a creepy son-of-a-bitch," she said finally. "That's why."

"He's dead?"

"Not that I know of. Why?"

"You referred to him in past tense, that's all."

"That's what he is to me, past tense."

"You want to talk about it?" he asked, turning her question from a moment ago back on her.

She grinned. "Nope."

Zach wanted to push. He knew to leave it alone. "Dropping it for now, partner."

CHAPTER ELEVEN

10:30 P.M.

MICKI ARRIVED HOME. TWENTY-FOUR HOURS without a break; she was toast. She'd had little to eat, no sleep, and way too much caffeine. She'd spent the drive home fantasizing about the moment her head hit the pillow.

Major Nichols had wanted them to follow up on every aspect of the nanny's story. And rightly so—crossing every "t" and dotting every "i" equaled good police work. They'd checked in with the criminologists; they had, indeed, collected a slip of paper with the name Brianna Heron written on it. From there they'd interviewed all parties involved.

Smith's story checked out.

Micki flipped off the porch light, dead-bolted the door, and made her way through the darkened living room, heading toward the kitchen and a peanut butter sandwich.

Angel had left the light above the sink burning. That was the habit they had fallen into—first to bed left the porch light and sink light on, last one turned them off.

Micki thought of the nineteen-year-old and felt a pinch of sympathy. Angel had been through so much in the past year, it was a wonder she was doing as well as she was.

If being the walking wounded could be categorized as doing well.

Micki reached the kitchen, shrugged out of her jacket and hung it over a chair. She longed to remove her shoulder holster, but thought better of it. As tired as she was, she couldn't trust herself not to forget and leave it behind, the kind of mistake a cop could die regretting.

She assembled the sandwich using whole wheat bread—Zach's influence, she acknowledged, making a face—and super-chunky peanut butter, then poured herself a glass of milk. Whole milk, thank you very much.

A hot shower, she thought, taking a bite of the sandwich. Followed by bed. And sleep, beautiful, beautiful sleep.

Micki carried the plate and glass to the table, another of Hank's hand-me-downs. She set them both on the scarred top, gaze going to the sketchbook at its center. Angel had left it behind, a highly unusual action for her young friend. Angel rarely let it out of her sight; she was intensely private about her drawings. To Angel, the sketches were like diary entries, she commemorated her days with images instead of words, recording her thoughts, feelings, and dreams.

And sometimes those dreams were precognitive.

"You can look if you like."

Micki glanced over her shoulder. Angel stood in the doorway, wearing over-sized dorm pants and a T-shirt, eyes red and puffy.

She'd been crying. Again.

"I wasn't going to without your permission."

"You have it." She crossed to the refrigerator and poured herself a glass of milk. "I'm not going to keep any secrets from you, not anymore."

"I appreciate that a lot." Micki motioned to the chair across the table from her. "Come and keep me company."

Angel shuffled over and sat, gaze going to Micki's plate and the half sandwich on it.

Micki nudged the plate in Angel's direction. "Go ahead."

"But you need to eat, too."

"Let's eat together."

Angel dug in, and without asking her if she'd want more, Micki stood and made another sandwich for them both. They devoured them quickly and in silence.

When Micki had drained the last of her milk, she broke the silence. "No secrets, right?" When Angel nodded, Micki went on, "Why were you crying?"

"You know why."

Seth. He'd both betrayed her and broken her heart. "I know it hurts."

"Do you?" Angel looked away, then back, expression remorseful. "Sorry. I know you do." She fell silent, then gestured to the sketchbook. "Please, I want you to."

Micki slid the spiral book over, flipped it open. As always, her breath caught at Angel's talent. At the raw power in her drawing hand—even in an unfinished sketch like this one.

It was of Seth, incomplete except for his mesmerizing gaze. The gaze, his beautiful eyes, were rendered with so much detail it felt as if he was peering into her soul.

She could only imagine how Angel had felt when she'd drawn them.

Micki flipped a page. Another drawing of Seth. This one dreamy. Another page, another drawing of him. Then another.

And another.

A knot of tears gathered in her throat. "Aww, hell, Angel. I'm sorry."

"It's okay. It's not your fault."

It wasn't, obviously. "You want to talk about it?"

"I thought he loved me," she said it softly, not meeting Micki's eyes. "I thought he'd be back for me."

Three months. That's how long it had been since that horrific day and the last time she'd seen him.

Micki searched for the right words. When they wouldn't come, she settled for her own—clumsy but honest. "Maybe his not coming back is his way of loving you? Maybe he knows you're better off without him, so he's staying away?"

"But I'm not better off without him."

In that, she and Angel disagreed. She reached out her hand to Angel's. "You're safer without him. You know *that's* true."

Angel was a powerful mixed being, part Lightkeeper and part Dark Bearer, with abilities useful to both sides battling for dominance over life on earth.

"They wanted to use you for their purposes, Angel. They wanted to turn you into something you're not."

"Not Seth," she said fiercely. "He saved me. He laid his life on the line to protect me."

"Yes," Micki said softly, carefully. "But first he tricked, lied to and used you."

"He wasn't all bad." She balled her hands into fists. "He wasn't."

"I know." Micki covered one of her clenched hands with one of her own. "I know you loved him—"

"Love him," she corrected. "I still love him."

"It hurts to hear, but you're better off without him, Angel."

"How can you say that?" She yanked her hand away. "How do you know that?"

"Because of what he tried to do. What he tried to turn you into—" What could she say? Into a monster? An agent of evil? She couldn't say either of those things, so said instead, "He wanted to bring out the worst in you."

"The worst in me? You mean my dark side."

Micki heard the bitterness in her voice, saw the tears sparkling in her eyes. How did you reconcile learning that a powerful darkness lived within you? A darkness you didn't ask for or deserve?

"He had good in him," she said. "Just like I do." She looked away, then back, defiantly. "We brought out the good in each other."

Micki couldn't agree with her, so she said nothing.

Angel lifted her chin. "I know what I am, Micki."

"And what's that, Angel?"

"Broken. Without Seth, I'm only half of what I'm supposed to be."

CHAPTER TWELVE

Monday, November 13
7:35 A.M.

MICKI SLAPPED THE ALARM CLOCK for the third time and forced herself to roll out of bed. Shrugging into her robe, she shuffled to the bathroom for the necessaries, then headed to the kitchen for the even-more-necessary coffee.

She spooned the grounds into the basket, then filled the carafe with water. Angel's cereal bowl was in the sink. She'd heard her leave the house a while ago. She must have had to open at the coffeehouse this morning.

For a moment she watched the coffee brew, then turned to the window above the sink, catching a glimpse of her reflection. She looked like hell. She pushed the hair away from her face and leaned closer. Bags *and* circles under her eyes; skin a rather ghastly shade of beige; cheeks hollow. Morning of the walking dead, for God's sake.

She felt every bit the way she looked.

And no wonder. Another night with little sleep. Another day ahead with too much coffee, stress, and crappy food on the fly.

When was the last time she'd enjoyed the morning?

She thought of Hank, the way he had gently admonished her. *"Girl, you're gonna blink and be an old-timer like me. Don't let your days pass you by."*

Micki smiled at the memory and grabbed a banana from the bunch in a bowl atop the microwave. She added a healthy dose of cream to her coffee, and took a sip, remembering. Sitting with him, letting the morning sun spill over her, and listening to the birds sing.

No one to sit with now. No one to enjoy those first few moments of the day with. The ache in the pit of her gut had nothing to do with hunger. She thought of what Angel had said last night, that she was alone without Seth. Was this what she meant? What she felt? A gnawing ache for soul-deep companionship? Was it why she had been dreaming of Hank almost every night?

She wanted to shake the thoughts off, but didn't have the mental energy. She could call Zach, he could distract her by making her laugh—or driving her crazy—but the blasted man could read her too easily. And the last thing she wanted was for him to know how she really felt.

Zach. He hadn't been quite the same since his mother's appearance. She drew her eyebrows together. He'd seemed preoccupied. Almost . . . aloof.

But she'd blamed that on herself.

There was something about Arianna that rubbed her the wrong way. In a nagging way, like a bug bite she couldn't reach to scratch.

Zach had picked up on it. He'd asked if she was jealous, because of the time he'd been spending with her. She'd denied it, of course. But maybe she was jealous? At the very least, resentful for Arianna's arrival screwing up their comfortable pattern of camaraderie.

If there was anything Micki Dee Dare resisted, it was change. She knew it about herself. She had her job, her circle of friends and colleagues, and her routine, and nobody better get in the way of it, thank you very much.

Micki finished the coffee and took the last bite of the banana, chewing thoughtfully. Her gaze landed on her running shoes, sitting by the door out to the back porch. When was the last time she'd gone for a run? Not because she had to keep fit for the job, but just for the pleasure of it. For the pounding of her heart and the rush of air into her lungs?

Another thing she and Hank used to do together. He had been amazingly fit for a man his age.

But he'd died from a massive coronary.

It didn't make sense. Not then. Not now.

Micki crossed to the trash, discarded the banana peel, and let out a long, even breath. Sense or not, she couldn't change the facts, as much as she wished she could. Hank was gone, six years now.

He would be disappointed with her. For not taking the time to hear the birds and feel the sun on her face. For not running, just because it made her feel good.

She glanced at her watch. She had the time. And as Hank used to say, *"The present is all you've got, girl. Tomorrow's not a guarantee. Not for you or anybody else."*

A quick run, she decided and smiled. She had the time. Besides, she'd probably be sucking wind before her time ran out.

⚜ ⚜ ⚜

Ten minutes later Micki was atop the levee on the Mississippi River Trail, feet pounding the paved path, the brisk morning air stinging her lungs. On one side of her lay the curve of the Mississippi River, on the other side rested her neighborhood, nestled up against River Road like a lover. The trail was a favorite recreational spot for New Orleanians. On a beautiful Saturday she'd be sharing this stretch with everyone from other runners to kids with kites.

But today, with the early hour and chill wind, she was nearly alone. Which suited her. She didn't want the distraction of others. She wanted to focus on the air filling her lungs to near-bursting, the hammer of her heart, and the burn of out-of-practice muscles.

No doubt she would pay the price later, but for now she was nearly giddy with pleasure.

Finally, Micki admitted she had no choice but to head back. As she neared her exit point, she slowed to cool down. Her street lay below, and she glanced that way, thoughts turning to the day ahead.

A man on the sidewalk, walking past her house. He glanced toward her cottage and the light caught his hair just so. It gleamed silver.

She caught her breath. That stance, the way he moved. She would recognize it anywhere.

Hank. The man was Hank.

Even as she told herself she was crazy—Hank was dead and buried—an involuntary sound passed her lips and she started to run, calling out as loudly and desperately as she could.

He wasn't dead. It couldn't be, but it *was* her Hank.

At the same moment she realized she was going too fast, she went down. Tumbling forward, hitting the ground with a thud that knocked the wind out of her. Pain shot through the side that took the brunt of the fall.

"Hey! Are you okay?"

Micki blinked, vision clearing. Another runner, descending in her direction. Micki sat up, wincing. "I'm fine," she called.

The woman reached her and held out a hand to help her up. "Think you can stand?"

Micki nodded. "The only thing that's really hurt is my pride. I feel like a total idiot." She took the woman's hand and cautiously stood. She was happy to find that, although a bit wobbly, she was fine.

"Thanks for the help."

"You were heading down the hill pretty fast."

Micki pictured the man with the silver hair. Hank? Come back to life? She was losing her freaking mind.

Choosing to scowl instead of cry, she shook her head. "Yeah, I feel pretty stupid. Worst part is, I know better."

The woman made a sound of sympathy. "It happens to the best of us. Don't worry about it." She indicated Micki's right arm. "You're bleeding, by the way."

Micki looked at her arm and frowned. A two-inch patch of her forearm oozed blood. "Scraped it pretty good, it looks like." She smiled ruefully at the woman. "I guess I'd better go take care of it. Thanks again."

She started down the embankment, then stopped and looked back. "I'm Micki, by the way."

"Paulette." She smiled slightly. "See you around."

Micki continued to make her way down to River Road, then across it to her street. By the time she made it to her cottage, she'd decided her mind had been playing tricks on her. A combination of fatigue and the morning's trip down Memory Lane.

Dead men did not come back to life.

She blinked furiously against tears. So much for Mad Dog Dare. From skull crusher to clumsy crybaby. Reputation shot.

When she reached her porch, she saw a padded mailing envelope propped up to the left of her front door. Angel had seen a shirt she'd really liked online, so Micki had ordered it, hoping to surprise her and maybe lift her friend's spirits.

Micki snatched the package up, thoughts still on her fall and runaway imagination. Hank, alive? Maybe she really did need some time off? Or an appointment with the department shrink?

No way. A shrink poking around in *her* head? Now *that* was a truly crazy thought. She dropped the envelope onto the entryway table and set her keys and sunglasses on top of it.

Her arm hurt. She looked at her wound. A single trail of blood ran down her arm, a few drops landing on the wooden floor.

Not a lot of blood. But enough for crime scene detectives to work with.

She shook off the thought. She needed to get her head straight, and fast. This kind of thinking sent cops to a permanent position riding a desk.

Micki headed to the bathroom. Her injury was only a scrape, mostly just nasty-looking. She cleaned it well, covered it, then noticed she'd torn a hole in her favorite yoga pants and gotten blood on her favorite Saints T-shirt.

Could this day get any more screwed up?

She stripped off the ruined pants, tossed them in the trash and jumped in for a quick shower.

Fifteen minutes later, she was dressed, shoulder-length, dishwater blond hair brushed and neatly tucked behind her ears.

She collected the package and headed to the kitchen to grab breakfast.

Poor envelope looked as if it had gotten stuck in a stamping machine, then been run over by a truck. She turned it over and frowned slightly. Not from the e-tailer where she'd ordered Angel's shirt. In fact, there was no return address at all. Her name and address had been handwritten in a familiar angular scrawl.

She grabbed a Greek yogurt and a hard-boiled egg from the fridge, eyebrows drawn together in thought. Where did she know this handwriting from?

"Old man, maybe you should think about a laptop and printer? Who can read this chicken scratch?"

She dropped the envelope as if it burned. Hank. It was Hank's handwriting.

No.

No . . . no . . . no. Stop it, Micki.

Somebody was messing with her. She took a deep breath. A perp with a grudge. Or someone in the NOPD she'd pissed off. She had a habit of doing that. She released the breath slowly, feeling calm coming over her. Or even J.B., the jokester from her unit at the Eighth. He'd think screwing with her mind this way was hysterically funny. Asshole.

Now she was mad. The son of a bitch, whoever it was, wasn't going to get away with it. In case she was dealing with somebody she'd put away, she ran to her car, retrieved a pair of scene gloves from her console and ran back. She opened the envelope as carefully as she could, preserving evidence her top priority—be it prints, hair, fiber or even saliva—just in case.

She unsealed the mailer and peered inside. A folded piece of paper and a small box, the kind department store jewelry might come in. With an abundance of caution, she grabbed a dishtowel and held it over her mouth and nose. She slid the folded paper out.

February, 23

Dear Michaela,

I knew this day would come, and I wanted you to have this. It has protected me all these years. Now it will protect you. Remember when you called me a silly old man for believing in the power of a "cheap, mass-produced trinket?" What you didn't understand is, I never believed the trinket protected me. What protected me was the power of what it stands for.

I believe in you. And not only because you are a warrior for what's right. You are a special person. You are here now, in this place and time, to fulfill an important purpose. Believe in yourself!

I love you, girl. You're the daughter I never had.

Hank.

Her mind went tumbling back. She remembered the conversation he'd referenced so clearly. It had been in the early years of their friendship. She'd been young. And self-destructive. He'd seen something in her she certainly hadn't seen in herself.

She'd asked him about the St. Michael medal he always wore. And laughed at his answer. She'd been so cynical and so sure of her own belief in nothing.

No one would know that but him.

She should open the box, Micki realized, a tear rolling down her cheek, hitting the paper. She carefully wiped it away, then set the letter aside. With shaking hands, she slid it out of the mailer and lifted the lid. Nestled inside was the necklace she remembered. She took it from the box, ran her fingers over the chain and across the stamped medal.

The chain was worn from being around his neck. She brought it to her nose. It smelled like him, she thought. She closed her eyes, breathed deeply and felt surrounded by him.

Like the chain, the medal was worn from wear, its edges softened from years of rubbing against skin and fabric. She curled her fingers tightly around it. The disk felt warm against her palm. As if, somehow, it thrummed with Hank's life force.

Memories swamped her. Tears with them. Of times spent together, of conversations, and of feelings. Of safety, comfort. Happiness.

Then of loss. Deep and shattering. Of losing Hank, yes. But ones that had come earlier and struck deeper: the theft of her childhood and her innocence.

Micki's knees gave and she sank to the floor, medal still clutched in her hand. Tears came. A storm of them. A tsunami of grief.

She couldn't fight it; she didn't have the strength. Not anymore. Not alone.

In her pocket, her cell went off. She managed to answer it, though she didn't know how, wasn't aware of what she said, or even if she spoke.

"Mick? Is that you?"

Zach. Concerned. "Yes . . . Something's . . . Hap . . . pened—"

"Angel? Is she—"

"Fine," she managed around sobs.

"Mick, talk to me. Are you all right?"

"I don't . . . No. . . I—" The last was swamped by a round of fresh tears.

"Hold on, partner. I'm on my way."

CHAPTER THIRTEEN

9:45 A.M.

ZACH MADE IT FROM HIS door to hers in record time. Micki stepped into his arms and he just held her. The tears had stopped but she trembled so violently, her teeth chattered. He'd never seen her this way, not even after she was shot or when Angel had gone missing.

Raw. Completely vulnerable.

What the hell did he do? How did he help her? People needing him wasn't his thing. Staying, being *that* guy, wasn't his thing.

But hadn't he longed to get a peek beyond her tough exterior, of the places she didn't share? A glimpse of what had made her into the woman she'd become?

He tightened his arms; instead of stiffening or pulling away, she seemed to melt deeper into him, accepting the security and comfort he offered.

Something pinched inside him. Deep in his chest. A catch that signaled something he didn't want and wasn't ready for.

He'd felt many things for this complex, sometimes infuriating woman. Loyalty and friendship. Respect, frustration. Sexual desire.

But this . . . softness? This protectiveness? No. Never.

He couldn't start now.

"Oh, Mick. I'm sorry." He murmured the words automatically, meaning to follow them by loosening his arms and stepping away. He knew her well enough to know she would rally at that. Pull herself together, fit her armor back in place. But instead of doing what was smart, he threaded his fingers through her hair, the strands silky against them.

She looked up at him, the expression in her eyes unbearably vulnerable.

Dammit. What did he do with that? With the way that vulnerability made him feel? With the pinch in his chest that had become a gnawing ache?

So, he kissed her. Softly but deeply, drawing her into him.

It'll be all right, the kiss said. I'm here. I won't leave. I'll protect you.

The lies a man told a woman when he didn't know what else to do. Or say. The lies they told when they might not stay, because leaving was always on the table.

Or because they were afraid. That they wouldn't go, not ever. That maybe, just maybe, he needed her just as much as she needed him. Maybe more.

He ended the kiss, rested his forehead on hers. Her trembling ceased. Bit by bit, he felt her transform back into the emotionally-controlled woman he knew. His Mick, he thought. The woman who needed—and depended on—no one.

Finally, she took an awkward step away. "I'm sorry, I don't, um . . . thank you for—"

"No," he murmured, "don't be sorry. And don't be embarrassed."

"It's just— Dammit!" She dragged a hand through her hair. "I hate this. I hate being weak."

He could have told her that falling apart, or needing someone, wasn't the same as being weak, but he didn't. "Tell me what happened," he said instead.

"It's crazy."

"I'll be the judge of that." He motioned toward the living room. "How about we sit down?"

She nodded and headed to the sofa, sank onto it, clasping her hands in front of her. He noticed an opened mailing envelope, a folded sheet of paper, and a small box on the coffee table in front of her.

He took the chair across from her and waited.

"It sounds . . . no, it is crazy. You're going to think I've lost it."

"Me, Mick? Mr. Crazy himself? C'mon, you can trust me. You know you can."

She nodded, averted her gaze a moment, then met his eyes again. "I think Hank's alive."

He hadn't expected that. How could he have? He cleared his throat. "You are talking about—"

"Yes, that Hank. The one who's been dead six years. Or at least I thought he was."

"You told me you were the one who found him, that you were there when the paramedics came—"

"And I was at his funeral. Yes, to all of the above."

He processed that. "Okay, Mick," he said, keeping his tone easy, "you're one of the most level-headed people I know, so you must have a good reason for even considering that."

"You're not supposed to encourage me, Zach." She shook her head. "You're supposed to tell me I'm crazy. That what I'm thinking is impossible, outlandish and—"

"I can do that, Mick, but I'd rather hear what you have to say first."

So, she began. He listened as she shared her thoughts upon waking, her memories of Hank, how they would sometimes, in the mornings, sit quietly and sip coffee; how they would go for runs, just because.

The Mick she described through those memories was happier, more relaxed, than the one he knew, and he wondered how one person could have had such a profound effect on another.

"I decided to go for a run," she told him. "The way he and I used to." Her voice deepened; her hand went to her bandaged forearm. "That's when I saw him. Or rather, thought I saw him."

"Hank?"

"Yes. Passing on the sidewalk in front of my house."

"So, you *don't* believe it was Hank?"

"I'm not . . . I don't." She clasped her hands together. "How could it have been him?"

"It couldn't have been. Just like the man you saw on the sidewalk outside the Eighth couldn't have been him."

"Right." She pointed at the open envelope, note paper and box. "That was on the porch when I got home."

"What is it?"

"A letter from Hank. And this."

She handed Zach the box. He opened it and took out the necklace.

"A St. Michael medal," she said. "He wore it all the time."

He drew his eyebrows together. "And this was delivered this morning?"

"Or it could have been yesterday or last night. I don't know for sure."

"Maybe it's not his. Maybe it's from someone who knows about your relationship with Hank and is trying to mess with your head?"

"It was his. Look how worn it is."

"So, somebody sent you a used medal. I doubt they're a rare item, especially in a predominantly Catholic city like New Orleans."

"I could buy all that, if not for the letter. It's his handwriting, Zach." She handed it over. "And that conversation he references, nobody else would know that."

He read the letter, frown deepening. She had a point. But what she was suggesting was impossible.

"Why have I been dreaming about him so much? Maybe it's because he's alive?" She dragged a hand through her hair. "I dream I see him, and then I see him. Crazy, huh?"

It was. Crazy enough to worry him. "Let's think this through. He's been dead six years."

"Exactly. So how can I be receiving this now?"

"Maybe it got lost in the mail. I saw a story not that long ago about a woman receiving a letter that arrived fifty years late. All because of transposed numbers and no return address."

She picked up the envelope. "No return address, but mine is correct." She frowned. "It's stamped, but it doesn't look like it was metered. That's weird."

"Maybe he meant to send it, but didn't, and the folks that bought his house ran across it and popped it into the mail."

"That could be," she murmured. "I sold them the house, they had my address. But it's been six years. How could they not run across it before now?"

"Call them and find out."

She picked up the letter. "Oh, my God."

"What?"

She met his eyes. "He wrote this the day he died. February twenty-third."

Zach reached around and plucked the letter from her fingers, read the date. "That's the day he died? You're certain?"

"We talked that afternoon." She brought a trembling hand to her mouth. "I remember, he was acting . . . I don't know, different. I wondered if something was wrong. I didn't ask because . . . I was working this case . . ."

Her words trailed off and her expression turned pensive. Zach frowned. "What case?"

She stood, crossed to the window. "The Three Queens. We had a strong suspect and had gotten a search warrant for her practice. She got wind of it and skipped town before we could bring her in for question-ing. It always felt like . . . somehow the perp—"

She bit the last back. He crossed to her, laid his hands on her shoulders and looked her in the eyes. "You're exhausted, your mind played a trick on you, and at the same time this long-lost package arrived."

She nodded. "There's no way Hank could be alive. Seeing his hand-writing . . . the medal— I just lost it."

"It's okay. Everybody loses it sometimes. The last thing you should be is embarrassed."

She stepped away. "Who said I was embarrassed? I'm pissed off."

She practically growled the words, and he grinned. "That's the Mick I know and love."

"You tell anyone about this, Hollywood, I'll kick your ass."

"I know you will." He scooped up his jacket. "Maybe you should take the day off? Get some rest? Clear your head."

"Hell no, that's not happening."

Zach started for the door, smiling back at her. "I'll tell Nichols you're having a nervous breakdown, and that you'll be in when you've got your shit together."

"Try it and die, Hollywood. Now, get the hell out of here. I've got calls to make."

Zach laughed, relieved. "Cussing and crabby, classic Mad Dog."

She followed him to the front door. As he started through, she stopped him. "Hey, Zach?"

"Yeah?"

"Thanks. For everything."

"Even the smooch?"

He wiggled his eyebrows in exaggerated lechery, and she pointed to his car.

"Go. Now. Before I lose my sense of humor."

As the door clicked shut behind him, Zach's smile faded. There hadn't been anything funny about that kiss—or the way it had made him feel. And they both knew where it might have led if he hadn't backed off.

It had been the elephant in the middle of the room. Taunting them both. So, he had addressed it.

The "what if" filled his head. He and Mick, naked on the bed, twined together. Hot and hungry. His mouth went dry and his blood began to thrum.

Thank God, he'd resisted. If he hadn't, the elephant in the middle of the room would have become the monkey on their backs. Or at least on his. Because he had a feeling that making love with Mick could become an obsession.

CHAPTER FOURTEEN

Noon

BY THE TIME MICKI ARRIVED at the Eighth, she'd talked to someone named Rhonda at the United States Postal Service Mail Recovery Center in Atlanta. From her, she'd heard why mail gets lost, how much gets lost, and how often the MRC actually locates the intended recipients. Rhonda had then directed Micki to call her local postmaster.

Which she did. A very friendly man named Pete. Not at all helpful, since he had no information about her package, but had agreed mail got lost all the time and shared how frustrating that was for all involved. They at the USPS were dedicated to getting every piece of mail delivered in a timely manner. And then he'd referred her to the MRC in Atlanta.

Micki had thanked him and hung up, feeling oddly reassured by the facts and more than a little bit foolish over her earlier histrionics. But not reassured enough to leave a thread dangling, so she'd taken a detour on her way in, stopping by Hank's old place. The curtains had been drawn, and no one answered the door, so she'd scribbled a note and tucked it into the mail slot.

Micki greeted Sue, collected her messages, and headed to her desk. Hank's medal hung from around her neck, nestled between her breasts and near her heart. She found its being there comforting. As if in some strange way, Hank was watching over her.

Zach was on the phone. He looked her way and pointed in the direction of Major Nichols' office, then hung up. "Big guy wants us. Pathologist's report is in."

He came around the desk. "But first, that was King's lawyer. Finally returned my call about the prenuptial agreement between Thom and Natalie King."

"And?"

"Just as the widow King said, there is one. Everything goes to his kids and grandchild."

"She doesn't get anything?" Micki sounded as incredulous as she felt.

"I'll read it to you." He retrieved his notes. "She keeps all her personal belongings, including any clothing and jewelry. She keeps her personal vehicle and anything they purchased during the marriage."

"What about the 2 River Tower and Hotel?"

"Nope. She gets nothing from the corporation. Only things they personally acquired."

"And that's it?"

"And a quarter of a million bucks."

To Micki, a lot of money. To someone who had been living the life of a billionaire's wife, not so much.

"And," Zach went on, "the lawyer confirmed the prenup was Natalie's idea. He's emailing a copy."

"Damn." She shook her head. "I called that one wrong."

"Trust me, you're not the only one. This also came in."

He handed her a file folder. "What is this?"

"Records of the electronic correspondence between Keith Gerard and Sarah Stevens."

The case they'd been working before King. It seemed like a month ago and it'd only been a few days. "And?"

"I didn't have time to take it all in, but in what I did read, there was nothing incriminating."

"Nothing?"

Micki opened the file, flipped through the pages, and stopped on the day preceding Stevens' suicide. She scanned the print-outs of their text conversations—Gerard came off as a model boyfriend.

She made a sound of disgust, closed the file and tossed it on her desk. "There's something there, and I'm going to find it."

He playfully elbowed her. "That's my Mad Dog. How about the package from Hank. Any answers?"

They started toward the major's office. "Apparently, some mysteries cannot be solved. Packages get lost. Sometimes for a very long time, and for a variety of reasons. No one knew how mine had gotten lost, but obviously it had."

"You okay with that?"

She wasn't okay with any of it. Not with thinking she saw Hank, or King's suicide, or a package from a dead man mysteriously showing up on her doorstep.

And not with the nagging feeling that she was missing something important.

She released a pent-up breath. "Do I have a choice?"

They reached Major Nichols' office and he waved them in. He started talking before they'd even taken their seats. "The coroner is classifying King's death a suicide." He moved his gaze between them. "Do you have anything that suggests that's the wrong call?"

Micki turned her gaze to the window to the right of the Major's desk. A crow sat on the ledge. It seemed to be staring at her.

A queasy sensation settled in the pit of her gut.

"Detective?"

She jerked her gaze back to Nichols. "Nada," she said.

Zach nodded. "Ditto, Major."

"Write it up."

"You want us to inform King's family?" Micki asked.

"The chief is handling that himself. I'd like those reports ASAP. That's all."

They filed out. Zach glanced at her. "You're quiet."

"Not much to say, is there?"

"You think there's more here?"

She shrugged. "It's one of those cases where what you see is what you get."

Even as she said the words, something tickled at her memory. Some-one had once said those exact words to her. Who?

"It's just so weird," Zach said. "A guy like King, killing himself? Why do you think he did it?"

She drew her eyebrows together. "Don't know. He didn't leave a note, so we'll probably never know."

"And that sits okay with you?"

It didn't. Not at all.

Better luck next time, Detective.

The hair on the back of her neck prickled. The Three Queens case. Again. Her first homicide investigation as a rookie detective, inextrica-bly tied to Hank's death.

It hadn't sat right. It had looked too easy.

In the end, she'd followed her gut.

And she had been right; there had been more to the story. Much more.

Better luck next time, Detective.

What was her gut telling her now? What wasn't sitting right with this case?

"Mick?"

She jumped as Zach touched her elbow. "Sorry. What?"

He frowned. "You okay?"

"Yeah. Of course."

He hesitated a moment, as if not quite convinced, then jerked his thumb in the direction of the door. "I'm going to head over to CE&P."

"Central Evidence? Why?"

"Before I write this up, I want to have a go at that Rolex."

"You're thinking there might be something there?"

"Truthfully? No. But I've got to do it anyway."

"Need me to come along?"

"I've got this." He grinned. "Besides, I know how much you enjoy working on reports. No way I'm going to keep you from it."

"You're not getting out of this, you know."

"Watch me."

She shook her head, amused. "Major expects a report," she called after him. "And not just from me."

He laughed and loped off, and Micki returned to her desk and started by assembling her notes on the King suicide, reading through and organizing them.

Suicide. Straightforward. Simple.

Not simple. Never.

Micki spun toward her computer to access The Three Queens file. She scrolled through, refreshing her memory. She wasn't exactly sure what she was looking for, but was confident she would recognize it when she saw it.

Similarities, she realized, switching back and forth between the two investigations.

Similarity number one. A case that had appeared simple but had proved to be anything but.

Similarity number two. Family members adamant that those involved would never do what they very obviously had done. In the one case, that was take another's life. In the other, take their own.

Similarity number three. Testimony from others that the mood or behavior of the individuals in question had recently changed, specifically growing darker.

Mick turned away from the screen and leaped to her feet. So, what? All three similarities could apply to numerous cases. She was wasting her time. The only reason she was thinking about The Three Queens case was Hank's letter. It had stirred up her memory of it, that's all.

The St. Michel's medal felt warm between her breasts. Crazy as it seemed, she sensed it was urging her on. She pulled it out from beneath her blouse and curled her fingers around it.

Carmine, she thought. When was the last time she'd been to visit her old partner? She answered her own question. When Zach had come on board, and Carmine had been assigned to the Cold Case Unit. Too long.

Snatching up her phone, Micki punched in his number. A brief conversation later, she was on her way headquarters.

CHAPTER FIFTEEN

1:30 P.M.

"MAD DOG," CARMINE SAID, GIVING her a bear hug. "How the hell are you?"

"Good." She eyed him. He looked ten years younger and thirty pounds lighter. "What's up, dude? You're like the amazing, disappearing man."

He laughed and struck a pose. "I look good, right? Wife and I took up yoga."

She almost choked at the image that popped in her head, of Carmine, aging goodfella, on a yoga mat in Downward Dog.

She cleared her throat. "Well, I've got to say, I didn't expect that."

He laughed again, motioned toward the chair across from his desk, then settled into his own chair. "Saw you and the hot shot pulled the King investigation."

"Sure did. Coroner's calling it a suicide."

"Was there ever any doubt?"

"There's always some doubt, you know that."

He shifted in his chair. "You and Harris make quite a team."

Micki wished she could share the truth about Zach with him, but she couldn't—no matter how much she trusted Carmine.

"We've had a lot of dumb luck come our way."

"A whole lot of it." It was obvious he didn't buy that and was hurt by her diversion, and she quickly added, "Harris has crazy good instincts. I've never seen anything like it."

"There's something different about that guy."

"You're telling me?" She leaned slightly forward. "He's out of his frickin' mind."

"Driving you crazy, huh?"

"And then some." She smiled. "You and I were pretty good, too."

"That we were." His expression turned serious. "You just here to shoot the shit, Dare?"

"Nope."

He settled back into his chair. "Didn't think so. What's up?"

"I've been thinking about The Three Queens case."

He inclined his head. "Any particular reason why?"

What did she say when she wasn't completely clear on that herself? She decided to start with the obvious. "I got a package today. From Hank. The letter inside was dated the day he died."

His expression registered surprise, then doubt. "That's not particularly funny. What's the punchline?"

"There is none. It looks like it got lost in the mail."

"For six years?"

"Apparently, that happens."

"Damn." He sat back, chewing on the idea of it. His expression turned sympathetic. "That must have been a shock."

"Big time. I'd been thinking about him a lot lately anyway, even thought I saw him."

She bit the rest back and held out the medal. "He sent me this. It was his, he wore it every day."

"And that brought you back to our Three Queens case."

"Yeah." She dropped the medal back under her shirt. "It's not just the package from Hank causing me to think about the Dead Queen."

"No?"

"No." She shook her head. "There's something about the King case. . . the way it makes me feel, that's the same."

"Like there's more to the story."

"Yeah."

"What does the hotshot say? You said his instincts are 'crazy good.'"

"I haven't talked to him about it, not specifically anyway." Carmine's eyebrows shot up, and she quickly went on, "He doesn't know the details of the case or how it unfolded. So, I came to you."

"Gotcha."

But he didn't. The easy word held a subtle condemnation. She'd shut her partner out, without valid cause. Not cool.

"I re-read the report, Carmine. How'd she know? How'd she get away?"

"Like you said back then, she anticipated your move. She had to know that someday, someone would catch on. And she was ready for it. That's why she left you that note."

"Better luck next time," Micki murmured. "You never noticed anything strange about her eyes, huh?"

He pursed his lips. "Nope. You did, I remember. Had an almost physical reaction to her. To her office even, the moment you walked in."

She remembered and thought of what Zach had said about King's daughters. "Like nails on a chalk board."

He smiled slightly. "I think she had a bit of the same reaction to you. You pushed her buttons, that's for sure."

"That I did."

"Where's all this leading, Dare?"

"Not quite sure. Maybe I just wanted your advice."

"On what to do about this case?" She nodded, and he leaned forward. "You're a good cop, Micki. Trust your instincts. Besides the badge and gun, that's pretty much all we've got."

Ordinary cops, like the two of them. Without super-mojo, bullshit powers. Didn't matter that Professor Truebell had "welcomed her to the club." Her tiny spark of light hadn't given her dip in the way of special abilities.

She looked down at her hands, then back up at him. "What if my instincts are wrong?"

"You cause yourself some extra legwork. Big deal."

More than that, she thought. Last time it had cost her Hank.

No. She rubbed her temple. Hank died of a heart attack. The pathologist had said so.

"Look," Carmine said, expression sympathetic, "there's nothing new on Blackwood. I check every so often. That same day we got the search warrant, she got on a plane to Costa Rica and hasn't returned."

"You're certain?"

"As certain as I can be. We flagged her passport; if she tries to re-enter the country, we'll be notified."

"But if she falsified her passport—"

"You think there's a chance she's done that?"

Falsified her passport. Completely changed her looks. And come back not just to the States, but to New Orleans?

Micki brought a hand to the spot between her eyebrows and the head-ache that had settled there. "Just throwing it out there. It's certainly a possibility."

He frowned, studying her. "Do you have some reason to believe she's stateside?"

Not just change her looks—but become a different person?

She couldn't be thinking that.

"No." She shook her head. "The whole thing—this case, the feeling that there's more to it—the package from Hank dredged it all back up."

"I get it, partner. It's tough."

It was tough. Losing Hank was the hardest thing she'd ever faced.

She stood. "Thanks, Carmine. I appreciate the time."

"Hey." He stood and came around the desk. "Are you kidding? Any-time." He gave her a quick hug. "Come to dinner sometime, bring the hotshot."

She forced a smile. "I'll do that."

"And Dare?"

She looked back at him. "Yeah?"

"Your partner. Maybe you need to fill him in?"

"You're right, I will. Thanks, Carmine."

CHAPTER SIXTEEN

2:10 P.M.

MICKI SAT IN THE NOVA, motor running. Thoughts racing. She breathed deeply, feeling calm—and common sense—ease firmly back in to place.

Whatever similarities she saw between King's suicide and The Three Queens investigation were coincidences. After all, how many times did the family members of perps swear up and down their loved one could *never* do what they very clearly had done?

Nine times out of ten. At least.

And how often did she hear testimony about recent changes to a perp's demeanor or personality? A lot, for sure.

Natalie King rubbed her the wrong way. So, what? She wasn't the first person to do that, she wouldn't be the last. Hell, she was Mad Dog Dare. *Most* people rubbed her the wrong way. That's what made her the crabby, skull-crusher she was.

Micki took in, then released, another series of long, deep breaths. Just like she'd said to Carmine, Hank's package had dredged up the past—and all the helplessness and hurt of Hank's death.

She thrummed her fingers on the steering wheel. Dr. Rene Blackwood had not somehow magically transformed herself into a completely different person. Of course, she hadn't.

She retrieved her cell, called Zach. "Hey, where are you?"

"Still at Central Evidence," he said, sounding frustrated. "They misplaced the watch. I'm going to wait around a little longer. How's our report coming?"

Amusement colored his tone. Usually she would play along, but Carmine's advice rang in her ears. "I had to run up to headquarters, but am returning now. When you get back, we need to talk."

"What's up?"

"Something my old partner, Carmine, said." He didn't like being put off, obvious by his long silence. "It's about an old case."

"The one you mentioned earlier today? The Three Queens?"

Of course he would guess it, right off. "Yeah, it's about that case." Another call beeped through. "I've got a call coming in. I'll see you back at the Eighth." Micki clicked through. "This is Dare."

"I can't believe you're letting her get away with it."

"Who is this?"

"Mercedes King. Porsche is here with me. Chief Howard called. Suicide? Really?"

"The pathologist's report—"

"I don't give a damn *what* that idiot says. She killed him!"

Micki heard Porsche murmur something. Probably admonishing her sister to calm down. Clearly, that wasn't going to happen.

"Ms. King, there's nothing to even suggest your stepmother—"

"Don't call her that. She was his wife. That's it."

"The coroner classified your father's death a suicide based on the pathology report. We've uncovered nothing to contradict their conclusions. If new evidence emerges, the coroner can reclassify. I'll stay on it, I promise you that."

"What about the five-million-dollar life insurance policy she took out on him? She may have had a prenup, but she's profiting big time from his death."

Micki felt the words like an electric spark. "She took out a policy on your father? When? Nothing came up in our search."

"It was taken out through the corporation and she's the sole beneficiary. I found out this morning."

"When was the policy taken out?"

"It activated the day they got married."

"A year ago?"

"That's right. Proof she's been planning this from the beginning."

In the mind of an angry, grief stricken daughter, but hardly a smoking gun. "Who authorized the purchase of the policy?"

For a long moment the other woman was silent. "My father authorized it, but that's only because—"

"Ms. King, I would love to help you, but I need something to work with."

"We're talking about five million dollars! That's something!" Again, Micki heard what sounded like Porsche trying to calm her sister.

"It *is* a lot of money," Micki said, "no doubt about it. And if you told me *she* took a policy out on his life a week or a month ago, yeah, I'd bring her in right now. But your father authorized his corporation to buy the policy the day they married. Sounds like a wedding present to me."

"You have to do something. You're the police, for God's sake! It's your job."

Micki counted silently to ten before replying. "I know what my job is, Ms. King. I'm a sworn officer of the New Orleans Police Department. I made an oath to protect and serve the people of this city and uphold the law. Without evidence suggesting otherwise, I have to accept that your father's death was a suicide. I'm sorry."

"She's moving out. Natalie is moving out."

"When?"

"I don't know. The bellman told me a representative from a moving company met with her this morning. Don't you find that suspicious?"

"If my husband jumped from the balcony of our home—"

"He didn't jump. She drove him to it!"

"—I'd probably move out, too. I'm sorry, Ms. King, but—"

"She got in his head, Detective. Somehow, she got in his head and made him do it!"

CHAPTER SEVENTEEN

2:45 P.M.

MICKI DROVE AIMLESSLY, THE RUMBLE of the Nova's powerful engine a backdrop for Mercedes King's words, ringing in her head.

"Somehow she got into his head and made him do it!"

Just like Rene Blackwood had gotten into her patients' heads and made them "do it."

Micki flexed her fingers on the steering wheel. But Natalie King wasn't Rene Blackwood. She had to remember that.

This case was, essentially, closed. It had been ruled a suicide; it was time to move on. No one, from the Chief on down, would support her spending one more minute on it.

"She's moving out."

Who could blame the woman? Her husband had taken a swan dive off a twenty-first floor balcony, his children despised her and were determined to make her life a living hell. What reason did she have to stay?

But once she left, she was gone. Out of reach.

The same as Rene Blackwood had been.

Micki shook her head. Not necessarily. Natalie King had no reason to leave the country.

Unless she was hiding something. Unless she had—somehow—helped her husband over the balcony.

Hank's advice sounded in her head. The medal warmed.

"Trust your instincts, girl."

Micki rolled to a stop at the traffic light. Up ahead she saw the jewel that was 2 River Tower and Hotel. It rose above the cluster of other buildings, seeming to beckon her.

Maybe she hadn't been driving aimlessly, after all. Maybe she should take one last crack at Natalie King.

Bounce it off Zach, she thought. If he bought into the idea, she'd do it. Maybe he'd even want in?

The light changed. She simultaneously inched forward and dialed Zach. It rang several times, then went to voicemail. "Hey, partner, just talked to Mercedes King. She told me the widow King is moving out. I'm thinking of taking one last crack at her. Just because. Call me back."

Micki ended the call and waited. She circled the blocks on either side of the hotel complex. Five minutes became ten. Then fifteen. Screw it, she decided. What would one quick visit with the woman cost her?

CHAPTER EIGHTEEN

3:05 P.M.

ZACH GAZED AT THE ROLEX, lying on the table in front of him.
It hadn't been misplaced, simply moved for pick-up by the family.

His hands were gloved. They still tingled from handling
the timepiece. His ears felt hot and his lips numb.

No chaotic energy had clung to it. No jumbled thoughts or
panic, no sounds at all.

Only the image of the dark-haired woman.

Smiling almost slyly, motioning him to follow her. That
smile had promised secrets shared, and he'd felt psychically
drawn to her. No, more than that, drawn *into* her.

The feeling had been bizarre, at once intimate and abhor-
rent. And he'd jerked his hand away.

Who was she? And what did she want from him?

He had to try again.

Zach reached out, floated his hand over the watch, then
lowered it until he curved his fingers around the gold case.
Nothing. No heat, no tingle. As if it had never existed—or
he was just an ordinary human being without any extraordi-
nary abilities.

He closed his eyes, cleared his mind, forcibly opening the
psychic channel.

I know you're there, he silently called. Come out so we can play.

He waited a moment. When nothing happened, he tried
again. *You want to play with me, don't you?*

With an audible crackle, energy gathered, then exploded

in his palm and raced up his arm. And there she was, the amber-eyed woman, motioning to him to come closer.

With his mind, he did, picturing himself walking toward her, taking her outstretched hand. As he did, the woman transformed. Mick was the seductress now. Mick from that night at the bar, her mouth hungry under his.

Once he steeled himself against that memory, another took over. Mick transformed into the woman from the other day, trembling in his arms. Open and totally vulnerable.

Her mouth clinging to his.

He felt her inhibitions fall away—and with them, all the reasons they shouldn't be together.

She didn't want to play it smart.

And neither did he.

Give yourself to me, Zach.

You want to . . . you know you do . . .

"Detective Harris?"

He opened his hand and sprang away from the table. He pulled himself together and glanced over his shoulder. "Yes?" he managed, voice thick, the word slurred slightly.

"Sorry to startle you, Detective. I wondered if you were going to be much longer. Mr. King's widow is here to collect his things."

"I'm done," he said, sliding the timepiece back into the bag, hoping the officer didn't notice the way his hand shook. "Thank you."

CHAPTER NINETEEN

3:35 P.M.

DESPITE THOMAS KING'S GRUESOME DEATH, 2 River Tower and Hotel had opened on schedule, not delayed by even one day. Thomas King, his board of directors had announced, would have wanted it that way. Judging by the number of people coming and going, the grisly publicity hadn't hurt business.

Micki sat on a bench with a clear view of both the building's entrance and the Tower attendant's desk. She'd been waiting forty-five minutes and wasn't giving up. Not yet anyway. This could be the only opportunity she got.

While she waited, the blue sky had become gray, then turned black. Rain had been in the forecast, coming ahead of a cold front, but Micki had hoped they were wrong.

They hadn't been, she acknowledged, wishing for rain gear as the skies opened up and the rain came down in sheets.

That's the moment Natalie King swept in, looking ridiculously glamorous in a shimmery, hooded raincoat.

At the sight of the woman, a sensation like cockroaches scurrying across a tile floor slid up her spine.

It wasn't the only time in her life she'd felt this way. At most of the others, however, she'd been much younger and way more vulnerable.

Micki stood. *I'm on to you, Natalie King.*

As if the woman had heard her thoughts, she looked directly at her. And smiled.

"Game on," the smile seemed to say.

Micki crossed to her. "Hello, Mrs. King."

"Detective Dare. This is a surprise."

"I was hoping we could chat a moment."

"Chat? That sounds fun. Like a couple of girlfriends getting together. Come on up."

They stepped onto the elevator. Natalie used her key card to access to the twenty-first floor. They didn't speak again until they were in the luxurious apartment.

Natalie slipped off her raincoat and laid it over the back of the couch, seemingly unconcerned about the wet coat on the velvet. She was a vision in a black jumpsuit cinched at the waist with a wide, red patent leather belt.

"I just saw your partner."

"Did you?"

"I was retrieving Thom's effects."

Natalie King positively glowed. Maybe losing the "love of your life," old fart husband had the same effect as a spa day? Who knew?

"Not much in there." She slid a manila envelope from her bag and tossed it to Micki. "Take a look if you like."

"No thanks." She tossed it back.

The woman caught it neatly and dropped it onto the coffee table. "Glass of wine? I have a fabulous French rosé."

"I'm working."

The widow cocked a perfectly shaped eyebrow. "Surely not? If so, you wouldn't be here "chatting" with me."

She crossed to the kitchen and the wine cooler, a sleek affair that matched the slick gray cabinets. She selected a bottle, then fetched two glasses.

"You're handling your grief very well."

"Why, thank you. You're so sweet."

Giddy, Micki thought. On top of the world—and completely in control of it.

The image of Rene Blackwood, her dark eyes devoid of emotion as she discussed her patients' psychotic breaks, popped into her mind.

"You seem so familiar to me," Micki said. "We must have met before the other night."

"Impossible. I'm not from around here."

"Where are you from, Natalie?" she asked.

"I spent a good bit of my youth in Trinidad. My father was in the oil industry." She handed Micki a glass. "What about you?"

"Mobile."

"Alabama?"

Micki set aside the wine. "You sound surprised."

"There's nothing soft about you."

"And you seem older than twenty-six."

"I've been told that before." She sipped her wine, made a sound of appreciation. "It's one of the things Thom loved about me."

"Makes sense. That face and body without the silliness of youth."

"The total package." She winked. "A dream come true."

"Or a fantasy come to life," Micki murmured.

"I like that even better." She held her glass up in a mock toast, then took a swallow of the wine. "To Thom."

"You're enjoying this, aren't you?"

"Enjoying what, Detective? Certainly not poor Thom's death. That would make me a . . . monster." She carried her wine to the wall of windows and gazed out at the sweeping view. "So wet, so dreary. I hate this time of year."

"Where are you planning to go? Someplace sunny, I presume."

Natalie looked over her shoulder at Micki. "Mercedes called you, didn't she?" She smiled and brought the glass to her lips, but didn't sip. "Or was it Porsche?"

"Mercedes."

"And so you raced right over, like the dedicated civil servant you are."

She left the window for the couch and sat on one end, curving her legs under her. She set her glass on the coffee table and scooped up the manila envelope.

She opened it and peered inside. "As I said, not much here. His wallet." She drew it out. "His wedding ring." She held the gold band up to the light, then tucked it into her pocket. "Such a lovely memento of our time together."

A chill raced up Micki's spine. Not a memento, a trophy.

"How many others do you have?"

"Wedding bands?"

"Trophies."

Something changed in her eyes. A flicker. Like a ripple in a dark pool.

Micki's mouth went dry. She had seen eyes like that before.

The truth of that would have knocked her to her knees if not for her steel will. She held tightly to it, grateful the woman had turned her attention back to the envelope.

"Ahh," she went on, retrieving the Rolex, "his watch, the thing that drew him back up here that night."

"I thought you didn't know what he came up for?"

"You and your yummy partner told me, remember?"

Then Micki realized that the widow King was enjoying playing with her. Like a cat, toying with a terrified mouse for a moment before it tore it apart.

But she was no scared, little mouse. She hadn't been in a very long time.

"You enjoy playing with people's minds, don't you?"

"Head games. Yes, very much."

"And do you always come out on top, Mrs. King?"

She smiled serenely. "Of course I do. Silly detective."

"You're so confident. To a fault, I think."

"Actually, I've earned it." Natalie King reached for her wine. "I'm gifted in that area."

"What area would that be? Fucking with people's heads?"

"Your description, not mine." She held up her glass in a second toast. "*Laissez Les Bon Temps Rouler.* Let the good times roll, Detective Dare."

Micki cocked her head. "Which are you? A narcissist or a sociopath?"

The woman laughed lightly and tapped her chin with her flawlessly manicured finger. "Let's see, the narcissist believes the whole world revolves around them and the sociopath will do whatever it takes to get what they want. Do I really have to choose?"

Evil, Micki realized, suppressing a shudder. Natalie King was pure evil.

Micki narrowed her eyes, motioned toward the watch. "Tell me about the Rolex."

"It was his wedding gift from me. I had it engraved on the back." She turned it over and read the inscription. "Our love. A dream come true."

Her exact words from a moment ago. Young, beautiful, and composed beyond her years, this woman had been Thomas King's dream come true.

"Another memento?" Micki asked.

"Oh no. I'll have it cleaned and sell it." She carelessly dropped it on the stone table top.

She was as much as telling her she was guilty, baiting her with the truth—and her inability to do a thing about it.

Time to strike back. "Has the insurance paid out yet?" There it was again, that liquid shift in her irises. "Five million dollars," Micki went on. "That's quite a payday."

"Yes, it is. I'm very thankful for Thom's generosity."

"I'll bet."

"You have something to say to me, Detective Dare?"

Go for broke, Micki decided. Lay all her cards on the table. "I met a friend of yours."

Those eyebrows lifted slightly. "A friend of mine? Really?"

"Mmm, a shrink. Her name's Rene Blackwood."

Micki waited, praying she took the bait. A moment later, she did.

"A talented therapist can be a woman's best friend, don't you think?"

"I try to stay away from them."

"Don't want someone poking around in that head of yours, do you? Wouldn't want someone to know all your secrets?"

"I think you're the one with secrets, Natalie. How'd you do it? Hypnosis?"

"Do what?" She drained her wine and stood to go for a refill.

"Get your husband to leap off the balcony."

The widow laughed, the sound bright, like the tinkle of wind chimes. "You're delusional, Detective. Thom committed suicide. Everyone knows that now."

"Thom wasn't the first person in your life to kill themselves, I'm certain of that. How many others have there been?"

Natalie poured herself another rosé. She looked at Micki over the rim of the glass. "We have many things in common, you and I."

"I doubt that."

"Oh, but we do. We're both confident in our abilities and will fight for what we want. And we've both suffered terrible losses. Me, my beloved Thomas and you, your beloved friend and mentor. What was his name?"

She was talking about Hank. The breath lodged in Micki's chest. How could she know about their relationship and how she'd lost him?

King pinned her with her malevolent gaze. "That's right, his name was Hank."

The blood rushed to Micki's head, and with it, a tidal wave of grief. She trembled with the force of it. She couldn't think, let alone speak.

"It hurts to lose the one you love most in the world, doesn't it? I'm sure you wouldn't want to experience that kind of pain again."

Mick curled her hands into fists. She pictured her gun, the shoulder holster nestled against her side. "Are you threatening me?"

The same thing she'd said to Blackwood. The same panic in the pit of her gut.

"What do you think?"

Micki saw herself reaching for the gun, curving her hand snugly around the grip, pointing and firing. She saw the woman's look of surprise, then disbelief. Then that beautiful face . . . exploding.

Get out, girl.

Now.

Micki reacted automatically to the voice in her head, turning, striding toward the door. She yanked it open and stepped out into the hall.

King followed her. "Thank you for stopping by, Detective. This was fun. So much fun, in fact, I don't think I'm ready for it to end."

King stopped in the doorway and she called after her, her tone amused. "Give my regards to your friends in your special little club. Tell them their secrets are not safe either."

She knew about Lightkeepers, Micki realized. Zach. Eli and the professor. Angel. Arianna. Which meant one of two things. She was one of them. Or she was a Dark Bearer.

The truth of that took her breath. It changed what was—and wasn't—possible. Micki lost her balance, stumbled, her hand going to the wall to steady herself.

Instead, she sagged against it.

Her heart pounded, as if she had just run a mile, flat-out. Her legs felt weak. Shaky. That day six years ago came thundering back. Everything—the sound of Hank's voice on the phone, how she had wondered if something was wrong. Realizing Blackwood was gone, that she had slipped through their fingers. The message Blackwood had left for her:

Better luck next time, Detective.

Finding Hank dead. The collapse of her world. How she had been certain Blackwood had gotten to him. Certain, anyway, until sanity sank in.

Hank had suffered a heart attack. Sudden and fatal. The only link between his death and Rene Blackwood was one of timing.

And she'd bought in to all that logic—until now.

Now, she knew Blackwood had killed Hank. And crazy or not, Blackwood and King were the same person.

How did she prove it?

The fury from minutes ago returned, full force, untempered by grief. Making her strong. And fearless.

This woman had killed Hank. She had orchestrated her own husband's death, and was now a threat to anyone Micki loved. She wasn't going to let her get away with it.

She flew back to King's apartment and pounded on the door.

"Open up, bitch! Or I'm going to kick this fucking door down!"

Natalie King opened the door. Her expression was expectant and pleased, as if she had been waiting at the door, expecting Micki back.

"I know who you are," Micki said. "And I know what you did."

"Is that so?"

King's subtle amusement made her blood boil. "You killed Hank."

"What if I did? How are you going to prove it?"

"I don't know, but I will. And I'm going to make you pay."

As Micki moved to take a step back; the woman grabbed her wrists, her fingers clamping around them like vices. She jerked her forward, across the threshold and into the apartment. "You have no idea what you've done," King hissed. "Or who you're messing with."

"Let me go, bitch. Now."

Instead, she pulled her closer. Her touch was cold. As if ice rather than blood ran through her veins.

"Who do you love most in the world, Michaela Dare?"

Almost exactly what Blackwood had said to her. And then Hank had been gone.

No. Not again.

Cold emanated from the woman's hands, crawling up her arms. The cold—like tentacles—circling, digging, creeping toward her bones, organs, the very center of her being. Soon they would reach her heart.

And it would stop.

And she would fall.

Is this what had happened to Hank? Is this how she'd killed him?

King's gaze had turned almost black. Micki tried to look away, but couldn't.

"Who would it hurt most to live without?" she asked.

Zach . . . Angel . . . Eli . . .

Micki sensed her glee. The white hot anger from moments before turned to icy cold terror.

More names, more faces.

Jacqui . . . Alexander . . . Professor Truebell . . .

She could target any one of them. Or all of them. A sound of horror rose up from the depths of her being. What had she done?

Micki told herself to fight—Natalie King and the cold. To fight the fear that held her frozen.

She thought of her friend and mentor, how much she'd loved him.

Hank, help me. . . .

Warmth rushed up from the vicinity of her heart, like a spark, growing and blossoming, doing battle with the cold, beating it back.

King's eyes widened in surprise. "You should be more careful with your secrets," she hissed. "You never know who might use them against you."

Then, as suddenly as she had grabbed her, she let go. Micki stumbled backward, into the hall. The door slammed shut.

From the other side came the sound of Natalie King's laughter.

CHAPTER TWENTY

4:40 P.M.

B Y THE TIME MICKI REACHED the Nova, she was soaking wet. She unlocked the car and climbed in, grabbing the blanket she kept for emergencies from the back seat.

She wrapped it around herself, shivering uncontrollably.

"You have no idea what you've done."

Micki brought her hands to her face. How could she have been so stupid? She should have left it alone. Moved on. This case, today. And the other case, back then.

Hank was dead because of her. She'd pushed Blackwood—and she'd paid the ultimate price.

"Who do you love most in the world, Michaela Dare?"

Who would it be this time? Who had jumped into her head first? Who second? A sob rose in her throat. She had to warn them.

Her phone went off. She found the device, checked the display. Zach. Again.

Zach. He'd been the first she thought of. She had to warn him. She went to answer, but missed him. She had hesitated too long.

She started to call back, then stopped. Calling would lead to questions, ones she wasn't ready to answer. Ones she wasn't sure she knew the answers to.

She decided to text instead.

Hey. I'm working out some stuff. Personal stuff. If you hear from Natalie King, don't talk to her. And whatever you do, don't meet with her. I'll tell you everything soon.

She reached to set her phone on the dash and her sleeve hiked up, revealing an angry red mark curving around her wrist. She looked closer. Not a bruise. She drew her eyebrows together. A burn.

She checked her other wrist. It, too, was red and felt numb and tingly.

It hadn't been her imagination or purely psychological. She imagined those icy tentacles reaching her heart. Her blood slowing. Her heart stopping.

Micki moaned. Hank's heart attack. Her fault. Her fault. Her best friend had died because of her.

She brought her right hand to her chest, to Hank's medal. Her eyes brimmed with tears she didn't allow to spill over.

I'm so sorry . . . forgive me . . .

Her hand warmed. The tingling in her wrists ebbed, then subsided altogether. She looked.

The red mark was gone.

Had she imagined it? No. But now, she had no proof. Not even to reassure herself she wasn't crazy.

Just like Hank. No marks. No bruises. Just stone cold dead.

Calm down, girl. Take a deep breath.

She responded to the voice in her head. A voice she recognized. Deep and kind.

Hank. It was Hank's voice.

She followed his instructions, breathing in and out. Again and again, in a soothing rhythm.

Figure it out. You're Mad Dog Dare. You can do this.

Calm began to overtake panic, reason to obliterate terror. She could do this. Last time she didn't know what was coming, didn't know who—or what—she was up against. But this time she did.

And this time she had friends to help her.

Eli. Professor Truebell. Parker.

And Zach. She squeezed her eyes shut. Not him. She couldn't lose him, too.

"You should be more careful with your secrets. You never know who might use them against you."

Her secrets. What did King mean? Her thoughts. Her fears. Her desires?

Who she loved?

Figure it out, she told herself again, fighting back a whimper. What secrets did she mean to exploit? And how could she use them against her?

Eli would know what to do. He and Professor Truebell would know what kind of monster she had unleashed.

She grabbed her cell, called up Eli's number. The call went straight to voicemail, and she wished she could communicate with him telepathically, the way he did her.

"Eli, it's me." She heard the edge of desperation in her voice and knew he would, too. "It's important. Call me back as soon as you can. I think I've done something . . . I'm not sure how bad it might be. I need your opinion. The professor's too. Call me."

CHAPTER TWENTY-ONE

7:20 P.M.

ANGEL SQUEEZED HER EYES SHUT, her heart thundering. The time was up but she was afraid to look. She knew in her heart what the answer was going to be, but a fervent, three-word prayer played over and over in her head anyway:

Please, God, no . . . Please, God, no . . .

She took a deep breath and opened her eyes.

A single, vivid blue line stared back at her.

The stick slipped from her fingers and clattered into the sink. She sank to the floor and brought her knees to her chest.

She was pregnant. At least three months along.

How could she have been so stupid? So irresponsible?

What did she do now?

The possibility she was pregnant had occurred to her only yesterday. She'd never had regular cycles, and had blamed her recent queasiness and lack of appetite on heartbreak. Then, yesterday, she hadn't been able to comfortably button her jeans. She hadn't been eating enough to gain weight; indeed, all her other clothes were too big.

So she'd started trying on other garments. All too big. Except for the waist. Then she'd realized her breasts were sore. The way they got before her period. The period that hadn't come.

Angel rested her forehead on her drawn-up knees. A sob came from what seemed like the center of her being.

Seth, she silently cried out, where are you? When are you coming back? You promised!

He wasn't coming back.

No. She shook her head against the thought. She wouldn't believe that. They loved each other.

Then, where was he?

She had risked her life for him. And he had deserted her. And now she was alone. And pregnant.

She imagined Micki's response.

"I told you he was no good."

"I warned you he would break your heart."

What was she going to do? A ragged cry spilled past her lips. That first sob led to another and another, and she curled into a tight ball on the cold, unforgiving tile floor. She cried until she was totally spent, until the harsh light of afternoon became the chill gray of evening.

Finally, stomach cramping from hunger, Angel pulled herself up. She gazed defiantly at her own pale reflection, wiping the tears from her cheeks.

Seth was coming back. He would collect her and their baby, and they would go somewhere safe. They would be a family.

Micki was wrong about him. There was a perfectly logical reason he hadn't come for her. He'd been hurt, escaping that day. Or he was being held somewhere against his will. Maybe he had amnesia.

Or he was dead.

Angel swallowed hard and shook her head. No. Wouldn't her dreams have told her? Wouldn't she have awakened compelled to draw what she dreamt?

But her dreams had been weirdly silent. They hadn't even revealed her pregnancy.

Maybe that part of her died with Seth?

She shook her head. She couldn't go on if he was dead.

But she'd have to. Because of the baby. *Their* baby.

She brought a hand to her belly, splayed it over the small swell. She turned sideways and squinted at herself in the mirror. She was definitely starting to show. Seth would know, if he was here. But nobody else would, not yet anyway.

Angel frowned. What was one supposed to do when pregnant? No drugging, drinking, or smoking, but she didn't do any of that anyway. Besides eating right, she seemed to remember something about special vitamins.

Her stomach growled at the thought of food and she headed for the kitchen. But what else was she supposed to do? Go to the doctor, she supposed. Have him check, make certain everything was all right.

She made a peanut butter sandwich and poured herself a big glass of milk. The sandwich made her think of Micki.

She'd been a good friend. She'd given her a home, believed in her art before anyone else, and had encouraged her to enroll at the University of New Orleans. She'd literally saved her life. Twice.

Angel took a big bite of the sandwich. The peanut butter taste filled her mouth and she realized how hungry she was. She gobbled down the whole sandwich, taking gulps of milk in between, then made herself another.

Micki deserved the truth. She'd be disappointed for her—but mostly worried. But wasn't that what family did? Worry about each other? Because they cared?

Micki was her family now. So was Zach. And Eli and the professor. Family stuck together. And they didn't keep secrets.

CHAPTER TWENTY-TWO

9:40 P.M.

ZACH COULDN'T SIT STILL. HE'D tried TV, then a book. Nothing took his mind off the questions he'd been asking himself since this morning.

Who was the amber-eyed woman? What part had she played in Thomas King's life—and death? What did she want from him?

And most pressing, why had she transformed into Mick?

The energy he picked up from crime scenes—and the images that energy manifested—were of the past, not the future. Static, not interactive.

The only exception had been the Dark Bearer's energy. It had been angry and aggressive; it would have killed him, if it could have. Which, even so, was much different than this sensual invitation.

As if the energy had become a manifestation of his own thoughts and desires.

He glanced at his phone, re-reading Mick's text message.

I'm working out some stuff. Personal stuff.

The letter from Hank? Probably. He understood that. But the last part of the text, about Natalie King. That, he didn't understand.

If you hear from Natalie King, don't talk to her. And whatever you do, don't meet with her.

The knock on the door wasn't totally unexpected, although it was late. Mick, no doubt. Come to make good on her promise to fill him in.

He opened the door, her name dying on his lips.

"Hello, son."

"Arianna. This is a surprise." He saw the flicker of hurt at his use of her given name, same as he always did. And same as always, he felt a pinch of guilt over it.

He stepped aside. "C'mon in."

"You were expecting Micki?"

"No, not expecting her. I just thought . . . we had a couple things to discuss."

"Are you two seeing each other?"

"No. Of course not." He shut the door. "Why would you think that?"

"I thought I picked up those vibes. I'm sorry if I . . . overstepped."

"You didn't." Zach jammed his hands in the front pockets of his jeans. "What's up?"

A small frown formed between her eyebrows. "I never heard back from you, so I took the chance and came by. I hope that's okay?"

"Sure. That's fine, of course. Sorry about the call. I got busy with the case and— Actually, I forgot."

"That happens. You've got a lot going on."

They stood that way a moment, just inside the door, awkwardly gazing at one another.

She cleared her throat. "Do you mind . . . could we sit? I wanted to talk to you about something."

"Sure. Sorry."

He led her to the living room and motioned the couch. "Can I get you anything? Coffee? Soft drink?"

"No, thanks. I'm good right now."

Zach shifted from one foot to the other. "How about a glass of water?"

"I'm fine, thanks."

They both sat. This time it was Zach who cleared his throat. "So, what did you want to talk about?"

She looked down at her folded hands, then back up at him. "Parker's offered me a job."

Her brother, his uncle and boss at the FBI. He frowned. "What kind of a job?"

"Training recruits."

"Sixers?"

"Yes." She refolded her hands. "He feels my experience uniquely qualifies me for it."

"Where? Not at Quantico?"

"No. Another facility."

"But not here?"

"No."

"I see."

"Do you?"

He got to his feet, suddenly angry. "Do what you need to do. You don't need to ask my permission."

"I wasn't. I thought we could discuss it."

"Why? What's the point? It sounds like a good gig."

"It would be," she said stiffly. "How do you feel about the idea?"

"I don't see why it should matter how I feel about it. We hardly know each other."

The words, their tone, were overly harsh. He saw her wince and wished he could soften them. But not take them back. Because they were true.

"All right, you want to know how I feel? I'm pissed off. You show up after thirty years, hang around a few months, then take off again. That's what I see."

"I'm not abandoning you."

"Sure as hell feels like it."

She tipped her hands, palms up. "There's nothing for me here."

"I got it. Go, take the job."

"That's not what I—" She pressed her lips together. "There's this distance between us—"

He cut her off. "You think?"

"Son—"

"Calling me that sounds like a lie."

"Is that why you don't call me mom?"

"I don't call you mom because you haven't earned it." She blanched, but he didn't back down. "I have a mother. She was there for me every day. When I was sick or skinned my knee. She was there at every game and every parent-teacher meeting. She held me accountable when I screwed up, which I did a lot. And through it all, she loved me."

"I loved you, too. Every minute of that time."

"Then where were you? Why did you give me away?"

"I told you, for your own safety. The High Council—"

"You know what? That all sounds like bullshit to me."

"I'm sorry about that, Zach. I'm sorry I hurt you. But I'd do it again to save you. Maybe one day you'll see that." She stood and started for the door.

Zach watched her go, the knot in his chest crippling. He felt like the hurt five-year-old kid whose best friend had just informed him, in the brutal way of childhood, of what "adopted" meant.

Your real mother didn't want you.

He felt like the determined eight-year-old who had wondered what he'd done wrong, and worked at being the best at everything, so when she came back, she would want him. And he felt like the angry teenager who wondered why he was so different and if she was, too.

And, Zach realized, he sounded like those boys just now. Young and petulant.

But he was no longer a boy, he was a man. He needed to act like one. "Arianna, wait."

She stopped, looked back, expression hopeful.

"Stay." He forced the word out; he didn't like the way it made him feel, exposed and vulnerable. "Please stay."

As the words passed his lips, the knot in his chest eased. He took a deep breath. "I'm sorry. I had no right to talk to you that way."

Her blue eyes, so like his, brimmed with tears. "Actually, you had every right."

He held out a hand. "Come on, let's talk. I feel like I don't know you at all."

They sat on the couch, each on an end, facing one another.

"What do you want to know?" she asked. "I'll tell you anything."

"I want to know the truth."

"About your dad?"

"Not about him, not now, anyway. About you. What happened to you that you could leave your newborn son with strangers."

She looked as if he'd struck her, but she nodded, head held high. "I fell in love with someone I shouldn't have. Someone who was off limits. The law forbidding Lightkeeper and human relationships had just been instituted and the council had spies everywhere."

"How old were you?"

"Almost twenty-five. He was older. I'd actually known him for a while, but one day, everything changed between us." Her expression grew faraway. "We had so much in common. Likes and dislikes, hopes and dreams. We both wanted to change the world, me through social work, he through the law.

"I had to hide it from everyone. But Parker was the hardest. We were so close." Her voice became thick. "I broke his heart."

"You told him you were pregnant."

"Yes. We had a terrible fight. He was scared for me. Disappointed. Angry and hurt."

"And he disowned you."

"He had to. If the High Council found out, I would be punished, excommunicated. Most probably imprisoned. If he'd sheltered me, the same would be done to him." She paused, took a breath. "That you would be taken away from me was a given, and I wasn't about to let that happen."

Zach curved his hands into tight fists. "I'll never understand that."

"As far as the High Council was concerned, I'd not only broken the law, I'd betrayed my race."

He frowned. "Betrayed your race? You were in love. Love's never wrong."

"No, Zach." She looked him dead in the eyes. "I went in with my eyes wide open. I knew what being with your father would cost me."

"And what did it cost you?"

"I was no longer fully Lightkeeper."

"I don't understand."

"My love affair with your father cost me some of my light force. Once it's gone, it's gone forever."

"That's . . . nuts. Love can't be a sin." His voice came out thick. "I refuse to believe that."

"Lightkeepers were sent to earth to stand with and work alongside humans, not to mate with them. Not to create a new race."

"And then, after all you sacrificed for him, he left you."

"No, I left him." She covered one of his clenched hands with her own. "Think about it. I'd not only put myself in danger, but my friends and family as well. My unborn child. I had to leave everyone behind."

She squeezed his hand, then released it. "I had a friend from Tulane who lived on the west coast. She offered me a place to live. I left without telling anyone where I was going."

Zach digested the information, struggling to come to terms with it. "You say you weren't about to let me be taken away from you. But then you just . . . gave me away."

Her eyes flooded with tears, the moisture turning them a brilliant sapphire. "Just? No, that word does not apply. Someone I trusted betrayed me. I thought she was my friend, but she was aligned with the dark. You weren't safe with me any longer. It broke my heart."

He'd always thought his bio mother had taken the easy way out. But it hadn't been easy; she'd sacrificed everything for him.

"I'm so sorry, Mom." The endearment slipped from his tongue. "That I said those things. That I've been so distant."

"You had the right to feel that way." She pressed her lips together a moment, then continued, "I hope you can forgive me."

"There's nothing to forgive." He stood, crossed to her, drew her up and hugged her.

She clung to him a moment, before easing her grip. She looked up at him. "Do you want to know his name?"

His biological father. Another connection he had longed for, one always out of his reach. Funny thing was, tonight he didn't.

Zach kissed her forehead. "Someday, Mom. But for now, this is good."

CHAPTER TWENTY-THREE

Tuesday, February 13
6:55 A.M.

MICKI SAT ON A SIDE-STREET, across from Lost Angels Ministry, a Venti coffee clutched in her hands. She'd come here the evening before in the hopes she would find the professor or Eli. Neither had answered her numerous calls or texts, and she'd gone from anxious to downright panicked.

But the center, except for safety lights, had been dark. No one had answered the bell.

Which in itself caused unease. Professor Truebell had created LAM to offer help for wayward Half Lights, the products of Lightkeeper and human matings. He insisted the center be available to youth in need twenty-four-seven, three hundred and sixty-five days a year.

Something was wrong. The professor was as dependable as the sun rising and setting.

So she'd spent the night in the Nova, parked here in front of the building. Watching and waiting. Sifting through scenarios.

The first one here would be the one who had left their post.

And now she saw who it was.

"Arianna!" Micki called, stepping out of her car and hurrying across the side street.

The woman stopped and whirled around, a hand to her chest. "Micki! You about scared the life out of me."

"I see that. Sorry, I didn't mean to."

"What are you doing here so early?"

"I need to see Professor Truebell or Eli."

"I'm sorry, they're not here."

"So I gathered. When do you expect them?"

She looked uncomfortable. "Not for a couple days. They had a meeting with the High Council."

"Did Zach know about this?"

"No one did. The Council likes the element of surprise. They summon, you drop everything and go."

"Where?"

"I don't know."

"You don't know?" Micki frowned. "That's a little weird, don't you think?"

"It's that way for the council's safety. They never gather in the same place, but move from one secure location to another."

"Wow. They're not only dicks, but paranoid dicks, too."

Arianna's cheeks reddened. "The Dark One and his army of Dark Bearers are real, Micki," she said. "He'd love to wipe them all out at once."

At her fierce defense of the Council, Micki cocked an eyebrow. "I thought your allegiance was to the professor?"

She stiffened. "Of course, it is. But agree with their policies or not, the Council is the Lightkeepers' governing body. We can't take any chances."

Something about the way she said it rankled, like the "we" was exclusive. "So, no communications to them, in or out. Am I right?"

"You are. And before you ask, not even telepathic ones."

Her response confirmed why neither one had answered her calls or texts. Micki nodded. "Thanks. If you happen to hear from them, let them know I was here."

"Wait! Your pendant, where did you get it?"

Micki's hand went to it. "It was a gift from a friend. Someone very special to me." She turned to go. "Be sure to tell them I was here."

"Maybe I can help you?"

She stopped, looked back. "I don't think so." The words came out more brusquely than Micki intended, so she added, "Thanks anyway."

"You don't like me, do you?"

"I don't know you, Arianna."

"I'm Zach's mother. That should mean something."

"That's between the two of you."

"And you're the kind of person who has to form your own opinions?"

"Yeah, I am."

"And you're very protective of the people you care about." She paused. "You can trust me, Micki. The last thing I want to do is hurt him."

Arianna was perceptive, she'd give her that. "That doesn't mean you won't."

Once more, Micki turned to go, but this time Arianna caught her elbow. "What about you?" Arianna asked. "Are you going to hurt him?"

"He's my partner. I'd put my life on the line to protect his."

"Not that kind of hurt."

"I don't know what you're talking about."

"Yes, you do." She held her gaze. "You're important to him. You know that, don't you?"

Arianna was trying to mind-fuck her. Not in the way Natalie King had the night before, but in the way Zach had that one time. Holding her gaze, seeming to reach into her brain and extract the emotional truth, like it or not.

Even knowing that, Micki couldn't *not* answer. "Yes."

"And he's more than a partner to you, isn't he?"

Micki couldn't break the hold of the woman's icy blue gaze. "Yes."

"You care for him. More than you should."

"I do."

"You might even be in love with him."

"Who do you love most in the world, Michaela Dare?"

Resistance rose up in her, rushing from a place inside her she hadn't known existed until yesterday, reverberating like a silent sonic boom.

Micki leapt away from her. "Who are you?"

"You know who I am."

"No." She shook her head and took another step back. "Have you done something with Professor Truebell? With Eli? Have you hurt them?"

"Micki, what are you . . . that's crazy. Of course not."

The woman looked shocked. And concerned. What if she was wrong, Micki wondered?

What if she wasn't?

Her head pounded. "Why'd you do that? Why'd you get inside my head like that?"

"I shouldn't have! I'm sorry."

"Drop the bullshit! Why'd you do it?"

The woman clasped her hands together. "Because I . . . I think Zach's in love with you and I wanted to know how you felt about him. That's all, I promise."

Her gaze dropped to Micki's hand, hovering over her holstered weapon. "Please don't shoot me."

Micki realized what she was doing and dropped her hand. She took another step back. If this was Arianna, her own behavior would be not only bizarre, but downright dangerous. And if this wasn't Arianna?

She should shoot her dead and face the consequences.

"Tell me what's going on, Micki. Why did you need to talk to Eli or the professor? Are you all right?"

Micki gazed at her, stomach going sour. No, she wasn't all right. Not at all.

This time, when she turned to walk away, Arianna didn't try to stop her.

CHAPTER TWENTY-FOUR

7:45 A.M.

THE NOVA'S ENGINE ROARED TO life. Micki found the deep rumble oddly reassuring. The way Hank's deep voice reassured. Familiar. And comforting.

Hank's voice. Twice now she'd heard it in her head. Both times warning her to move away from where her thoughts were taking her. Both times had been since she'd started wearing Hank's medal.

Or had his voice always been there? Could it be the medal only made her more aware of it?

What was happening to her? She'd imagined shooting Natalie King. She'd almost pulled her gun on Arianna. She'd accused the woman of doing something egregious to Eli and the professor.

Micki curled her fingers around the mahogany steering wheel, the wood warm from the sun. Eli and Professor Truebell weren't going to be able to help her, not right now anyway. She thought of Zach and Angel, the things Natalie King said. They were in danger, but she didn't know how to protect them.

She had to find a way. She couldn't lose them. It would kill her.

Her cell phone went off, startling her. She grabbed it. "Detective Dare."

"Detective, it's Cyndi Stevens. Sarah's sister."

It took Micki a moment to make the connection. Sarah, who committed suicide. Her grieving sibling.

"Yes, Cyndi," she said, her own voice sounding unfamiliar to her ears. Tinny and breathless. "How can I help you?"

"You told me I could call if . . . anytime to check . . ."

Her words trailed painfully off. "Of course," Micki said. "Unfortunately, as of this moment, I don't have anything new to share."

"It's his fault she's dead, Detective. You have to prove it!"

Micki thought of Mercedes' call, of the bizarre similarities between the two situations. "I understand your feelings, I do. But unless we find physical evidence that links Keith Gerard to your sister's death, our hands are tied."

"Are you even looking?" Her voice rose slightly. "I'm sorry, I'm just so . . . Sarah was my only family and my best friend."

Her voice cracked on the last, and Micki's heart went out to her. "It's okay. You're upset. I get it."

"Cyndi thought he was cheating on her. With someone from the ad agency."

"People do that sometimes, Ms. Stevens—"

"She was there, the night Sarah did it."

"Who was there?" Micki asked.

"The woman he was cheating with. A neighbor saw her."

Micki sat up straighter. "This is new information."

"I just learned it myself. I'm here with her neighbor now."

"Stay put," Micki said. "I'm on my way."

⚜ ⚜ ⚜

Cyndi Stevens was a waif-like woman, made more so, it seemed, by grief. She sat on the front steps of the fourplex, another woman beside her, arm around her shoulders.

They both stood as Micki climbed out of the car and started up the walk. One maple tree stood in the small patch of yard, and birds flitted around a feeder hung from a low branch. A large blackbird seemed intent on ruffling the others' feathers by swooping this way and that, shooing the others away, but not feeding itself.

"He's a troublemaker, that one."

Micki looked at the older woman. "Pardon?"

"The blackbird. He comes around every so often, just to stir up trouble."

She clapped her hands, and he flew to one of the upper branches and perched there, seeming to watch them.

"Detective Dare, this is Geri. She's the neighbor I told you about."

"How do," the woman said, holding out her hand. She wore a colorful housecoat and slippers; gray hair peeked out from under a pink spa turban. "Came out to feed my birds this mornin'—" she pointed to the bag of seed, "—and ran into Cyndi. I had to offer my sympathies."

"That's when she told me about seeing a woman here Thursday night."

"Yup, I saw her." She nodded and the turban bobbled. "Thursday night."

"What time was that?" Micki asked.

"'Bout eight, I think. Me and my fella had been out for a bite."

Micki made a note in her small spiral.

"How did you recognize her?"

"Didn't. Never seen her before."

Stevens jumped in. "She described her to me. It sounded like the woman, so I showed her a picture from Facebook."

She took out her phone, tapped the screen, then held it out. "That's her."

Micki studied the image a moment. "And that's the woman you saw here, Thursday night?"

"Yes, ma'am." Again, the turban bobbled.

"You're sure?"

"One hundred percent."

Stevens jumped in again. "Geri saw her leaving Sarah's apartment. Her name's Tara Green. Like I said, she works with Keith at the ad agency."

"Here's the thing," Micki said. "Even if her being here is proof Keith was cheating on Sarah, how does that support your theory that he's partly responsible for your sister's death?"

"Maybe they were working together?"

"To do what?"

"Get her to kill herself."

Micki shook her head. "But why? What would they get out of it?"

Stevens stared blankly at her. "I don't know what you mean by that."

"Gerard and your sister weren't married, so he was free. There's no insurance money, bank accounts or property to be gained. Nor kids to fight over. So why do it? And not just one person, but two? I'm sorry, it doesn't make any sense."

"Maybe they're just evil?" Steven's voice shook. "Rotten, horrible human beings who get off on hurting people? Please, Detective Dare, you have to help me!"

She started to sob. Pinned by the neighbor's accusing glare, Micki agreed. "Okay, I tell you what. I'll talk to her, see what she has to say and and get back to you."

CHAPTER TWENTY-FIVE

ANGEL HEARD MICKI MOVING AROUND the kitchen. She'd waited up as long as she could the night before, wanting to tell her about the pregnancy as soon as possible.

Instead, she'd fallen asleep, sketchpad in her lap, charcoal smeared on her fingers. Her sleep had proved fitful, her dreams populated with Seth and their baby.

And nightmares, too. Of the baby being taken—snatched from her arms in one and stolen from its crib in another.

Angel set aside her sketchpad and climbed out of bed. She still wore her sweatpants and T-shirt from the day before. She glanced in the mirror and made a face. She had a charcoal smudge between her eyes and on both cheeks.

She tiptoed to the door, cracked it open and listened, using the moments to mentally prepare herself. Now or never, she decided. She had to do it. This particular issue wasn't going anywhere—for about six months, anyway—and she certainly wasn't going to be able to hide it.

She darted into the hall and ducked into the bathroom. She took care of the necessaries, including washing her face and combing her hair, then headed to the kitchen.

"Morning," she said.

Micki looked over her shoulder at her and smiled. "Good morning, sweetie!"

Sweetie? Not quite Micki-like, but maybe she and Zach had finally done something about that thing that was always simmering between them?

Angel frowned slightly. "Are you okay?"

"Fine. Why?"

"You just seem a little . . . off. You sleep okay?"

"Great. Want some breakfast?"

"I'll get a bowl of cereal. How about you?"

"Already ate." She smiled. "A peanut butter sandwich and a glass of milk."

"Your go-to." Angel pulled out a bowl and the box of cereal. "Are you on your way out?"

"I've got a few minutes. Why?"

"I wanted to talk to you about something."

"Good, because I wanted to talk to you about something, too."

"About what?" Angel added milk to her cereal and carried it to the table.

Micki poured herself a cup of coffee, then came and sat across the table from her. "I heard you cry out last night."

"You did?" The cereal turned to ash in Angel's mouth, and she had to force herself to swallow. "What did I say?"

"You were calling for Seth."

"Oh." She set down her spoon. "That's kind of what I want to talk to you about."

"Good." Micki reached both her hands across the table. "Take my hands."

Angel hesitated. "I don't know what's going on, but you're sort of—"

"Humor me. Take them."

Feeling a bit foolish, she did. Micki grasped them and looked her in the eyes. "You need to let Seth go."

"What?"

"He's not coming back, Angel."

"You don't know that."

She went to pull her hands away, but Micki grasped them tighter. So tightly it hurt. "He would have come back by now if he was going to."

"Something could have happened to him. He could be hurt or—"

"Grow up, Angel! I hate to say this, but I have to. He doesn't love you. He never did."

Tears burned her eyes. Angel blinked furiously against them. "Why are you doing this?"

"It's for your own good. This brooding isn't healthy. It's time to move on."

Angel yanked her hands free and jumped to her feet. "You don't know anything! You don't know—"

"I know enough." Micki got to her feet, rounded the table. "I know he lied to you. Manipulated and used you. You're lucky he didn't get you pregnant."

Angel backed away from her. "Why are you being so awful?"

"What's on the inside of your thigh, Angel? You carry the mark of the beast. Because of him."

A triple six, tattooed in that sensitive spot. Against her will. And Seth had watched. And done nothing.

Angel felt sick to her stomach; the tattoo burned. Something seemed to glow in Micki's eyes. Like she was pleased with herself. Almost . . . happy. That hurt most of all.

"I can't believe I trusted you." Angel backed away from her. "I can't believe I thought of you as my family."

The contents of her stomach rushed up to her throat. Hand over her mouth, she ran toward bathroom.

Micki called after her. "You're only upset because you know I'm right. You'll thank me someday."

Never, Angel vowed, slamming the door behind her and twisting the lock. She made it to the commode just in time. Dropping to her knees, she retched until she had nothing left but tears.

CHAPTER TWENTY-SIX

11:00 A.M.

ANGEL HOPPED OFF THE STREETCAR, calling goodbye to the driver, who knew her by name. She rode his route three times a week, always alighting at the Telemachus Street stop.

She adjusted her loaded backpack and darted across Canal Street, heading for Lost Angel Ministries. Eli would know what she should do. He would understand. He always did.

Micki had left the house shortly after their argument, not even checking on her or calling out goodbye. Angel supposed that small slight shouldn't hurt, but it did. It hurt a lot.

Micki had said those things about Seth before, from the very beginning. That he couldn't be trusted, that he didn't love her and wasn't coming back.

But never that way. Almost gleefully, as if she knew how much her words were hurting Angel, but didn't care. No, worse than that. Like she was getting off on Angel's pain. And her whole "take my hands" thing had been so creepy. And condescending. Like Angel was a stupid little girl.

Angel unlatched the iron gate and stepped through, securing it again behind her. The rain of the night before had left the brick steps littered with leaves and other debris. She would sweep the porch, she thought, pressing the call-buzzer and looking up at the camera, as soon as it was dry enough.

A moment later the lock turned over and she stepped inside. It was unnaturally quiet, especially for this time of day.

"Professor!" she called. "Eli! It's me, Angel." She stopped at the foot of the stairs. "Where is everybody?"

Arianna emerged from Professor Truebell's office and came to the top of the stairs. "Hey, Angel. It's just me here today. We canceled classes."

She looked up at Arianna, battling the urge to cry. "You know when Eli's going to be back?"

"I'm not sure. It could be a couple days."

She tried to hide how devastated she was at the news. She'd really counted on Eli being here. She shrugged with forced nonchalance. "Okay. I guess I'll see you around."

"Don't go." Arianna came down the stairs. "It's really lonely around here, and it's almost lunchtime. How about I fix us something? There's leftover pizza."

Angel eyed her suspiciously. Arianna had always seemed nice enough, but she had never really talked to her. Pizza sounded good. And she had nowhere else to go.

"Sure." She dumped her backpack, followed the other woman into the kitchen and plopped onto a chair.

She tilted her head. "You and Zach look so much alike. Not the smile though. His is different."

Her expression altered slightly, and she looked quickly away. "No, not the smile."

Then Angel understood. "That's from his dad, isn't it?"

"It is."

Arianna laid half a dozen pieces of the pizza on a baking sheet and slid it into the oven. "How about a salad? I have everything we'd need."

Angel automatically started to refuse, then thought of the baby. "That'd be great."

She watched Arianna get the lettuce, tomatoes and a bag of shredded carrots out of the refrigerator. "My mom dumped me, too. But you probably know that already. Mine's never going to show back up, though."

"You don't know that for sure."

"I kind of do. It's okay. I think it's cool that you came back for Zach."

"Thank you," Arianna said, her voice sounding thick. "I appreciate that."

"I couldn't give my baby away like that. I mean, if I had one."

Arianna joined her at the table, taking the chair across from hers and looking her directly in the eyes. "Sometimes in life, you have to do things you would have never thought you could. And when you're a mom and it comes to your kids, you find this incredible strength to do whatever is necessary to keep them safe."

Angel nodded. "I get that."

"Good." She patted her hand. "How about we start with our salads?"

Angel watched as she picked through the lettuce leaves, discarding the ones that looked spent before putting them in a bowl, dropping in the chopped tomato and sprinkling shredded carrots on top.

Angel tilted her head. There was something reassuring about the woman. And comfortable. Like a mom was supposed to be.

Arianna looked over her shoulder and caught Angel studying her. She smiled. "Ranch or Caesar?"

"Ranch, please."

Arianna set the salads on the table, then went back for forks and napkins.

"Is it true you were held prisoner at a Dark Bearer prison?" Angel asked.

"Yes, it is."

Angel brought a forkful of lettuce to her mouth, frowning as she chewed. After a minute, she looked back up at Arianna. "It was one of those birthing compounds, huh?"

Arianna nodded.

"It must have been pretty awful?"

Arianna was quiet a moment, then met her eyes. "It was . . . hell on earth."

Angel swallowed hard. She didn't know what to say, so she reached over and touched the other woman's hand. "I'm sorry that happened to you."

"Thank you." She turned her hand over and gave Angel's hand a squeeze, then stood up. "How about I get us that pizza?"

Angel watched as she took it out of the oven and transferred it onto plates. She gave herself two pieces and Angel four, and they ate in silence for several minutes.

"How did you escape?" Angel asked, picking up her last slice.

"I don't actually remember." She wiped her mouth with a napkin. "I woke up in a hospital in Washington. I was found half dead at the side of the road with no memory of what happened."

Arianna pushed her plate aside. "I only remember some of my time at the compound. The doctors say there's a chance more memories will return. But it's far from a sure thing."

"Would you even want them to?"

For a long moment, Arianna was quiet, the expression in her eyes far away. "No," she said, "I don't think I do."

Angel finished off the slice. "I don't know how you got through it."

"It's that strength thing." She looked her in the eyes again. "You do what you have to do. That's what you did, right, Angel?"

The intensity of Arianna's gaze made her uncomfortable. "You know my story?"

"Some of it. I know about you going to save those kidnapped girls yourself. And I know about how you wouldn't leave your boyfriend and went back to save him from that Dark Bearer."

"Seth," she murmured, dropping a hand to her belly.

"Why did you come here today, Angel?"

"To talk to Eli."

"I know that. But why?"

Angel shrugged and looked away.

"You're pregnant, aren't you?"

Angel's eyes widened. "How did you know?"

"You forget where I've been. I recognize the signs. How far along are you?"

"Three months."

"Does Micki know?"

"No." The word came out harshly. "And I'm not telling her."

Arianna frowned slightly. "Is the baby—"

"Seth's, yes. And he's coming back for me, no matter *what* Micki says."

"Micki doesn't think he's coming back?"

"Why would she? According to her, he never loved me at all."

Arianna seemed to ponder that a moment. "What are you going to do now?"

Angel let out a ragged breath and folded her arms protectively around her middle. "I don't know."

"That's why you came here today, isn't it? For help?"

Angel nodded, tears stinging her eyes. She didn't know if it was Arianna's gentle voice or the tenderness in her eyes, but the story poured out of her. How her jeans wouldn't snap and she'd bought the test, how she meant to tell Micki, only to have her say the most hateful things to her about Seth. How she had seemed to enjoy hurting her.

"I can't live there anymore," she said. "Not after that."

"Are you absolutely sure he's coming back?"

"Yes. I know he is. I know he's good . . . our love changed him."

Arianna was quiet a long moment. "Angel," she said finally, softly, "please listen to me. Your baby is in danger."

Angel recoiled. "No . . . Seth would never—"

"Not from Seth." She paused, reached across and caught Angel's hands. "From the Dark One."

"Why?" She searched Arianna's gaze. "It's just a baby."

"Born of two who are both dark and light."

She was right, Angel realized, mouth going dry with fear. She hadn't even considered that. Seth was just Seth.

"You have a tremendous gift. I imagine Seth does as well. Everyone is going to want this baby. The bad guys and the good ones."

"No." She shook her head. "It's ours. I won't let them have it."

"They won't give you a choice." She leaned forward. "They will take it, by any means. They would even cut it from your womb and leave you to die."

Angel felt lightheaded, sick to her stomach again. Angel recalled her dreams from the night before—of her baby being yanked from her arms.

This was worse. So much worse.

"What do I do? I don't know what to do." She squeezed Arianna's hands tighter. "Will you help me?"

"Of course I will. But you have to trust me. Completely. You'll have to do whatever I say. Can you do that?"

"Yes." Angel let out a long breath and said it again, forcefully. "Yes."

"Good. First rule, we keep this a secret as long as possible. Do you understand?"

She swallowed hard. "Yes," she managed.

"From everyone. Even Eli and Professor Truebell."

"But why? They'd never—"

"Maybe not. But what if they're compromised? Think about it." She searched Angel's gaze. "What if you're carrying The Chosen One?"

CHAPTER TWENTY-SEVEN

12:15 P.M.

ZACH PARKED BEHIND THE NOVA. He was actually on the clock, but when he'd checked in at the Eighth and learned that Mick had requested a couple of personal days, he knew something was bad wrong.

She didn't answer his repeated calls, so the moment he could break away, he headed to her place. He'd stopped for her favorite coffee, and grabbing it, stepped out of the car. She came to the door wearing sweats and a wrinkled NOPD T-shirt. She looked like hell.

"Hey," he said.

"Hey."

"Are you sick?"

"No."

He frowned. "So, what's up?"

"Nothing."

He would have laughed if he wasn't so worried. "Since when aren't we partners?"

"We're partners."

"You've got a funny way of showing it. Personal days, Mick? Without telling me? What the hell?"

She indicated the Venti. "That for me?"

"Yeah."

"What is it?"

He cocked an eyebrow. "Your favorite, what else?"

"What is my favorite, Zach?"

He laughed. "You're serious? Quad Venti Latté, extra hot. No sugar, no syrups. But you don't get it until you let me come in."

She reached for the coffee and eased the door the rest of the way open with her foot. He followed her in, closing the door behind them.

"Angel here?"

"No. She was gone when I got back this morning."

"From where?"

"LAM." She crossed to the couch and sank onto it, cradling the cup.

"Lost Angel Ministries? This morning? How come?"

"To see Eli and the professor, but they're out of town. At least that's what she said."

"Who said?"

"Arianna. But I don't know if it's true."

"You think Arianna lied to you? Why would she do that?" When she didn't respond, he frowned. "What's going on, Mick? You text me a message warning me to stay away from Natalie King and that you'll explain why. Then you disappear. I'm here to collect on that explanation."

She nodded and took a swallow of the coffee, then set it aside. Zach watched as she brought her right hand to her chest and curled her fingers around Hank's medal.

She'd been doing that a lot, he realized.

"I don't think I should be talking to you," she said.

He frowned, concern growing. "Why not?"

"If I care about you or Angel . . . or anyone else—" She stopped, took in a deep breath, then released it. "You might die."

In another situation, he'd laugh, make a joke. Not this one, not today. "Die, Mick? You don't think that's just a little nuts?"

"It sounds that way, but it's not." She looked him in the eyes, dead serious. "I think she means to kill you."

He went from worried to deeply concerned. Not about his own safety, but about her state of mind. "Who might kill me?" He tipped his head. "Natalie King? That's where you're going with this, right?"

She nodded. "The way she killed Hank. Only it was my fault. Because I pushed her into it. I wouldn't let go. And now I've done it again."

He crossed to the couch and squatted down in front of her, taking her hands. The one that had been clutching her medal was warm. "Mick, look at me. Hank died six years ago. Natalie King would have been practically a teenager. Think about it."

He felt her resistance and tightened his fingers. "Getting that package from Hank, mailed on the day he died, it was a shock." He brought her hands to his mouth. "Sweetheart, you're—"

"Don't call me that. You can't care about me. And I can't— I *don't* care about you."

He was surprised how much those words, coming from her, hurt. "You're overwhelmed and exhausted," he went on. "Take a few days off, maybe make an appointment with the department shrink—"

"No. Not the shrink. She was a shrink last time. She could do it again."

"Partner, you're starting to scare me. For real."

"Good. Because she could be anyone, Zach. Even me."

CHAPTER TWENTY-EIGHT

2:40 P.M.

AFTER LEAVING MICK'S, ZACH WENT back to the Eighth and hopped on the computer. Mick had called the case tormenting her The Three Queens investigation. Cross-referencing the date with the details he knew, he found it.

Two homicides. One attempted. The only thing the three perps had in common was the shrink they'd been seeing. Mick had been convinced the psychiatrist had used hypnotherapy to turn the three into killers.

By the time she got a search warrant, the shrink had bolted.

But not before leaving Mick a message that read: *Better luck next time, Detective Dare.*

There'd been nothing in the file about Hank's death. And nothing to suggest a connection to Thomas King or his young, beautiful wife.

Yet Mick believed they were all related.

"She could be anyone, Zach. Even me."

He had been unable to get anything more out of her. She'd gotten agitated when he tried, and told him to go. She couldn't bear to have his death on her hands.

Zach decided to pay her old partner, Carmine Angelo, a visit. He'd met the man once several months ago, an affable guy with a mile-wide protective streak toward Mick.

Zach greeted him now. "Hey man, how's it going?"

"Can't complain. It's pretty chill here in the Cold Case Squad."

Zach laughed. "Good one. Mick said you were a funny guy."

"Yeah? She's says you're a pain in the ass."

Zach laughed again. "That's my Mick. She doesn't pull her punches."

Angelo cocked an eyebrow at his word choice, but didn't comment. "What can I do for you, Harris?"

"I had some questions about The Three Queens investigation."

"Everything's in the file."

"This isn't."

Angelo folded his arms across his chest. "Maybe you'd better elaborate."

"What did the case have to do with her friend Hank's death?"

His expression turned wary. "Why do you want to know?"

Zach understood the man's hesitation. "Anything you tell me is completely confidential. I'm trying to help Mick, not the other way around."

Angelo studied him a moment, then nodded. He motioned toward the hallway. "Let's take a walk."

They strolled down the hall to an empty interview room and stepped inside; Angelo closed the door behind them, leaned against it. "What do you know so far?"

"Mick's friend Hank had a massive heart attack and died the same day your suspect skipped town."

"Rene Blackwood. Yeah. She was one creepy bitch. But she bothered Dare way more than me. Just gave her this feeling—"

"Like nails on a chalkboard."

"Yeah, that's it." He shook his head. "Schools today have those Smart Boards, can you believe that shit? Anyway, the woman had called that morning and threatened her."

"What kind of threat?"

"This veiled threat, something about messing with the people Micki loved most."

"Then Hank was dead."

"And Micki was convinced that somehow, she killed Hank. At least until the path report came in." Angelo shrugged. "You know how tough Mick is. She gave it up and moved on. Never got over Hank's death, though."

Zach looked him dead in the eyes. "You think this shrink could've had anything to with his death?"

"Don't see how. Path report was pretty straightforward." He stopped, his gaze just as direct. "I talked to you, you talk to me. Why do you want to know all this?"

Zach lifted a shoulder. "If my partner has a problem, I've got a problem. You know what I mean?"

He obviously did, because he simply nodded and stepped away from the door. "You need anything else, I'm here."

"Appreciate it, man."

"By the way, Micki was here the other day. Asking about Blackwood, if I thought she could be back in the States."

"What did you tell her?"

"Anything's possible, but it's not probable. We flagged her passport."

Not probable.

Unless she wasn't human.

CHAPTER TWENTY-NINE

8:00 P.M.

LIGHT TUMBLED FROM ARIANNA'S FRONT window. Zach took the three steps up to the porch and crossed to the door. She wasn't expecting him; he hadn't wanted his stopping by to feel like a big deal.

But now, it sort of did. And he wished he'd called first.

He knocked on the door; she answered, looking surprised, but pleased. "Zach," she said.

"Hey. I hope my just coming by this way is okay."

"Of course it is. C'mon in."

He stepped inside. He'd been by twice before, the first to help her move in the secondhand furniture she'd bought, and the second for the small, housewarming pizza party she'd had a week later.

The TV was on. The Food Channel. He wondered if she liked to cook and if she was good at it.

She waved him in. "Have a seat." She moved aside a ball of buttercream yellow yarn and knitting needles, dropping them into a big basket with balls of other colors of yarn.

"I didn't know you knitted," he said, taking a seat on the couch.

She hit the remote, silencing the television. "I learned from my mother—your grandmother. She made beautiful throws and sweaters. I took it up again after my capture. It was something I could do for the babies."

He drew his eyebrows together. "I don't understand how you can remember some things and not others."

"Nor do I."

Her simple response rang true and he thought of what had brought him here tonight—Mick's comment about Arianna lying to her.

"Mick told me she stopped by LAM today and that the two of you spoke."

"So, that's why you're here. I thought maybe you'd . . . " She shook her head. "Yes, she was waiting for me when I got there."

"What time was that?"

"Early. Before seven, I think. Although she wasn't there to see me."

"You told her Eli and Professor Truebell were out of town."

"Called in to see the High Council. Yes." Arianna looked away, then back. "She was acting so strange."

He frowned slightly. "How so?"

"She seemed sort of unraveled. Not her usual self, all business and totally in control."

Unraveled. That's the way she had seemed to him as well.

"She asked if I'd done something with Eli and Professor Truebell. Like I'd hurt them or something."

"She said that?"

"Yes." She laced her fingers together. "I know you care a lot about her and I hate to say anything that might come between you—"

"Nothing is going to come between us." The forcefulness of his own response took him aback. "But I am worried about her. So, don't filter. Just tell me, flat out."

"Okay." She laced her fingers together in her lap. "She accused me of not really being . . . your mother. And for a moment, I thought she was going to shoot me."

"Shoot you? Mick?"

She tipped her chin up. "You don't believe me?"

"It's not that. Frankly, I'm shocked. That's not the Mick I know and have worked with for almost a year."

"And you don't know me at all."

"I didn't say that."

"I see it in your eyes. And I feel it. Our light force connects us, son, whether you want to acknowledge it or not."

"But you know me, Zach."

He looked over his shoulder in surprise. Angel, head phones looped around her neck, charcoal smudges on her chin and cheeks, stood in the doorway to the kitchen.

He stood and gave her a hug. "What're you doing here, kiddo?"

Angel looked at Arianna, as if seeking help. Arianna stepped in.

"Angel's decided to move in with me for a little while."

He looked from one to the other, a sinking feeling in the pit of his gut. "Why?"

"Micki," Angel said. "She said some pretty mean stuff to me."

"Like what?"

"That I was stupid for loving Seth, that he never loved me and wasn't coming back. She told me I needed to grow up."

That sounded blunt, even for Mick. "Maybe you just took it wrong?"

"I know I have in the past, but this time was different. It was like she was *trying* to hurt me. Like she enjoyed it. She's never been like that before."

Her eyes filled with tears, and he hugged her again. "Let's sit down, kiddo. We need to talk."

When they had, Zach turned toward Angel. "I think she may have been trying to drive you away. In her mind, for your own good."

"My own good?" Angel looked at Arianna, then back at Zach. "What do you mean?"

How did he explain and still protect his partner? He decided to keep it simple and vague. "She thinks there's someone out to hurt the people she cares about."

"Like a perp?"

"Yeah, like a perp. I don't know much more than that, but I will. Until then, you need to stay away from her. Both of you. Don't let her in, not here or at LAM. You think you can do that?"

Arianna looked uncomfortable. "Are you sure about this?"

"Honestly? No. But this way, I'll know both of you are safe. There's something strange going on with her."

"Could it be a dark force?" Arianna asked.

"I thought no, but now I'm not so sure."

"Okay." Angel nodded, looked down at her hands, then back up at him, gaze defiant. "She's wrong, you know. He is coming back for us."

It wasn't until Zach pulled away from the curb that he realized Angel had said Seth was coming back for "us," not for "me." Even as he told himself it'd been a slip of the tongue, he wondered if it could have been a different kind of slip—one that revealed a secret she was keeping from them all.

But not from Arianna. He pictured the knitting needles and yarn, the baby soft yellow of it.

"It was something I could do for the babies."

Angel, pregnant? He counted back, and his stomach sank. It was possible. Angel could be pregnant with Seth's child.

CHAPTER THIRTY

10:10 P.M.

ZACH'S MARIGNY NEIGHBORHOOD CAME ALIVE at night, with folks from all around the city drawn to the eclectic eateries, funky bars, and off-beat music venues. Zach had been forced to park several blocks away from his place, but he didn't mind the walk, especially tonight, with his thoughts churning.

And most of them revolved around Mick.

Most. But not all. One of his questions could be dispelled with a phone call. He dialed Parker. Last he'd heard, the Bureau had sent him to the U.K. to meet with Scotland Yard.

He answered immediately, though it was obvious he'd been sleeping. "Special Agent Parker."

"Uncle P, it's your favorite nephew."

"Zach," —he all but growled his name— "do you know what time it is here?"

"Nope. Don't care."

Parker groaned. "Why am I not surprised by that?"

"Got a question for you."

"Make it quick, if you don't mind."

"You happen to know how I can reach the professor and Eli?"

"Come again?" He suddenly sounded way more alert, which was definitely not a good sign. "They're not at LAM?"

"Or responding to calls, texts or emails. Arianna said they were summoned by the High Council. I figured you knew about it."

Silence. Then, "Shit. That's not good."

"No?"

"No. When?"

"I'm not certain. A couple days ago, I think. Do we need to be worried?"

"Not yet. I'll make some inquiries and get back to you." Then, in typical Parker fashion, he hung up without saying goodbye.

Frowning, Zach pocketed his phone. That hadn't gone as planned. Parker wasn't a worrier, so for him to sound that concerned, something was most definitely up.

Zach reached his building and buzzed himself in. Halfway up the stairs, he met a neighbor coming down.

"Hey, Zach," the neighbor said. "How're you doin' tonight?"

"It's all good, Steve. How 'bout you?"

"Can't complain." Steve stopped, and looked back at Zach. "I let your friend in. She seemed cool. Hope that's okay."

When Zach reached his door, he saw the friend in question was Mick. She looked more than a little lost, sitting on the floor with her knees drawn to her chest, back against the wall. "Hey," she said. "Steve let me in."

"Yeah, I just saw him. He told me."

"Can we talk?"

He frowned. Something about her didn't seem right. "I thought you said we shouldn't talk right now? That being together would be dangerous for me?"

"I need your help, Zach."

She never asked for help. She'd go down first, fists swinging. He experienced a little pinch in his chest. "Sure. C'mon in."

He unlocked the door and snapped on the light; she followed him in. "You want something to drink? A glass of wine or a beer?"

"I might need it for what I have to say. So, yeah, a glass of wine. Whatever you have."

"Being awfully mysterious, Mick." He motioned toward the living room. "You know where the couch is."

He returned moments later with her wine and a glass of water for himself. She wore that same pensive, vulnerable expression she had earlier. It still felt like a surprise, and he wondered if he'd ever get used to this Mick.

She took the glass, noting his water. "You're not going to have one?"

He took the chair across the coffee table from her. "You know drinking's not my thing. Plus, I have the feeling I'm going to need to be clear-headed."

"I was kind of out there earlier, huh?"

"A little bit, yeah."

"Getting that package from Hank . . . it stirred up so many memories. And a lot of pain. And I guess I just . . . lost it."

She lifted her gaze, her eyes brimming with tears. "The past got all mixed up with the present and I was afraid."

"Of what, Mick?"

"Of being alone again. And" — she paused to take a deep breath— "of losing you."

He stood, came around the couch and sat beside her. "You're not going to lose me." He put his arm around her and she laid her head on his shoulder. "I think you're kind of stuck with me."

The citrusy smell of her shampoo wafted up to him. It shouldn't have turned him on, but it did. As did the soft sound of her breathing and the way she curled into his side.

Dangerous territory indeed. Lines that shouldn't be crossed between them. Not here. Not now.

Even so, he tilted her face up to his and kissed her. Softly at first, then deeper, as she melted into him.

"We shouldn't do this," he murmured against her mouth.

She slid her hand under his shirt and caressed his chest. "Yes, Zach, we should."

"Not when you're like this, Mick."

"Like what?" she whispered against his ear, then nipped his lobe. "This? Or" —she moved her mouth lower, trailing kisses and nibbles along his neck— "this?"

He groaned. "Yes. I mean, no—"

"You want me, don't you?" She pushed him backward against the cushions. She hovered above him, eyes smoky with passion, mouth ripe from their kisses. "Isn't it good?"

It was. Very good.

But wrong. He didn't know why, but it was.

Zach sat up, easing her off him. "This isn't why you came here, Mick, and I—"

"Yes, it is. It's why I came here." She started to unbutton his shirt. "I wanted to talk about us."

He caught her hands and lowered them to her lap. "Us?"

"Mmm-hmm." She leaned toward him, laying a hand on his thigh.

"You and me—" She slid the hand up, finding his erection. "Us. Simple as that."

Zach caught his breath as a wave of pleasure washed over him. She moved her fingers, stroking and massaging. His head fell back.

"Let's take care of this thing between us tonight. You feel it. Tell me you do."

He felt a lot of things at that moment, not the least of which was white hot arousal. But crazy as it seemed to him, it wasn't enough.

"No." He moved her hand. "Stop."

"You're not serious."

He sat up, forcibly setting her away from him. "Oh yeah, I am."

Angry color flooded her face. "I wouldn't have guessed you to be a liar."

"Actually, I'm being completely honest with you."

"Bullshit." She jumped up, straightening her clothes. "To pretend you don't feel the heat between us makes you a liar."

Mick was blunt. Except about the awareness that crackled between them. That was always off limits.

He didn't know who she was right now.

"Oh, I feel it. But you are not okay right now. So, this isn't okay. Not with me. And like you've said a dozen times, we're partners and can't cross that line."

"I changed my mind."

"Why?"

"Because I want you and you want me. So, what's the problem?"

"Why now, Mick?"

She looked annoyed. "Why not now?"

He arched an eyebrow. "Maybe because you're acting totally whacked out."

She narrowed her eyes. "If you turn me down now, Harris, it'll never happen."

"Now or never, is that what you're saying?"

"Maybe it is."

"Okay, I choose never." He stood. "Time for you to go, partner."

Her face went momentarily slack with surprise, then tightened with fury. She jumped to her feet. "You're going to come crawling to me. You know that, right? And I'm just going to laugh."

She stalked to the door and he followed. "Mick, wait."

"Too late, Hollywood."

"Look, I'm not taking advantage of you when you're obviously—" he thought of Arianna's word, "—unraveled."

"Whatever. You lose."

A moment later, she was gone, slamming the door behind her.

CHAPTER THIRTY-ONE

Wednesday, February 14
3:25 P.M.

ANGEL PEERED OUT THE APARTMENT'S front window. High school boys in khaki pants and navy blazers streamed toward cars parked along the side streets. The Catholic boys' school up the street must have just let out for the day.

They laughed and called to one another, and Angel wondered what it would be like to feel so free, to have not a care in the world except a backpack full of homework.

Arianna rented one side of a Banks Street double, within walking distance of LAM. Arianna said there was a place she could go, away from New Orleans, where she and her baby would be safe. From the Dark One and his army of Dark Bearer lieutenants. And the High Council as well.

But it would mean going into hiding. Leaving everyone and everything she knew behind. Including Seth. He wouldn't be able to find her.

The thought of it hurt almost more than she could stand. She curved her arms around her middle, imagining her arms were Seth's, that he was holding her.

Where are you, Seth? I need you.

We need you.

She blinked. One of the school boys had stopped on the sidewalk outside the window and was staring at her. When she realized he'd been caught, he moved on. That's when she saw him. Seth. On the opposite side of the street, walking toward Canal Boulevard.

Her heart seemed to stop and she raced to the door. "Seth!" she called as loudly as she could. "Seth!"

But between the traffic noise and the jostling boys, he didn't hear her. There was no way he could, she thought, panicked. Even if she screamed at the top of her lungs.

Angel darted outside, slamming the door behind her. She leapt down the porch steps and across the sidewalk, then ran into the road. A car laid on the horn and she heard the sickening crunch of metal meeting metal.

Someone was yelling. She didn't pause or even glance in that direction. She couldn't lose him. Not when she'd finally found him again.

She reached the sidewalk in one piece and ran as fast as she could, calling his name. She felt the stares of people around her, but didn't care. The only gaze she cared about was Seth's.

He'd reached Carrollton Avenue and was in the crosswalk, nearly to the other side. The crosswalk signal began to flash. The light was about to change. Traffic was stacked up and waiting. Impatiently inching forward.

She wasn't going to make it.

No! She couldn't lose him. She wouldn't.

Angel sped up. She reached the curb and stepped off. Suddenly she was stumbling backward, landing against the chest of a burly-looking man wearing a leather jacket and a Hell's Angels T-shirt.

"Stupid girl," he said, voice gruff. "You could've gotten yourself killed." He set her away from him, making sure she was steady before he let go. "You be more careful, you hear?"

Dazed, Angel nodded, and then he was gone, crossing in the other direction. She turned back to the traffic whizzing through the intersection, scanning the other side of the road and sidewalk beyond, searching frantically for Seth.

A cry bubbled to her lips. She'd lost him.

The sun was going down by the time Angel made it back to Arianna's place. She was exhausted and heartsick. She had gone up and down all the side streets, had popped into shops, restaurants and other businesses along Canal Street, hoping to catch sight of him again. She'd turned back when she reached LAM, worried someone would see and recognize her.

Angel let herself into the apartment, realizing she hadn't even locked the door when she left. She stepped inside, stopped and listened. There was something different in the air, she thought. As if someone—or something—had just passed through, leaving a psychic trail.

That was Zach's area, not hers. She was imagining it. She closed the door behind her, the snap of the latch resounding in the quiet.

Gooseflesh ran up her arms and she rubbed them, chilled. Irresponsible, she thought, leaving the door unlocked. And ungrateful. If Arianna had gotten home before her, she'd be pissed—and Angel couldn't blame her.

But she wouldn't have done anything differently either.

"I'm home," she called tentatively, peeking around the corner into the living area. "Arianna?"

Empty. Nothing different since she charged out the door after Seth. Nothing but the atmosphere.

She ran a hand wearily across her forehead. If that had even been Seth. Maybe her thoughts and longings had conjured him? Maybe she had been running after some dark-haired stranger. He'd probably wondered who the crazy chick behind him was.

The crazy, pregnant chick. Not that he would have known that.

But she'd do well to remember it, she thought, suddenly realizing she was not only exhausted, but chilled to the bone as well. And if that biker dude hadn't grabbed her, she—and her baby—would most likely be dead.

Tears stinging her eyes, Angel dragged herself to the bedroom Arianna had set her up in. She crossed to the bed and stopped. Her sketchpad lay open on top of the quilt, to a drawing she'd done three months ago, before Seth had disappeared. It showed the two of them together, their torsos joined, their lower bodies depicted as twisting roots planted deep into the earth—a portrayal of their fierce connection, physical and spiritual.

But that wasn't what made her heart skip a beat. Someone had used her charcoal pencil to leave her a message:

I'm coming for you.

Not someone. Seth.

Angel sank to her knees beside the bed. She hadn't been wrong. Seth loved her. He'd loved her then, and he loved her now.

And they would be together again soon.

CHAPTER THIRTY-TWO

10:45 P.M.

HEART IN HER THROAT, MICKI stared at the note propped up on Angel's pillow. The note, written on a piece of paper ripped from her sketch book and written in charcoal, looked as if it had been the last thing Angel had done before she left.

After all the things you said to me about Seth, I can't stay here anymore. I'm living with Arianna until I figure out what to do next. Thank you for everything you've done for me.

Angel

When did she leave? The days had begun to run together, but Micki was certain she'd seen her the other morning. Hadn't she?

No, Micki remembered, she hadn't actually seen her. Just her empty cereal bowl—evidence that she'd been there.

Micki told herself it was for the best. Considering what was going on, and Natalie King's threat against those Micki cared about, the last place Angel needed to be was here.

But still, it hurt. She hadn't even bothered to say goodbye.

How would it feel to lose those you love most?

Natalie King's words rang in her ears and she wondered if this was what she'd meant. Her friends deserting her, turning on her, rejecting her. She could live with that, Micki decided. As long as King didn't hurt them.

Micki propped the note carefully back in its original spot. She had planned to talk to Angel, suggest she stay somewhere else for a while, someplace safe. Until Eli and the professor returned and helped her figure out what to do.

Micki started to pace. *If* they returned.

Stop it, Micki. They're coming back.

A couple days, Arianna had said.

Arianna, who now had Angel.

Micki stopped short, heart lodging in her throat. What if she didn't? What if Angel was in trouble? Tricked by Natalie King or whatever she was?

Micki glanced at the clock. Nearly eleven o'clock. Late to be calling anyone, but she couldn't not call. Micki dug her phone from her pocket and punched in Arianna's number.

The woman answered, sounding wary.

"Is Angel with you? This is Micki."

Silence.

"Is she?"

"Angel's with me, yes."

"Thank God, I was afraid—"

"I can't talk to you, Micki. I'm sorry. Good night."

She ended the call and Micki was left holding the dead phone to her ear. Mad Dog Dare didn't cry, Micki reminded herself, fighting the urge to do just that. Mad Dog crushed skulls.

But that wasn't the way she felt. She felt wounded. And alone. In a way she hadn't since Hank's death.

His medal warmed and she curled her fingers around it. The warmth seemed to sink into her, reassuring her she wasn't alone. That he was still with her.

The feeling was so real that at the knock at her door, his name jumped to her lips. Catching herself, Micki retrieved her service weapon and made her way to the door. She peered through the peep hole.

Eli. It was Eli. She tucked her gun into her waistband and flung open the door. He folded her in his arms, and she clung to him, relief spilling over her like the sun.

"When did you get back? Arianna said you and Professor Truebell had been called to the High Council."

"Tonight."

He held her at arms' length and looked her in the eyes. Their blue was exactly how she remembered.

"I'm sorry it took so long for me to come."

"Is everything okay?" she asked.

"Fine." He smiled reassuringly. "Routine business."

"Is Professor Truebell with you?"

"He's still there."

"But he's okay?"

"Yes, Michaela. There's nothing to worry about, at least with us."

His mouth curved into that gentle, infinitely wise smile of his. Micki realized how much she identified Eli by both that gentleness and the wisdom. "Come." He caught her hand. "Tell me what's causing you such distress."

They went to the living room and sat together on the couch, their bodies angled to face one another. She opened her mouth and the story spilled out. All of it, from Thomas King's suicide and the investigation, to her confrontation with Natalie King. And also of the past, The Three Queens investigation, Rene Blackwood's threat, and Hank's sudden death.

"I don't know how it's possible," she said, "but Natalie King and Rene Blackwood are the same woman. She killed Hank six years ago, and she means to hurt the people close to me again. She can't be a Dark Bearer because Zach didn't pick up any energy from her, but I got the feeling she knew about the Lightkeepers and their special abilities. I feel like I'm losing my mind!"

"You're not losing your mind, Michaela. I promise you that."

A sound of relief spilled past her lips. "That's good news, at least."

"Don't start celebrating yet, Michaela, because what I'm going to tell you now is not good news. What you're describing is a powerful force for darkness, a creature we call a Chameleon."

"A chameleon? Like the garden lizards that change color to camouflage themselves?"

"Exactly."

"They change their appearance?"

"Completely, yes. Age, race, gender. Everything. Some are tricksters and troublemakers, others are driven to darker acts. Those are hunters."

"What do they hunt for?"

"Pleasure."

Gooseflesh raced up her arms. "What do you mean?"

"They take pleasure in causing pain, both physical and emotional. They do what they can, because they can. They act without regard for the feelings of anyone but themselves and their own desires." He looked away, then back. "All that pain and chaos, the lives ruined. That gives them great pleasure."

Micki acknowledged her heart was racing with excitement. "That's the definition of a psychopath."

He didn't correct her and went on, "What makes these creatures particularly dangerous isn't that they can change their appearance. It's their ability to access their victims' deepest desires or fears, their most closely held secrets and memories, and imprint them to use against you. They become what you most desire—or fear."

Answers, Micki realized. Finally, after six years, she was getting answers. "And they can use this ability to drive someone to kill themselves or others?"

"Among other things, yes." He paused to let that sink in, then went on, "In the case of King, she became everything he always dreamed of."

Micki nodded. "The inscription on his wedding band was 'Our love. A dream come true.' It was right there, exactly what she was doing."

"Yes. And once she had him, she began orchestrating his death." He paused. "Did she touch you?"

"Yes." Her heart sank. "That's how they do it, isn't it? How they access your hopes and fears? The way Zach can shake your hand and know if you're telling the truth?"

"Zach's abilities are insignificant compared to those of this chameleon. Don't underestimate her. It would be a mistake."

Micki thought of Hank. That's how Blackwood had known about Hank, that he was the person she loved most, that hurting him would hurt her more than anything.

A knot of tears formed in her throat. She forced it back. Everything she'd thought all along had been correct—her loving Hank had caused his death.

Micki squeezed her hands into fists. "I won't. I've seen how destructive she is."

"Good."

"You called her a dark force. She's not a Dark Bearer?"

"No. Dark Bearers are part of the Dark One's army. Their allegiance is to him, his desires and agenda. For chameleons, their allegiance is only to themselves and their own pleasure."

Micki let out a thoughtful breath. "When I confronted her, she grabbed both my wrists. Her touch was as cold as ice and it felt as if it was penetrating my flesh and bone. Making its way to my heart. That's how she killed Hank, isn't it?"

"Probably." His expression turned pensive. "She could have killed you then, but she didn't. What you need to ask yourself is why."

"Why she let me live? Or why she's singled me out?"

"Both."

Micki thought a moment. "She's doing this to me because I threatened her. For whatever reason, I picked up things about her that other humans don't. And I vowed to stop her."

"So, she wants to punish you."

"No," Micki countered. "She's afraid of me."

He looked skeptical. "Then why did she let you live? If she was afraid of you, why not kill you?"

"That would've been too easy," Micki said. "Too painless. I think she wants me to suffer. Like you said, hurting others is pleasurable to her. So what would be more pleasurable than watching your adversary suffer?"

"I believe you're right about that, Michaela."

Micki stood and crossed to the window. She stared out at the dark street. "She's overconfident."

"Be careful," he said, the slightest edge in his voice. "It's *you* who's sounding overconfident."

"How do we stop her, Eli? I'm afraid she's going after Zach or Angel."

He looked away for a moment, then back at her. "They're very clever. And very difficult to stop or kill. But we can do it, if we work together."

Something in his voice suddenly sounded different. Then he spoke again, and it was gone. "Don't worry about it. The professor and I will figure it out, come up with a plan. Until then, just be cautious."

She went weak with relief. "When will the professor be back?"

"In the morning." He stood and started for the door. "In the meantime, get some sleep, then go back to work tomorrow. I'll talk to Zach and Arianna, get things straight with them. By tomorrow afternoon, I'm sure we'll have something for you."

"Thank you, Eli." She gave him a hug at the door. "Seriously, if you hadn't come here tonight, I don't know what I would have done."

CHAPTER THIRTY-THREE

Thursday, November 16
9:05 A.M.

THE NEXT MORNING, MICKI ARRIVED at the Eighth a few minutes late. She felt a hundred percent lighter in spirit than the day before. Eli was back. She knew what she was dealing with. They could beat this together.

"Morning, Susan. Any messages?"

"Just one." Sue's gaze darted from Micki back to her computer screen. "Major Nichols wants to see you right away."

"You okay?" Micki asked.

She kept her gaze trained on the screen. "I'm fine. Just busy this morning."

"Is Zach in?"

"He was here earlier, then left again."

Micki frowned. "Did he say where he was going?"

"He didn't say, I didn't ask."

Micki had a hard time believing that. Susan made it her business to know everybody's everything. "Should I wait for him before I go see Major Nichols—"

"No." Susan looked up, but didn't meet her eyes. "Only you this morning."

Only her? A queasy sensation settled in the pit of Micki's stomach. She thanked the woman and started in the direction of his office. Susan stopped her, looking flustered. "Not Major Nichols' office. The war room. Sorry."

The war room? Just her, not Zach? Susan's nerves and the pin-drop quiet squad room? Whatever was about to go down, it smelled like an ambush—and she had a good idea who they were gunning for.

A moment later, Micki saw that she was right. Three men sat at the table, but the one who spelled the biggest trouble for her was Captain Pete Newman, head of the Public Integrity Division, the unit that investigated complaints against NOPD officers *and* presumed you guilty until you proved yourself innocent.

What the hell did they have on her?

She took a deep breath and strode confidently into the room. "Major Nichols, I understand you wanted to see me."

The chief answered for him, another bad sign. "That's right, Detective Dare. Have a seat."

He indicated the chair at the head of the table.

"Thank you, Chief." She took it and moved her gaze between the three men.

"You know Captain Newman, of the PID."

"Of course. Captain." She nodded in his direction, then redirected her attention to Chief Howard. "What's this about?"

Her stomach took a nosedive when Newman, not the chief, took over. "Detective Dare, on Monday, February twelfth, did you, without your superior officer's permission, go to the 2 River Tower and Hotel to interview Mrs. Natalie King?"

"Yes, sir, I did."

"And did you go on your own and without Detective Harris' presence or foreknowledge?"

"Partly, Captain. I left Detective Harris a voice message telling him what I meant to do."

"I believe your message said you were"— he looked at his notes— "going to take one last crack at her."

They'd spoken to Zach already, she realized. Of course they had. They always interrogated the partner first. "That's a figure of speech, sir. But yes, I imagine I did say that."

"You don't remember what you said? This was only three days ago."

"It was a voicemail, sir. How many voicemails do you leave in a day?"

He pinned her with his gaze. "This isn't about me, Detective."

"No, sir."

"So, again, did you leave Detective Harris a voicemail saying you meant to take another crack at Natalie King?"

"And again, yes, I left a voicemail, but I don't remember the exact wording of it."

"I'm confused by your actions, Detective. The case was closed, was it not?"

"We received the path report that morning, yes. The Coroner's office ruled King's death a suicide."

"And neither you nor your partner, during the course of your investigation, uncovered anything that might contradict that ruling?"

"That's correct."

"Hence my confusion, Detective. Why did you feel the need to re-interview Mrs. King?"

Her palms started to sweat. Obviously, Natalie King had registered a complaint. The big question was, what had the woman said about her? And now, how did she answer the question honestly without revealing the truth and looking like a total nut job?

"Before writing my report, I wanted to confirm a few case details," she replied evenly. "I wanted to make certain it was done right before we closed the book on it."

"I see." He looked down at his notes, then back up at her. "Why did you decide to act without Detective Harris?"

"He was over at Central Evidence. He wanted to take a last look at the evidence before writing his report."

"You both seem extremely concerned with double-checking the details of a case that turned out to be pretty clear cut. Is there something you're not sharing with us?"

"Absolutely not. We're both extremely thorough, Captain Newman."

"I'm glad to hear that. And I'm sure the Chief is, too." He cleared his throat. "But still, you couldn't wait for your partner?"

"I didn't think this was a big deal. A few simple clarifications. That's it." She looked at Major Nichols. "I had orders to write up my notes and move on. That was my focus."

"What did you do immediately before making that call on Mrs. King?" Newman asked.

"I don't understand."

"You left Major Nichols' office at approximately twelve-thirty. Then what?"

They knew about Carmine. She'd signed in at HQ. "I went to my desk and reviewed the case."

"Is that the only case you reviewed?"

"No, sir. I reviewed an unresolved, six-year-old case."

"The Three Queens investigation."

"Yes."

"Why was that?"

"What is this about?" she asked again.

"Your thought process, Detective Dare? If you don't mind?"

"The King case caused a similar gut reaction in me that The Three Queens case did. As you know, good cops sometimes have to go with their gut."

"Is that why you went to see your old partner, Detective Angelo?"

"Yes."

"And?"

"We discussed the case. That's all. It was good to see him. What do you want from me, Captain?"

"The truth, Detective."

She was pretty damn certain he couldn't handle the truth. Lightkeepers? Dark Bearers? Creatures that steal your most closely-held secrets and transform themselves into anyone? Hardly.

"That is the truth."

"Mrs. King has filed a complaint against you. She charges that you harassed and bullied her."

"That's not true."

Major Nichols stepped in. "Detective Dare. Micki. This is me you're talking to. For over a year, the pressure on you has been intense. You and Harris have worked some very high-profile cases. My God, in one of them you were wounded in the line of duty. In another, your partner was."

"Your point, Major?"

"Police officers are human beings. Meltdowns and burn-outs happen. It's to be expected."

"I'm fine," she said. "No burn-out, no meltdown. Grateful for the opportunity to serve the people of this great city."

She sounded like an advertisement, and a corny one at that. But sometimes corny sentiment proved to be just what the doctor ordered.

Not this time, she realized, as Newman started up again.

"So, you wouldn't describe your behavior with Mrs. King—or any of your colleagues—as outside the norm?"

"I would not."

"Not in any way unraveled?"

"Is that how she described me?" Micki asked. "If so, this is starting to sound like a 'she said/she said' situation. With all due respect, I would hope that my years of loyal and exemplary service would carry some weight here."

"In a 'she said/she said situation,' it definitely would. However, Mrs. King provided us with video of the incident."

"Video?" she repeated, her lips going numb and the beginnings of a vicious headache exploding at the base of her skull. "I don't under-stand."

"Provided by security footage from the hallway outside of Mrs. King's apartment. Let's have a look, shall we?"

She didn't need to have a look. She had a pretty good idea what the camera must have caught.

She was screwed.

He opened his laptop and spun it toward her. Her mouth went dry as he hit play. Even as she told herself she didn't want to see this, she couldn't look away.

The video was black and white, the picture quality poor. Still, there was no doubt it was her and King entering the apartment. No drama at all.

Yet.

Newman fast-forwarded. This, she knew, was where it got dicey.

And then there she was, leaving the apartment, expression dazed. Weaving slightly, sort of collapsing against a wall. Her mouth moving, like she was talking to herself.

It was painful to watch. Then it got even worse. Her, charging toward King's door. Pounding on it. Even though there was no audio, it was obvious that she was shouting for the woman to open the door.

Micki felt sick, but she couldn't drag her gaze from the grainy image. She anticipated each moment of the footage: her face twisted with fury; King tugging her inside, away from the camera's eye. But that's not the way it appeared. No, the video made it look like she pushed her way in.

Outplayed, Micki thought. Every step of the way. When King grabbed her wrists and yanked her over the threshold, she'd known the camera would be blinded to her vicious grip on Micki's wrists, her sly smile and obvious glee as she threatened Micki. Without audio, they wouldn't hear her laughter after.

And a picture was worth a thousand words.

Suddenly, Micki appeared back in the frame, stumbling backwards out of the apartment, righting herself as the door slammed shut behind her, then turning and running for the elevator.

Her face burned with embarrassment. She'd looked and acted like a crazy person.

But she'd had reason. Good reason.

One she couldn't explain.

"Had enough?" Newman asked.

Micki nodded. "More than."

"Would you like to change your response to the question about your behavior of late?"

Someone having a meltdown. A major one. Nichols had been offering her an out, she realized. The pressure. The pace. Being wounded.

She should have taken it. God, she wished she'd taken it. It was too late now.

"You're not hearing what she's saying to me. She threatened me. She threatened people I care about. I know that's probably hard to believe—"

"Yes, it is," Newman said quietly. "And I don't."

Micki's mind raced. Eli would have spoken to someone by now, Zach for sure.

She looked at Major Nichols. "There's more to this story. Talk to Detective Harris. He'll back me up."

"I'm afraid he won't. I'm sorry, Micki, but I spoke with him early this morning. He described your recent behavior as erratic and your state of mind as dangerously fragile."

"What?" She couldn't believe what she was hearing—or how much the words hurt. Like a stake being driven into her heart.

She'd trusted him. Believed he had her back, one hundred percent.

"He's worried about you," Nichols said softly. "So is Detective Angelo. They're on your side, Micki."

Carmine, too? "Right," she said, the word coming out choked.

"You've been through a lot in a short period of time. And Hank's death was a terrible shock. We feel for you, we understand and support you."

Chief Howard stepped in. "But we cannot, I cannot, have one of my detectives in the field while in such a precarious emotional state."

"You're . . . firing me?" She could hardly say the words. The NOPD was her family. Her job was her life.

"For now, it's just a suspension. Mrs. King was gracious—and very kind. She doesn't plan to pursue action against the department, on the condition we relieve you, at least temporarily, of your duties and you seek psychological help for your problems."

Micki struggled to keep her emotions in check. What had Eli said the night before? That chameleons could get in your head, learn your most closely held secrets. They could read your soul—what you loved most, and hated most. What you feared, and how to break your heart. Even your darkest longings.

She'd been completely outmaneuvered, Mick acknowledged. She had no job, so no family, to rely on. She'd broken trust with those she cared for most. And as a final twist of the knife, if she wanted her job back, she had to see a shrink.

The chief continued, "And I need your assurance you will not contact her again, not in any way." He paused as if to let that sink in. "Can I get that assurance from you?"

"Yes, sir."

"And you understand your conditions for reinstatement?"

"Yes, sir."

"I'll need your firearm, Detective. And your badge."

The words echoing in her head, Micki stood. She removed her shoulder holster, laid it and the gun on the table. Her badge was next, and she slid it across the table to him, hand rock steady even though she felt as if her world was collapsing around her.

"Get help, Micki," Major Nichols said. "Rest. Get healthy. I want you back. I need you on the street."

"May I get something from my desk?"

"Of course. I'll get someone to accompany you."

A moment later, Stacy Killian met her at the war room door. "I'm sorry," she said softly.

"There's more to the story than their version of events."

"There always is."

They made their way into the squad room. Zach was at his desk. He looked stricken when he saw her. She strode over, stopping directly in front of him. She shook with the force of keeping her emotions in check.

"How could you?" she asked, voice low.

"I'm worried about you, Mick."

"Bullshit." She placed her palms on the desk and bent to look him square in the eyes. "You didn't stand up for me. Partners have each other's backs."

"You're not yourself, Mick. The last two days proved that, don't you think?"

"I should have known not to trust you. I should have stuck with my gut. You're a—"

"Micki," Stacy said softly, touching her elbow, "you don't want to do this. Not here."

Micki stopped. Stacy was right. Everyone was watching them. Everyone was listening, taking notes. She'd be at the top of everyone's list to talk about over a beer at Shannon's Tavern later.

Proving the validity of the reason for her suspension.

Screw all of them. She wouldn't give them the satisfaction.

Without another word, she collected a few personal items from her desk, turned and left the building.

As the Nova roared to life a few minutes later, she wondered if she'd ever be back.

CHAPTER THIRTY-FOUR

10:35 A.M.

"YOU OKAY?"

Zach glanced up. The question had come from Stacy. She'd returned from accompanying Mick downstairs, and was looking at him, her expression concerned.

"Yeah," he said, "I'm fine."

"That's bullshit," she said, voice low. When he didn't respond after an awkward moment, she added, "Something's not right here. And you know it."

He could hardly meet her eyes. Micki's words from this morning—and her actions of last two days—collided in his head.

He cleared his throat, not wanting her to know how unnerved he was. The words Mick had hurled at him had hit their mark. He should have had her back, no matter what.

"Look, Killian, I'm not sure what all Mick's dealing with, but I am sure she needs some time to sort it out."

She drew her eyebrows together. "This way? A suspension? I don't know everything she's going through either, but I know Dare. And she's a straight shooter. And you're supposed to be her partner."

Zach watched her walk away, the truth of her words thundering like a drumbeat in his head. Mick was a straight shooter. By the book, dedicated to the force and the job. If the major hadn't shown up at his apartment early this morning with the tape, he wouldn't have believed the accusation.

But he did see the tape. It had been incredibly damning.

And the way she'd come on to him, that wasn't the Mick he knew.

And her anger when he'd refused her advances? Her all or nothing ultimatum? Where had that come from? Never, not in a million years, would he have expected that behavior from Mick.

Not the Mick he knew anyway.

But she wasn't the Mick he knew. He massaged his right temple, and the knot of pain that had settled there. He thought back, piecing together the timeline of the last few days. Mick had been fine until that package from Hank arrived.

Or had she? She'd thought she'd seen Hank before she got the package. Twice—once Friday afternoon, then the morning of the delivery. She'd admitted having had dreams about seeing him. Angel had heard her call his name in the middle of the night.

She was either having a psychological break, or something had gotten to her. Something supernatural.

If a Dark Bearer was involved, he'd have picked up the energy.

Zach pushed away from his desk and headed for the major's office. He tapped on the door, then stuck his head in the office. Nichols sat at his desk, staring out his partially opened window. The building that housed the Eighth pre-dated air conditioning, and the nearly floor to ceiling windows were designed for maximum circulation. His looked out over Royal Street.

"You have a minute, Major?"

Nichols tore is gaze away from the view and waved him in. He sighed. "Tough morning."

"Yeah." Zach sank onto one of the chairs facing the major's desk. "How'd she take it?"

"Faced with the video, there's wasn't much she could say. She claimed King threatened her by threatening the people she cared about."

The same as she'd said happened with that shrink four years ago. The same as she'd said the other day.

"I think she means to kill you. The way she killed Hank."

She'd warned him to stay away, then hours later, had come to his place and tried to seduce him? It didn't make sense.

Zach kept his gaze focused on Nichols. "It could be true, Major. There's no audio on that tape."

Nichols folded his hands. "Even if it was—which I find hard to believe—there's an appropriate way to respond. The behavior I viewed was far from appropriate."

"I'm just . . . struggling to come to grips with this. It's just not . . .

Mick."

"You agreed with me this morning, Zach."

He had. After seeing the video, and still feeling unbalanced from their last two interactions. Should he have fought for her? Had her back despite her volatile behavior?

As if reading his thoughts, Major Nichols leaned forward. "Nothing you could have said would have changed the outcome of this, Harris. Natalie King is a powerful woman, and she has proof to back up her charges against Dare. Our hands are tied."

Zach frowned, recalling the other morning. *What is my favorite coffee, Zach?*

Like she'd been testing him. As if she doubted who he was.

But why would she?

"A full suspension?" Zach asked.

He inclined his head. "Return possible only with the department shrink's blessing."

It might not happen, Zach realized. Mick hated shrinks. So, which was stronger—her dislike of shrinks or her love of the job?

He didn't know if he wanted to do this without her.

"Major, you mind if I take the rest of the day? Get my head on straight?"

"Go ahead. The last thing I need is you unraveling, too. But look—" He tapped his index finger on the desktop. "I'd give her some time and space. She was pretty pissed off this morning."

Zach nodded, stood and crossed to the door. Nichols stopped him and when he looked back, a movement caught his eye. A sparrow, perched on the bookcase behind Nichols' desk.

Zach indicated the bird. "You have a visitor."

Nichols swiveled in his chair, startling the sparrow. It burst into flight, flapping wildly, and Nichols jumped to his feet. "What the hell!"

It took a couple of minutes, but between the two of them, they shooed the creature out the window.

Nichols looked sheepish. "I guess I should keep the window closed, but this office is like a furnace this time of year."

And the squad room was like a refrigerator. "If there's nothing else, Major, I'm going to head out."

"Just one thing. I know what you did today wasn't easy. But it was the right thing to do."

Was it? Zach wondered. Because it sure as hell didn't feel like the right thing.

Zach went back to his desk for his keys and jacket, then signed out. He passed Susan on her way into Nichols' office.

"I'm out for the day," he said. "I've got my phone for emergencies."

She nodded, looking as troubled as he felt.

CHAPTER THIRTY-FIVE

11:15 A.M.

ZACH WAS ON THE STAIRS when he heard the scream. Before he could return to the squad room, Stacy Killian burst through the stairwell doors.

"Major Nichols fell out his window!"

Zach all but flew down the rest of the stairs, Killian with him. A commotion greeted them as they charged out of the building. Officers shouting, pushing the curious back, already setting up a perimeter, the wail of an ambulance, the cluster of NOPD officers.

"What the hell happened?" Zach asked as he and Killian pushed their way through. "I was just with him."

"I don't know. Susan was nearly incoherent, just something about him falling out the window."

Zach's first look at his commander was a shock. He wasn't moving. Didn't seem to be breathing. As he and Killian knelt down beside him, his eyes popped open and he arched up with a terrible, primal sound.

"Keep him still!"

"Until we know what his injuries—"

Zach, Killian and several other officers circled him, holding him down firmly but as gently as possible.

"Don't move, Major—"

"Ambulance is on its way—"

He fought them, writhing and twisting, the sounds coming out of him like those of an animal in pain.

Finally, the paramedics arrived. Zach and the others stepped back, standing in a silent circle, watching the EMTs work. Little by little, they peeled away—crime in the Eighth didn't stop because one of their own was hurt.

Zach's phone went off; he moved away from the scene. "This is Harris," he answered.

"Detective, this is Porsche King! I need your help."

"What's happening?"

"It's Mercedes." Her voice rose, taking on a hysterical edge. "She got into a fight with Natalie and now she's talking crazy." She drew in a ragged-sounding breath. "She says she'll only talk to you."

He frowned. "To me?"

"I don't know why, but she said you would know the truth!"

"Put her on the phone."

"I can't. She's barricaded herself in Dad's apartment and won't come out!"

"Porsche, listen carefully. Do you think she might harm herself?"

"Mercedes? Oh, my God . . . you mean kill herself? No, at least I don't think so, but—"

"She hasn't said *anything* like that?"

"No." Porsche's voice rose. "But I've never heard her this way, like she's lost it. One minute she's yelling, cursing Natalie, the police, even dad, the next she's crying and begging me to do something. That's when she said to call you."

Zach glanced toward the crowd gathered around the ambulance. "Try to keep her talking. Tell her I'm on my way, and that together we'll get this worked out."

He hung up and found Killian. He touched her arm. "I've got to go. Keep me posted. If he needs anything, call me."

⚜ ⚜ ⚜

Porsche met Zach on the twenty-first floor, outside her father's apartment. "I told her you were coming and it seemed to calm her down."

"That's good." He moved close to the door, tapped on it. "Ms. King, Mercedes, it's Detective Harris. I'm here to help you."

"Go away! No one can help!"

"You told me to call him!" Porsche cried. "You said he was the only who *could* help!"

"You never cared about any of this, Porsche. And now, it's all going to be yours."

Zach didn't like the sound of that. He looked at Porsche. "You don't have a key?" he asked, voice low.

She shook her head. Her face had gone white.

"The building manager must have one. Get him up here."

She nodded and hurried out of earshot to make the call. Zach turned his attention back to the door and Mercedes on the other side of it. He could hear her agitated breathing.

"Hey Mercedes," he said, pressing closer to the door. "Tell me what's going on. What's happened?"

"You let her walk away. Free as a bird."

"We had nothing we could charge her with, so there was nothing we could do."

"Free as a bird," she said again, tone changing, becoming high and brittle. "She laughed at me. Told me 'better luck next time.'"

The phrase tugged at his memory, but he couldn't put his finger on why and didn't have the time to try. "Look, let me in and we'll talk some more about it."

She went on as if he hadn't spoken, "I told her I would *never* stop trying to prove she killed him. I vowed to use every cent of my inheritance on private detectives, and she laughed at me. Told me I was pathetic. That I was nothing without him. She was right."

"No," Zach said quickly. "She's not right."

"I was never good enough. Not smart enough. God knows I wasn't pretty enough—"

"That's not true."

"I tried and tried . . . I worked so hard . . . But I was always a disappointment."

"If you don't want to come out, Mercedes, let me come in. Just you and me. We'll make a plan."

"That's all I wanted. Him to be proud of me. To love me. And now he's gone. It's pointless."

He laid his palm flat on the door, near where her breathing was the loudest. "Mercedes, you had Porsche call me because you said I could help. So let me help. Open the door and we'll figure it out."

"No. I had Porsche call you because she told me I should."

"Who told you that? Porsche? Natalie?"

"No. The other woman."

"Who?"

"You know her." Her voice grew distant. "She said so."

He racked his brain for who she might be referring too. "Is she there with you now?"

"She's in my head. She says it's time to go."

"Mercedes—" He grabbed the door handle, and then he knew. The energy raced up his arm and her image exploded in his head.

The amber-eyed woman. Laughing at him.

He rattled the knob. "Mercedes! She's not real. Let me in!"

"Goodbye, Detective Harris."

"No!" He pounded on the door. "You were right! I do know the truth. We're going to get her. But we need you! You're the only one who can help!"

She didn't respond. Zach put his ear to the door. He could no longer hear her breathing and knew she'd moved away from it.

Toward the sliding glass doors, he thought. To the balcony beyond.

Porsche came running down the hall. "I reached him! He's coming up! It'll be just a couple minutes."

They didn't have a couple minutes. He knew what Micki would do—kick the damn door in.

Working to remember his training, he reared back and landed a good, square blow. It hurt like hell, but he did it again. This time the wood splintered. Then, with another blow, it gave.

He burst through the door to see Mercedes King crouching atop the balcony rail, holding on with both hands but teetering precariously.

She looked over her shoulder, but not at him. She nodded her head, as if agreeing with something someone was saying to her.

"Hold on, Mercedes!" he shouted, starting for her, hand out. "I'm coming for you."

She still didn't look his way. Instead, a small, strange smile curved her lips. "You're right," she said. "It's better this way."

And then she let go.

CHAPTER THIRTY-SIX

12:10 P.M.

MICKI DUG HER TOES INTO the sand and breathed in the cold, damp air off the Gulf of Mexico. When she'd left the Eighth earlier that day, she'd climbed into the Nova, hopped on I-10 East and headed for the Mississippi Gulf Coast.

The hour drive from New Orleans wasn't a pretty one—mostly highway lined with "progress," an outlet mall, gas stations and fast food stops. Chain retailer after chain retailer.

Finally, those had given way to small coastal communities, then this expanse of sand, water and sky.

Micki popped a French fry into her mouth. It was crispy and salty, just the way she liked them. She'd stopped at the diner just up the beach highway and got herself the fries and a chocolate milkshake. She figured she was on vacation—sort of—so she might as well make the best out of it.

She pulled another out of the brown paper sack and bit it in half, chewing thoughtfully. Was she stupid to expect Zach to call? Not to apologize—no, she wasn't certain she deserved one—but to talk it out? Hear the whole story? Surely, he realized there was more happening here than a meltdown?

But maybe not. She'd seen the recording. She had no illusions about how bad it looked for her right now.

The shake was thick, and Micki sucked in several strawfuls of the concoction. Eli said he and the professor would come up with a plan, and she trusted him. Hour by hour, minute by minute, that's how she was going to get through this. She wasn't about to let this chameleon creature break her.

Her cell went off and she dug it out of her pocket. It was the first time it had rung since she'd exited the Eighth. She checked the display and was disappointed to see it wasn't Zach. She started to refuse the call when she heard Hank's voice in her head, clear as a bell.

"Aren't you going to answer it, girl?"

So she did. "Hello?"

"Detective Dare?"

A woman's voice, though she couldn't place it. "This is Micki Dare. Who is this?"

"Cyndi Stevens. Sarah's—"

"Sister," Micki finished for her. "I remember. How can I help you, Cyndi?"

"I didn't hear back from you . . . I was wondering if you had a chance to question the woman my neighbor told you about?"

"I have not. I'm so sorry, Ms. Stevens, my partner and I have been hung up in another investigation. And in fact, I'm afraid I won't be able—"

She didn't finish the thought because Cyndi Stevens burst into tears. A lump formed in her throat—she understood what it was like to feel helpless against the world.

What the hell, she decided. She'd already been suspended. Why not go for impersonating an officer, as well? "I'll do it today," she said, "and get back to you with what I learn. But please, don't get your hopes up. The coroner ruled your sister's death a suicide. That's difficult to overcome."

"Thank you, Detective. Thank you so much!"

Micki ended the call and tucked the phone back into her pocket. She stood, brushed the sand off her pants and collected the remnants of her makeshift lunch.

Was she crazy? Micki wondered, tossing her trash in the receptacle at the sidewalk. She unlocked the car and slid behind the wheel.

"What do you think, Hank?" she asked, starting the engine.

The medal seemed to warm and she smiled. Hell yeah, crazier than a tourist in the French Quarter during Mardi Gras. "That's what I think, too. Let's do this, Hank, you and me."

⚜ ⚜ ⚜

The ad agency Keith Gerard worked for was located in Place St. Charles, a swanky commercial building in the heart of the downtown financial district. Micki made one quick stop on the way—the Big Easy Costume Company.

Five minutes later, she'd emerged from the store with a shiny new police badge. Now, badge affixed to her belt, she fed the parking meter in front of Place St. Charles.

She'd been a cop long enough to know that police work was as much about attitude as firepower.

Good thing, she thought, and stepped onto the elevator. Moments later she alighted on the fifteenth floor. Double glass doors announced Walton & Johnson Advertising.

As she approached the receptionist, she opened her jacket to reveal her badge. The young woman saw it, Micki knew, because her eyes widened slightly.

Micki stopped at the desk. "Detective Micki Dare, NOPD. I'm here to speak one of your employees. Tara Green."

"Tara?" The young woman's gaze darted past Micki, down at the phone, then back up at her. "I'm not sure—"

Micki looked her dead in the eyes. "It wasn't a request."

She nodded and made the call. A minute later, a pretty, young blonde approached her.

"I'm Tara Green," she said. "Can I help you?"

"Micki Dare. NOPD. I need to ask you a few questions."

She frowned. "I think you must have the wrong person."

"Perhaps." Micki motioned toward the doorway the woman had emerged from. "I suspect you'd appreciate it if we spoke somewhere private."

"Sure. My office is this way."

Green led her to a small, functional office. She closed the door behind them. "I hope this won't take too long, I've got a big media buy to finish by five."

"You're a media buyer?"

"That's right." She clasped her hands nervously together. "I have a degree in marketing."

"Good for you." Micki smiled. "Do you know someone named Keith Gerard?"

She looked surprised by the question. "Of course. He works here."

"How would you describe your relationship with him?"

"With Keith? We're co-workers. Friendly, but that's it."

"Are you saying you two are not romantically involved?"

"Me and Keith? Romantically involved? No way." She shook her head for emphasis. "Where would you get an idea like that?"

Micki ignored the question and asked another of her own. "Does the name Sarah Stevens mean anything to you?"

"No. Should it?" She stopped, biting back the words. "Wait. Keith's girlfriend's name is Sarah."

"That's right," Micki said. "Sarah Stevens."

Her eyes widened and she brought a hand to her mouth. "The other night . . . I heard she killed herself."

"Yes, Thursday the eighth. She slit her wrists."

Green found her chair and she sat down. Her hands shook. "It's so horrible."

"What would you say if I told you a witness can place you at the scene at the night of her death?"

Green looked up. Her lovely brown eyes were filled with tears. "What?"

"A witness," Micki said, "placed you at Sarah Stevens' apartment that night. Thursday, February eighth."

"That's not possible."

"Why is that, Ms. Green?"

"I was on vacation last week. My sister in Phoenix just had a baby and I was visiting her."

CHAPTER THIRTY-SEVEN

3:30 P.M.

MICKI FOUND A PARKING SPOT just around the corner from LAM, under the shade of a big oak tree. Ignoring the squawks of the birds disturbed by her arrival, she swung open the car door and stepped out.

She breathed deeply, the cold air clearing her head. Before she left Tara Green's office, the young woman had insisted on digging her boarding pass stub and several travel receipts out her purse, then calling up the dated photo stream on her cell phone.

Tara Green had been hundreds of miles away from New Orleans the night Sarah Stevens killed herself.

The lead had proved a dead end, and when Micki called Sarah's sister to let her know, she'd been crushed by the news. With nothing else to offer her, Micki hung up.

Promising herself that as soon as she was able—if that ever happened—she would review Gerard's correspondence records. She locked the car, and headed for the center. She hadn't heard from Eli, so she'd decided to check in with him. He had probably heard about her suspension, and she hoped he and Professor Truebell had some sort of an idea about how to get her out of this nightmare.

A couple minutes later, she rang the bell and looked directly into the camera.

Arianna came over the intercom. "I'm sorry, Micki, but I can't let you in."

For a split second, Micki thought she had misheard. When she realized she hadn't, she had to struggle to find her voice.

"Why not?"

She paused a moment. "I just can't."

"I need to speak to Eli."

"He's not here, Micki."

"The professor then. We'll get this sorted out."

"I told you, they were summoned to the High Council. I haven't heard from them since and don't know when they'll be back."

"I saw Eli last night," Micki said. "He told me Professor Truebell was arriving this morning." Her voice rose. "He said everything was going to be fine."

"If they're back, they haven't contacted me or been by LAM."

"I'll wait. Let me in."

"I can't do that. I'm sorry, but Zach made me promise—"

"Zach?" Micki took an involuntary step backward. She felt as if she'd been slapped in the face. "Zach told you not to let me in?"

"Until we figure out what's going on with you. To keep Angel safe and protect the center."

They thought—Zach thought—she could hurt Angel? And that she would do what to the center? Steal Lightkeeper secrets? Or come in, guns blazing, and blow it apart? It was inconceivable to her.

But apparently, not to Arianna. Micki turned and walked away before the woman could say that she was sorry again. Her hand shook as she unlatched the gate and stepped through. She was out of moves, plain and simple. Everyone she trusted, it seemed, had turned against her. Except Eli, who'd disappeared.

She cycled through ideas, eliminating one after another. Confronting Natalie King again would be disastrous. Calling one of King's daughters would do nothing—except backfire. Running away seemed equally as ludicrous as hiding out at home.

Zach, she thought. He was the only one who might listen.

Despite everything, she still believed in him. In their partnership. The question was, did he believe in her anymore?

As she neared her car, she saw a crow had perched itself on the Nova's hood. It seemed to spy her at the same time and flew back into the tree she had parked under. A good thing, too, because she wasn't feeling charitable this morning.

She shifted her gaze; her steps faltered. Someone was sitting in the Nova, behind the wheel. She'd locked it; she always did. Her pulse quickened, and she automatically went for her gun, simultaneously realizing it wasn't there.

Dammit. She had a personal weapon stashed in the Nova's locked glove box, but it wasn't going to do her any good now.

She slowed her steps, moving her gaze from left to right, assessing her surroundings. She had two choices: turn and walk away, or confront whoever it was without knowing if they were armed.

The UNSUB made the decision for her. The driver's side door opened, and a man stepped out and turned toward her.

Her heart stopped when she saw who it was. "Professor!"

She closed the distance between them and he gave her a quick, hard hug. He held her away from him, mouth curving into the elfin grin that always managed to transform his middle-aged, bearded face into that of a mischievous boy. "Michaela. You knew I'd come."

"Eli told you everything?"

"Yes. You've been having quite a time."

"It's worse than you know. I was suspended from the force this morning."

"I know that, too."

"How?"

"Back channels." He motioned toward the car. "Let's ride and chat, just in case we're being watched."

"Are we?" she asked. "Why?"

"I don't trust anyone right now. And you shouldn't either."

They climbed into the car, she inserted the key and the engine rumbled to life. "Where to?" she asked.

"Anywhere."

Micki took a left on Canal Street, heading west, toward Lakeview and the West End.

After they'd gone a couple blocks in silence, she glanced at him. "Arianna wouldn't let me into LAM. She said Zach warned her against it. To protect Angel. And the center."

He didn't respond, and she went on, "Why's he doing this? I don't understand."

"Look at it from his point of view, Michaela. He saw the videotape."

"You heard about that, too?"

He nodded. "The fact is, right now, you can't trust him."

"I don't understand," she said again.

"It's not him, it's her. The chameleon." He angled in the bucket seat to face her. "You thought of Zach first, when she asked who you cared for most. Am I right?"

She stopped for a red light. "Yes."

"And who was second? Angel?"

"Right again."

"So, she knows how much it hurts you to be without them."

The light changed, and Micki rolled through the intersection. "That's why I'm afraid for them. I think she's going to . . ."

"Kill them?" he said.

She thought of Hank. How his loss had stripped her of something essential. Something she'd only just started to get back. She nodded. "Yes."

"She'd have done that already, don't you think? If it was her desire."

"What is her desire, then?"

"You already know."

"To punish me for challenging her. To prove she's all powerful and that I'm helpless against her."

"Very good, Michaela." He paused a moment, then went on, "She's taking your loved ones from you, just in a different way. And it hurts, doesn't it?"

"Yes." Her throat nearly closed over the word.

"She'll do anything, become anyone. She won't stop, until she wins."

"What does that mean, Professor?" Micki looked at him, then back at the road. "What's a win for her?"

"To break you."

The stark intention of those words took her breath. She almost missed the light ahead turn red, and had to slam on the breaks. They jerked against the safety belts. The medal, she realized, had gone cold.

"I think she's already done that." Micki gripped the steering wheel tighter. "She's won."

"Michaela," he chided gently, "you're so much stronger than that. You've lots more fight in you."

He knew her well. "Why can't I just go to Zach, tell him everything. He'll believe me. I know he will."

"What if it isn't Zach? And even if it is, what if he thinks you're falling apart, having a breakdown. You might never be reinstated."

Could she stand it? she wondered. Fired. Most likely never able to work in law enforcement again. Certainly, never for the NOPD.

"You have to understand what you're dealing with. How clever this creature is. Brilliant, like a master chess player. And she could be anyone right now."

"Even you?"

He smiled slightly, like a proud parent. "That's the way to think, Michaela. But no, she can't imprint a Full Light." He paused, as if to let that sink in. "That's why Eli and I have to be the ones to stop her."

"Then do it, please. I don't know if I can take much more than this."

"It's going to take some time. I'm sorry."

"I feel like I'm almost out of time."

He turned away from her, his gaze toward the side window. When he turned back, his expression looked resigned. "Go home," he said softly. "Stay there. Don't go out. And don't let anyone in."

Shut up in her house. Alone, nothing to help pass the hours.

It sounded like a death sentence.

"Anyone, Michaela. Especially Zach. Or Angel. Eli or I will contact you soon."

CHAPTER THIRTY-EIGHT

8:45 P.M.

ANGEL AWAKENED WITH A START. She'd fallen asleep while sketching and as she sat up, the drawing pad and bag of charcoal pencils slipped off her lap and fell to the floor. She pushed her hair away from her face. Seth. In her dream, he had been calling to her. Outside, he told her. He was waiting for her outside.

She slipped quietly out of bed, stepped into her jeans and grabbed a sweatshirt. Then, after quickly lacing up her Nikes, she tiptoed to her bedroom door.

Angel eased it open, peered down the hall. Arianna's bedroom door was shut. Except for the glow of the nightlight in the hall, the house was dark.

She darted into the hall and unarmed the alarm, holding her breath, praying the telltale beep didn't awake Arianna.

All remained quiet and she hurried to the front door, unlocked it and stepped expectantly out into the night.

At the sight of the empty porch, her hopes plummeted. She had *known* Seth would be there waiting.

"Seth," Angel whispered, "where are you?"

Not even the chirp of crickets or hoot of an owl answered her. She crossed the porch and descended the steps, scanning the sidewalk and street, to the right, then left.

Nothing.

Angel called again, but this time silently. *Seth, I'm here. Where are you?*

Around back. By the empty tool shed.

She took a step, then stopped. It could be a Dark Bearer waiting for her. A trap set by the Dark One who claimed to be her father. She shivered and hugged herself. He had sent others to collect her before.

It was how she had met Seth.

Angel swallowed her fear. She couldn't *not* go. Not if there was even the smallest chance it *was* Seth. Besides, her dreams were never wrong. That was her gift.

She went around the side of the house. The air changed, seeming to become charged with some sort of energy. The hair on her arms prickled, then stood on end.

Seth. I'm here.

And then, there he was. Stepping out from the shadow of the shed. He opened his arms and she ran to him, clinging as he held her tightly, and feeling the missing piece of her click back into place. In her womb, their baby stirred, as if recognizing its father.

After several moments, he eased her from him. Cupping her face in his hands, he studied her.

"What?" she asked, voice thick.

"I missed you so much."

Tears flooded her eyes. "I missed you, too. But I knew you'd come. No one believed me."

"I'm sorry it took so long."

She shuddered with longing as he trailed his thumb across her bottom lip. "Where have you been?"

"Everywhere but here. On the move, in hiding." He rested his forehead against hers. "When I chose you over Will, I betrayed the Dark One and his forces. I have an army after me now."

Fear nearly choked her. An army of Dark Bearers? Some with power enough to bring a building down, turn it to rubble? Or the kind with power that couldn't be overcome by less than a dozen Full Lights?

She trembled. What chance did they have against such forces?

"Hey," he said, tipping her face up to his. "It's going to be all right."

"How?" Her eyes filled with tears. "Where can we go? How do we hide from an army?"

He kissed her, once, then again. Softly at first, then deepening with passion. And something more. Urgency, she realized. They didn't have much time.

When he ended the kiss, she whimpered in protest anyway.

"Do you trust me?" he asked softly.

"Yes."

"I have a place. It's for beings like us. We'll be safe."

Beings like her and Seth—half light and half dark, products of obscene experiments enacted by the forces of darkness.

She had to tell him about the baby. She wished she didn't have to, not now, like this.

He felt her stiffen and frowned. "What's wrong? If it came to it, I'd lay my life down for you, Angel. You believe that, don't you?"

"I do. But there's something I have to tell you." She took a deep breath. "It's not just me anymore, Seth. I'm pregnant."

He looked stunned. Then disbelieving. "Are you sure?"

She wanted to cry. "Yes, I'm sure."

"Have you been to a doctor?"

"No. Just a home test. But I know I am. There are . . . changes. In me. My body. How I feel."

She took his hand, laid it on the gentle swell of her abdomen. He splayed his fingers, expression changing from disbelief to wonder.

"We're having a baby."

She nodded, her tears spilling over. He kissed them away, kissed her so tenderly and deeply, it took her breath away.

"Do we have to go?" she asked. "I feel safe here."

"I get that, babe. But I can't stay here. It's not safe for me. And it never will be."

He cupped her face in his hands once more. "And you won't be safe either, not if we're together. Because they'll know they can get to me through you."

She knew he was right, but didn't want to face it. "We have powerful friends here, Seth. They'll help us. I know they will."

"I don't think so, babe. I'm not one of them."

"But neither am I!"

"It's different for me. You've never been controlled by the darkness. It's a battle for me, every day. And they'll never trust me because of it."

She opened her mouth to argue, but he stopped her. "We've got to think about our baby now. They're going to want it. And if they get the chance, they'll take it from us."

She would do whatever necessary to ensure that didn't happen. "I'll get my stuff."

He stopped her, drawing her against his chest once more. "Not yet. The baby changes things. I'm not certain they'll take us now."

Angel couldn't believe what he was saying. "You're leaving me?"

"I have to, babe. Trust me."

"You say you'll keep me safe, but if anyone tried to hurt you, I'd do anything to protect you. Anything," she finished, surprised by the ferocity in her voice.

He laid a finger gently against her lips. "Don't say that. That's the dark in you talking. If you give hatred even a toehold, it makes you vulnerable to them."

She looped her arms around his neck. "Please take me with you."

"I can't. Not yet." He unwound her arms and set her away from him. "But I'll be back."

She felt as if she was dying inside. "Promise me."

"I promise." He kissed her again. Hard. Then took a step back. "Don't tell anyone I was here, Angel. Anyone."

And then he was gone.

CHAPTER THIRTY-NINE

9:20 P.M.

MICKI PACED FROM ONE END of the house to the other, like the lion she'd seen at the Mobile Zoo when she was six. Pacing back and forth. Planning its escape. Deciding who would be the first to pay the price for its imprisonment.

Inaction wasn't her style. Cooling her heels made her want to kill someone. Just like it did that lion.

Take charge and move the situation forward. That's what she did. That was one of the reasons she was a good cop.

Was a good cop. Past tense.

For how long? she wondered. The professor had said to wait for his call. Eli had promised the two of them would take care everything. But when?

The hours had crept by, her mood growing darker as they did. Her phone had gone silent. She'd tried to distract herself with TV and the Internet. She'd talked to Hank, but he had been silent.

So she'd returned to pacing.

Something was wrong here. It nagged at her, like an insect flying around her head, but every time she went to swat it, it darted out of reach.

Hank's medal had begun to chafe. It had started in the car with Professor Truebell, and gotten worse as the day progressed. So much for feeling wrapped in the warmth of Hank's presence. It had become another irritation in a day brimming with them, and, muttering an oath, she took it off.

Immediately, she felt bereft. And vulnerable.

Stupid, she thought. Maudlin. Ignoring the urge to put it back on, she marched to her bedroom and laid it on the nightstand by the photo of her and Hank. She gazed at the photo, tears gathering in her eyes, then shifted to another one, of her and her friend, Jacqui. Jacqui cradling Xander in her arms. Micki wondered how they were, if they were safe. Alexander was a special child, maybe the most special. He and Jacqui had had to go into hiding, to protect Xander from the Dark One and his army.

More loss, she thought. And now Angel. Micki turned her gaze to the hallway and Angel's bedroom door. Closed, shut tight. The way she felt, closed off from everyone—and everything—she cared about.

She made her way to Angel's room, stopping at that door, an ache in her chest. What did she say to Angel that was so awful? That caused her to pack up her stuff and just . . . go?

Micki thought back to the last time they'd really talked, exchanging more than a "Hello," "Goodbye" or "Have a great day."

The night they'd shared a peanut butter sandwich, she recalled. Sure, she'd been honest about her feelings—and her worries. But she'd been gentle. Respectful of Angel feelings. At least she'd meant to be.

Out of habit, Micki tapped on the door, waited a moment, then opened it. Neat and tidy, bed made, everything in good order—just as it had been two days ago. She crossed to the closet. A few of Angel's things hung there, summer items, mostly. She went to the dresser next, opening each drawer. Like the closet, they contained items Angel left behind.

Micki found them reassuring. Angel would be back, even if only to retrieve her things. Whatever happened between them, they'd work through it. Eventually. She had to believe that.

As she turned to go, Micki noticed the small trash can by the desk was full. She snatched it up and a wadded piece of paper tumbled out. She bent to retrieve it, then smoothed it out.

Nothing on either side but a few strokes and smears of charcoal, the beginning of something gone bad.

Like her and Angel's relationship.

Micki re-crumpled the paper, tossed it in the can. As she did, she noticed a pink and white stick peeking out from a wad of Kleenex.

A pregnancy test? It was, she saw, as she plucked it out of the trash. The display window was empty, whatever the results were, now long gone.

Micki sat on the edge of the bed, the stick still held between her thumb and first finger. Her mind raced. Could Angel be pregnant? If she was, it had to be Seth's. She was crazy in love with him—she wouldn't have been with anyone else. So, how far along would she be? Micki counted back.

Three months, give or take a few days. That was a long time to keep that kind of secret. Unless she hadn't known. If Angel's periods were irregular, that could happen. It happened all the time.

Angel had been moody, Micki realized. A couple times over the past weeks she'd mentioned feeling queasy, that she didn't feel like eating. In retrospect, she should have suspected.

Micki stood up and headed to the kitchen. How long had Angel known? Not long, judging by test result's location near the top of the waste basket—and the fact that she'd been gone three days.

Which meant she'd discovered she was pregnant and, basically, run to Arianna. That hurt. A lot.

But why? Micki wondered. Why not share the news with her? And who else would she tell? Surely not Zach? They were close, but he would have urged Angel to tell her. Eli and Professor Truebell, according to Arianna, were unavailable.

Micki found her phone, punched in Arianna's number. Nearly eleven, the woman answered, voice sleepy sounding.

"It's Micki," she said.

"I can't talk to you—"

"Don't hang up. I just need to know one thing. Did Angel tell you she's pregnant?"

"I guessed and she confirmed it."

"Is she awake? I want to talk to her."

"She doesn't want to talk to you."

She shouldn't care, Micki thought. It shouldn't hurt. But it did. Another rejection in a long list of them.

But that didn't matter. Angel's health and her baby's safety did. "I need to know that she's okay."

"She's fine."

"Has she been to the doctor?"

Arianna's silence was her answer.

"Why not?"

"I didn't think it was safe. Considering."

Considering The Prophesy. That the Chosen One was coming: a

being half light and half dark who would bring lasting peace or final destruction. Whoever controlled that being controlled the fate of the world.

"How did you find out?" Arianna asked.

"The home test was in her trash can. Who else knows?"

"No one. I think we should keep it that way. I've got to go."

"Wait! Have you spoken with Eli or Professor Truebell yet?"

"No. Good night, Micki."

Micki held the phone to her ear for several moments after Arianna hung up. Suddenly exhausted, she made her way to Hank's old recliner. She sank into it, the worn leather cushioning her like a hug.

Neither Eli nor Professor Truebell had been in contact with Arianna yet. Yet Eli had contacted her twenty-four hours ago? They were both back in town, yet they hadn't been by LAM?

Something was wrong. She rested her head back and gazed up at the ceiling. A long, thin crack ran from the fan at the center to the far edge. Arianna said no one else knew about Angel's pregnancy. Which meant she hadn't shared the information with Zach, her son, or Parker, her own brother.

None of this made sense. And until Eli or the professor got back to her, there wasn't a damn thing she could do about it.

CHAPTER FORTY

10:30 P.M.

MAJOR NICHOLS HAD BEEN TAKEN to University Medical Center. Zach met Susan in the ICU waiting room. She looked ragged with worry and fatigue. Even her usually teased-up do had fallen.

"How is he?" he asked.

"In a lot of pain." She clasped her hands in front of her. "They have him pretty heavily drugged now, so he's out of it."

"What are his injuries?"

"A punctured lung. Shattered all his ribs on his right side. Broken collar bone. It could have been much worse."

She started to shake and Zach helped her to a seat. "It's late. You need to go home."

She nodded, chin quivering. "I know. I just . . . I feel so guilty."

He took the chair next to hers and angled toward her. "Why's that, Sue?"

"I should have done something. If I'd reacted quicker . . . maybe I could have kept him from falling."

He thought of Mercedes King. That moment when she'd gone over the side and he knew he was too late. He'd lost her. That moment would haunt him for a long time. "I understand feeling that way. But sometimes there's simply nothing you can do."

She nodded and looked down at her hands. Her cat's-eye glasses slid down her nose.

"What happened?" he asked gently. "I was just there with him, and he was fine."

She pushed her glasses back up her nose; her hand shook. "He was at the window. He'd pushed it all the way up—you know how big those old windows are."

"I do," he said softly.

"He was looking down at the street. And . . . he just fell."

"Just fell out the window?" Zach said.

She glanced at him, then looked back down at her hands. Again, the glasses slipped. "Uh-huh. Just fell." She cleared her throat. "They think he may have had a seizure or blacked-out or something."

"What do you think, Susan?"

"I don't know what to think." She looked fully at him then. "He's the best boss I've ever had. And he's a good man. A really good man."

She wasn't telling him everything. But not to protect herself, to protect Major Nichols.

"When I was going through my divorce, he was so kind. He made accommodations for me. If it was a particularly bad day, he'd tell me to go home. Take some time. But he never counted it against me, never docked my pay." She nudged the glasses up. "Today was . . . it was so horrible, Zach."

"Yes," he agreed, "it was." He paused. "Think for a moment, Sue. Was there anything else, something that might have spoken to his state of mind?"

She shook her head. "He was fine. You said so yourself." Her chin inched slightly up. "He didn't deliberately fall out that window. He didn't jump."

"I'm not suggesting he did."

She went on, expression adamant, "He was in good spirits. He smiled at me when I came in the room. That's not suicidal. Right?"

Zach pictured Mercedes, that strange, chilling smile the moment before she let go of the balcony rail, and a bitter, metallic taste filled his mouth.

"Right?" she asked again.

"Right." He reached across and covered her hands with his. "Look at me, Susan."

She did and he held her gaze. He felt the connection, like the tumbler of a lock, clicking into place. He ignored the pinch of guilt—Sue was a friend, traumatized and because of that, particularly vulnerable to him. He concentrated on using his light force to overcome her resistance.

His fingers tingled slightly, then his palm. "You're exhausted," he said.

"Yes." Her lips trembled. "I'm so tired, Zach."

"You know you can trust me." She nodded. "You know I have Major Nichols' back, just like you do."

She nodded again and he held her gaze. "Was Major Nichols' falling out that window an accident, Sue?"

Tears flooded her eyes, and she slowly shook her head. "No, it wasn't an accident."

"When you walked into his office, tell me exactly what you saw."

"He was perched there at the window. Talking to himself and staring down at the street. I said his name. In a question, you know? Like what's going on? He looked at me and—" she shuddered, "—and grinned. Then he just . . . fell. On purpose."

Talking to himself, the way Mercedes had been. The way her father had been. Both immediately before plunging to their deaths.

Zach swallowed hard, feeling sick. Killian was right this morning, when she said something didn't add up. Partially right, anyway. Because it wasn't something that didn't add up—it was everything.

He had to go back to the Eighth and confirm what he suspected—that the amber-eyed woman had visited Major Nichols.

"Sue," he said, "has anyone been in the major's office since the fall?"

"No. I closed the window and locked the door before I left."

He tightened his fingers around hers. "This doesn't add up. I know he'd want me to search for clues to what really happened. You want that too, don't you?"

A tear slipped down her cheek and her lips quivered. "I do."

"I need to get into Major Nichols' office. Can you help me do that, Sue?"

"I keep an extra key to his office in my desk. It's taped to the underside of the middle drawer."

"Thank you, Sue. You did the right thing." He stood, helping her to her feet. "You need to get some sleep. I'll walk you to your car."

Twenty minutes later, Zach's suspicions proved correct. The amber-eyed woman had been here. He picked her up on the arm of one of the chairs in front of Nichols' desk, and again on the stand of a display baseball he kept on his desk, engraved with the logo of Nichols' favorite team, the Chicago Cubs.

Zach crossed to the window and slid it up. He poked his head out the opening and the energy hit him. Not the woman. Something different. Dark. Mercurial and threatening.

Zach jerked away from the window, disturbing a feather resting on the ledge, sending it over the side. A black feather, he realized. Like the one Micki had found at King's the night of his suicide? He couldn't be sure, but his gut told him yes.

Zach shut the window. The amber-eyed woman hadn't been alone. Not at King's. Not here. And whatever he'd picked up was every bit as dangerous as the woman. And maybe more.

Because this creature had the ability to fly away.

CHAPTER FORTY-ONE

Friday, November 16
12:01 A.M.

"COME, MICHAELA, LET'S PLAY A little game of make-believe."
Uncle Beau. His voice in her ear. The smell of his bour-
bon-sweet breath filling her senses.

Micki's eyes snapped open. Not her childhood bedroom. Her cozy
living-room. The TV was on.

*"In other news, Mercedes King, the daughter of developer Thomas King, has
died. This afternoon, in a tragic turn of events, Ms. King leapt to her death from
the same high-rise balcony her father had only six days ago."*

Micki came fully awake. She shook her head in an attempt to clear
away the nightmare.

*"Detective Zach Harris was at the scene. He endeavored to save the woman
but was too late."*

Micki snatched up her phone to send Zach a text message. *Just saw the
news,* she typed. *Heard you were there. Call me when you—*

She stopped. The professor had told her not to talk to anyone. Especially Zach. Zach, who had told Major Nichols she was emotionally
fragile and acting erratically.

He was her partner. He was supposed to take her side, no matter
what.

She deleted the text and tossed the phone aside, her attention turning
back to the television. The segment had been edited to jump from an
interview with one witness after another: the couple who had been sip-
ping cocktails on the patio below, the housekeeper cleaning a room five
floors below, a mother and daughter on their first trip to New Orleans.

She should have been there, Micki thought. Maybe she could have stopped it from happening.

But here she'd sat. Doing nothing. Disgusted, Micki grabbed the remote and silenced the TV.

And as the room went quiet, she became aware of the rhythmic squeaking of the front porch swing. With it came the scent of tobacco, one she remembered from her childhood.

And from her nightmares.

Micki broke into a cold sweat. Slowly, carefully, she reached for her gun, there on the side table beside the recliner, then eased out of the chair. She tucked the weapon into the waistband of her pants. And only then, with its cold weight pressing into the small of her back, did she take a breath.

It couldn't be Uncle Beau. Her stir-crazy mind was playing tricks. He would be an old man now. She could take him, easily—with or without the firearm.

On bare feet, she went to the door, slid the dead bolt back, inched the door open.

She was wrong. The devil had, indeed, come to call.

"Hello, Michaela," he said, stopping the swing and standing.

He hadn't changed. Hadn't aged. Her breath lodged in her lungs. She felt seven years old again, frightened and helpless. She felt his hands on her, his sweaty body touching hers with hair that rubbed her raw, his weight smothering her. Heard her silent screams for help and tasted her own vomit.

"You're not welcome here," she said.

He stopped directly in front of her. "I'm family, Michaela. I'm always welcome." He moved around her and into her house.

And like the child she'd been back then, she didn't stop him.

"Close the door, Michaela. You'll let the moths in."

"Yes, Uncle Beau."

She curled her hands into fists. "Why are you here? Is it about mother? Aunt Jo?"

He looked at her. His grin was straight out of her nightmares. "You know why I'm here."

"Come Michaela, let's play a little game of make-believe . . ."

She started to tremble. From the inside out, core deep, until even her teeth chattered.

"No, Uncle Beau. Please don't."

He held out his hand. "Come along. Be a good girl."

She stared at the short, pudgy fingers, stomach lurching to her throat. Knowing his palm would be damp as she slipped her tiny hand trustingly in his.

Not.

This.

Time.

She reached behind her. "This ends now." Gripping the gun with both hands, she aimed at his chest.

He laughed. "You're not going to shoot me."

"Oh, yes, I am. I should have done it a long time ago."

"But you didn't. Because you're weak, Michaela. You always were."

"Maybe then. Not now."

"You liked it. You liked the attention. My attention."

"No." She gripped the gun tighter. Sweat slid down her spine. "I hated it. And I hated you."

"But you never told anyone, did you?" He leaned closer. "Our little secret to share. Just the two of us."

"Shut up."

"It's still our little secret, isn't it? You've never told anyone. Why's that, Michaela?"

Shame. Guilt. Her fault Mama was so crazy. Her fault her daddy left. Her fault Uncle Beau hurt her.

Sweat formed on her upper lip. "No." She shook her head. "You're a monster."

She squeezed her eyes shut. And when she opened them, it was Hank standing before her.

"Hank!" she cried, and dropped the gun. He held out his arms and she threw herself into them. "What's all the fuss about, girl?" he whispered, holding her tightly.

Micki pressed her face into his chest, her memory and senses swamped with him—the feel of her cheek against his chest, his clean, masculine scent, the cadence of his breathing.

"I miss you so much! Why did you have to go, Hank? Why'd you have to die?"

"Because of you, Michaela. It's your fault."

Uncle Beau's voice again. Not Hank's. His comforting arms—gone. She was in the grip of a fiend.

With a cry, Micki pushed away, stumbling slightly. She righted herself. "You're not Uncle Beau, or Hank. You're a fabrication from my memories. You can't hurt me."

"Really?" He laughed. "A fabrication?"

"A thing called a chameleon. A type of Dark Bearer that uses a person's dreams, desires and nightmares to control them."

"Bravo! And where did you get all this information?"

"A friend. One with the ability to stop you."

"A friend? With abilities? Which one?"

Transfixed, Micki watched the vision transform in front of her eyes. Like a snake shedding its skin, the shedding layer folded back into itself, at once horrible and fascinating.

"This friend?"

The elfin Professor Truebell stood before her.

"Or this one?"

The transformation happened again, more quickly this time, in the blink of an eye. So fast she could have imagined it.

Except there stood Eli, tall and classically handsome, close enough to reach out and touch. Eli, the healer, who would never hurt anyone. Her senses flooded with him and his brilliant blue eyes seemed to reach in to touch her soul.

He was so real. Both of them were. Micki took a step back, feeling as if the very foundation beneath her was crumbling. "But you can't imprint a Full Light."

"But I haven't. I imprinted *you*. All of this, every detail, I got from *you*."

Almost like a bird ruffling its feathers, the chameleon transformed back into Uncle Beau. "You didn't even see it coming. You didn't even question why Eli had to knock on your door that night. Like a mere human. He can communicate telepathically with you, Michaela. He can place his fingertips on your temple and access all you have to tell him. But did he do that?"

He leered at her. "No. But you didn't wonder about that, not even once."

Stupid, Micki realized. Gullible. She'd wanted so badly for Eli to come fix everything, she had never questioned if it was truly he.

"Even after I told you what I could do, what I could become, you still believed. That night, as Eli, today as your precious professor, all you had to do was put two and two together. But you didn't. It always works, no matter whether my chosen victim is a captain of industry or a disillusioned police officer."

"Big problem for you," Micki said, voice shaking. "Now I know you're not real, you can't hurt me."

"Oh, but I can. Because I'm as real as your memories. And like them, I'm always with you."

Her gun lay on the floor between them. Micki calculated her best move for getting her hands on it before the chameleon did.

"I'm not going to fight you for that," he said. "Go ahead, take your time."

Micki snatched it up, curling her fingers around the grip. "You need to die."

"You're the one who needs to die, Michaela. No one cares about you. No one wants you around."

"That's bullshit."

"You didn't even know Angel was pregnant. Why is that?" Micki didn't respond, and he went on, "She told Arianna, and Angel hardly even *knows* her. But when she needed understanding, that's who she went to.

"And what about Zach?" Uncle Beau grinned; sweat beaded his upper lip, the way it always had, no matter the temperature outside. "He betrayed you, didn't he? Like all the others. Your father first, just up and left you without a goodbye. Your mother was next, wasn't she? Oh, she stayed in body. But her soul checked out. She didn't care enough about her little girl to notice . . . things. Even your old partner turned on you. Everyone, Michaela. Why is that?"

Every word felt like another piece of flesh being brutally ripped away. No, worse than that. Pieces of her soul.

"And what about your precious Hank?"

"He never left. He loved me and believed in me."

"Then why didn't he tell you the truth?"

"What truth?" Her gun bobbled. "We shared everything."

"Not everything, Michaela. You didn't tell him about me. You didn't tell him about *us*."

His voice was suddenly everywhere. Booming off the walls and resounding in her head. Over and over.

You didn't tell him about us.

"Stop it!" she cried.

"And he didn't tell you everything, Michaela. He had secrets from you. Big secrets."

She tightened her grip on the gun. It seemed to have no effect. "Is that why you killed him?"

"I didn't. You did. You killed him."

The last was like a damning hiss. Micki felt it to her soul.

"You wouldn't back off. You forced my hand. And now you're doing it again. The same mistakes, over and over. You're stupid and weak."

"I'm taking you out. This stops today. Now."

"I agree. It should stop." Her uncle's thick drawl deepened. "But my death won't stop it. Only yours will."

Micki struggled to clear her head. To stop his words from seeping in and sounding . . . right. Because they were making sense. The logic of them was bringing a sort of peace.

"No," she managed. The Glock's grip was slippery with sweat. Sweat rolled down her spine and pooled in the small of her back. "Dead is dead, no matter what kind of monster you are."

He laughed. "You can't shake this off, because I'm in control. We're joined now. That day, the cold. I know you felt it. I slithered into your head. I live there now, Michaela. Just like I lived in Thom's and Mercedes' heads. Just imagine me, there in prison with you. And every day, every moment, I'll remind you of who and what you really are."

"Come, Michaela, let's play a little game of make-believe."

"The instant you pull that trigger, I transform into Natalie King and you become a murderer. You're the cop who went off the rails and murdered an innocent woman. What a blight on the NOPD. Her estate will sue, of course. Her attorney will see to that. Think about the future, Michaela. About just how awful it would be for everyone and everything you care about."

Micki did, ideas and images running wild through her head, stealing her ability think clearly, let alone fight. Her legs gave, and she dropped to her knees.

"Only you can stop our little game of make-believe."

Him, his voice, in her head forever. Her reputation ruined. A cop gone bad. The police department punished. The people she cared about hurt.

Micki looked at the gun, held now with limp fingers. It would be so easy. So quick. And then, no more pain. No more nightmares.

She curved her fingers around the grip. Tears slipping down her cheeks, she turned the barrel on herself.

"That's my good girl," he said softly, starting toward the door, and pausing when he reached it. "You don't get out of this alive, Michaela. You never could."

CHAPTER FORTY-TWO

12:59 A.M.

ZACH TURNED ONTO MICKI'S STREET. The arc of his headlights illuminated a man climbing into a car parked directly in front of her place. Zach frowned. From the man's hulking silhouette, he appeared middle-aged and overweight.

It was well after midnight. What business could he have had with Mick?

Zach didn't like any of the answers that popped into his head. He eyed the car as it passed him; the driver didn't glance his way. Just in case the man checked his rearview, Zach drove past Mick's, pulling over only when the other vehicle turned off.

Zach wasted no time, setting off for Mick's at a dead run. He reached the entrance, rang the bell. After several moments of silence, he pounded on the door. "Mick! It's me. Open up!"

"Leave me alone! I don't want you here."

Her voice sounded strange, wild and uneven. "Mick, sweetheart, you're talking crazy. Come to the door. It's me."

When she didn't respond, he grabbed the door handle. A sensation like poker-hot pinpricks ran up his arm. The image of the woman exploded in his head. Her amber eyes seemed to glow as she laughed.

At him. As if she had *known*. That Zach would come. But that he would be too late. That she had bested him—both of them—and had known the outcome of the game before it had even started.

Fear nearly strangled him. He pounded on the door. "Dammit, Mick! Open the door."

Nothing. He peered through the sidelight—the foyer was clear. He went to the front window. The shade was drawn, save for an inch at the bottom. He squatted, peered inside.

The sliver revealed Mick, on her knees. Holding something to her head. No, not something. Her gun.

As if she sensed him staring, she turned toward the window. And smiled. That same flat, expressionless grin that Mercedes King had turned on him just hours ago.

Panic propelled him back to the door. He pounded. "Open this goddamn door right now, or I'm going to kick it in! Five . . . four . . . three . . . two—"

For the second time in less than twenty-four hours, Zach found himself rearing back, then driving his heel into a door. This time, he placed it perfectly. The wood splintered. With the second blow, a panel cracked, then, with the third, shattered.

Zach reached through, unlocked the deadbolt and burst into the house.

Mick was on her feet then, eyes wide, gun aimed directly at him. He stopped short, lifting his hands in surrender.

"Whoa . . . put the gun away."

"Stay away from me. You're not real."

"Mick, sweetheart . . . if I'm not Zach, who would I be?" She was looking at him as if he was a monster. "It's me. Your partner. Your friend."

"Prove it."

"Seeing me's not enough?"

"No."

"Who was that man I saw leaving?"

"My Uncle Beau. But he wasn't real either."

He took a cautious step toward her. "I saw him, Mick. Big guy. He climbed into a car and drove away."

"You don't understand." Her eyes filled with tears. "He's in my head. I can't live with him in there."

Zach took another step and held his hand out. "Mick, I can't do this job without you. Give me the gun. We'll work it out."

"I don't think we can." She shook her head. "No. I don't think *I* can."

She turned the gun on herself and his heart jumped to his throat. "It's Natalie King," he said quickly. "She's some sort of dark force. I think she can change shapes."

Zach tried to calm his voice. "I picked up her energy on the door handle."

Mick's expression changed, as if something he said struck a chord.

"Remember the dark-haired, amber-eyed woman I picked up at the King scene? Mercedes King killed herself this afternoon—she was there, too. And at the Eighth, in Major Nichols' office."

He took another step. He was almost close enough to grab the gun. Problem was, if he made that kind of move, she might pull the trigger.

"And just now, I picked her up from your door handle. She was laughing. At me. At *us*, Mick. Because she thought she'd beaten us."

She hadn't moved, so he pressed forward. "I think she masks her true physical identity somehow."

"She's a chameleon," Micki said. "And she has beaten us, Zach. She's won."

"She's hasn't beaten me, Mick. How about you?"

She didn't respond. He was losing her, he realized. "That's not you, Mick! You're a fighter. Mad Dog Dare, remember?"

She shook her head. Time seemed to slow. Every sound magnified in his head—the rustle of her hair against her neck, the faint creak of the gun's firing mechanism, her exhalation of breath.

Something bright, hot, and primal rose up in him. He felt it pour forth from his being. A sound rent the air between them, the ceiling fan spun wildly, and light exploded around them. No, not around them—from him. The gun flew from her hand, hit the wall and dropped.

In the next moment, he had her cradled in his arms—and encased in a cocoon of light. For long moments, she shook uncontrollably; her teeth chattered, and her hands were like ice.

Slowly, warmth seeped into her. Her body stilled, then softened, as if whatever evil had held her in its grip melted away. Until she was Mick again.

His Mick.

He closed his eyes and breathed her in, the realization of how close he'd come to losing her sinking in. Zach pressed his lips to the top of her head, and she tilted her face up to his in an unspoken question.

He decided on honesty. "I almost lost you."

"Yes," she said.

He shuddered and pulled her closer again. He rested his cheek against her hair. "Don't ever scare me like that again."

"I was . . . going to do it." She looked up at him. "I couldn't get his voice out of my head. And hers too, the chameleon's, telling me it was the best way. The only way." Her eyes flooded with tears. "You saved my life, Zach."

They stayed that way, gazes locked and clinging to one another—contemplating the horror of what could have been—and almost was.

He thought of those moments, his to-the-core terror followed by that explosion of light. His light. So forcefully directed, it ripped the gun away from her. He'd seen Full Lights with that kind of power. But Half Lights like him couldn't do things like that.

A fluke, he decided. Born of terror and desperation.

"How did you get the gun away from me?" Mick asked.

"You don't remember?"

"It was like I blinked, and I was in your arms."

A discussion for another time, he thought, and tucked her hair behind her ear. "They don't call me Hollywood Harris for nothing."

She smiled and laid her head against his shoulder.

"I have a question," he said.

"You just saved my life. Ask away."

"The other night, at my apartment—"

"Your apartment?"

"Yeah, you know. When you said . . ."

He realized she didn't have a clue what he was talking about, and let the last trail off. He'd been about to ask if she'd meant what she said about "now or never."

That hadn't even been her, he realized. It must have been the thing she'd called a chameleon.

He wanted to laugh. That night, he'd known that wasn't Mick. On some cellular—or chemical—level. That's why it had been as easy as it'd been to turn her down.

Even knowing all that now, he felt almost comically disappointed.

"What's wrong?" she asked, frowning slightly, in that totally Mick way, two small furrows forming between her eyebrows.

One corner of his mouth lifted in a lopsided grin. "Just thinking that you and I have a lot of talking to do."

CHAPTER FORTY-THREE

2:40 A.M.

MICKI TOWEL-DRIED HER HAIR. IT fell in loose waves to her shoulders. Funny how she'd hated those waves as a teenager. How she'd fought them. Now, she was so grateful she had them because they made her life easier.

She thought of Zach, waiting for her in the living room. How she'd fought him becoming her partner. How pissed off she'd been.

And how grateful for him she now was.

She stepped into her lightest sweatpants, the soft, clingy fabric somehow reassuring. As was the ancient denim shirt she donned, the fabric worn threadbare in places from years of washing.

Zach wasn't in the living room, she discovered moments later. He was in the kitchen. She stopped in the doorway, a greeting dying on her lips. He stood with his back to her as he gazed out the window above the sink.

A lump formed in her throat as an unfamiliar feeling washed over her—like the sun peeking out from behind clouds on a chilly day.

And something more. From deep inside her. A place that had been long closed seemed to unfurl.

Her breath caught. This belonging, this need, was dangerous territory. She told herself to shut it down, clamp a lid on whatever this was happening between them.

She couldn't do it. Maybe later, but not now. For this moment, she couldn't bear to lose what she'd just found.

Zach looked over his shoulder at her and smiled. "You okay?"

"Yeah." She smiled. "Happy."

His eyebrows shot up in mock shock. "I don't know that I've ever heard you say that before."

She didn't smile. "I'm glad you're really you."

He was silent. Their gazes held. Something crackled between them, like a high voltage wire.

He broke the connection. "I'm mostly glad you're really you."

A combination of relief and disappointment skittered through her. "Mostly?"

"Yeah." He crossed to the refrigerator and opened the freezer. "While you were in the shower, I ran to the grocery." He took a bag out and carried it to the table. "I didn't know what your favorite flavor was, so I got several."

"You got ice cream?"

"Yup." He took a pint of Blue Bell from the bag. "Sweet and Salty Crunch," he said, setting it on the table. He reached for another. "Rocky Road." He took another pint from the bag. "Cookies and Cream."

"What? No vanilla?"

"I'm not a vanilla kind of guy." He met her eyes. "And I didn't think you were a vanilla kind of girl. Was I wrong?"

They both knew he wasn't really talking about ice cream flavors. And God help her, he wasn't wrong.

"No, you were right."

He grinned. "I covered my bases anyway." He took a last tub out of the bag, held it up.

"The Great Divide," she read aloud, then laughed. "Sounds a bit like us."

She grabbed a couple of spoons and they sat across from each other at the table, the four pints between them. She pried the lid off the Sweet and Salty Crunch and dug in.

"Oh, my God," she said around the sweet, melting mouthful, "this is so good." She went for another.

He laughed and opened the Rocky Road. "Reminds me of being a kid. It wasn't Blue Bell. Haagen Das."

"The fancy stuff." She licked her spoon. Then her lips.

He watched her. "You might want to stop doing that."

"What?" She licked the sweet, sticky residue from the corners of her mouth.

"That."

She realized what he meant, and knew she had a choice. Tease him by doing it again—and take what was happening between them a step closer to its natural conclusion. Or take a giant step back to reality.

Micki laid down her spoon. "You ready to talk?"

"Only if the party's over?"

She wished the situation was different or that she was another kind of woman. "Seems that way, Hollywood. Sorry."

"It's okay, Mick. I consider it a temporary delay." He stuck his spoon in the Rocky Road. "You go first. I'll appease myself with ice cream."

"Where should I start?"

"Start with that chameleon thing. What the hell is that?"

So she told him about Eli coming to see her, how he had told her Natalie King was a chameleon. How they got in your head and could transform themselves into that which you most desired. Or feared. And anything in between.

It was his turn to talk around a mouthful of ice cream. "That case you told me about, The Three Queens investigation—How does it fit in?"

"That shrink who skipped the country, she's the very same creature who is now Natalie King. I crossed her then and she took the person I loved most in the world. I've crossed her again, but this time she means to take everything from me."

"Even your life."

"It looks that way." Micki took a cleansing breath and went on, "Even knowing all that, I was one hundred percent fooled. First by Eli, then Professor Truebell. Until tonight, I thought they were both back in New Orleans."

She shook her head. "I should have spotted the ruse right away, that both Eli and Truebell were manifestations, but I didn't because I wanted so desperately to believe. I just . . . let myself overlook the obvious."

"Which was?"

"They had no powers. Couldn't read my mind or communicate telepathically. None of it."

"You said 'until tonight.' What changed?"

"She came as Uncle Beau, then transformed into Hank. And back. She admitted it all, totally revealed herself."

"But you weren't supposed to live to tell the tale."

"I wouldn't have, if not for you." She cleared her throat, hating the tremor. The show of weakness. "That place she took me, I never want to feel that way again."

Zach reached across the table and laced his fingers with hers. "What did she do to you? How, Mick?" He searched her gaze. "You're the strongest person I've ever met."

She forced a weak smile. "I guess I've blown my skull crusher image."

He didn't return the smile. "That's not the kind of strength I mean."

"She knew all my secrets. My darkest fears and deepest wounds, and she used them against me. It was psychological warfare, and it was . . . brutal."

Micki looked down at their joined hands. "I was defenseless. It was like she stripped me of everything good and strong." She lifted her gaze to his. "Everything worth living for was gone."

He reached his other hand across the table. She grasped it.

"I'm sorry," he said. "I should have stood up for you. I should have gone in there and made them understand the kind of cop you are."

"You have nothing to apologize for, Zach."

"Don't I?"

She winced at the bitterness in his tone. "No, you don't. I saw that video. What were you supposed to think? I looked completely deranged."

"Nichols came to my house yesterday morning, early. He told me about King registering a complaint against you. She provided video, he wanted me to look at it." He paused. "I was worried about you. I told him so."

She pushed back from the table, stood and crossed to the sink. "You said I was acting erratically and was" —she made quote marks with her free hand— " 'emotionally fragile.' After seeing the video, I deserved that."

"I didn't say that, Mick. I told him I was worried about you, that's it. He promised me nothing was going to happen fast and that I would be formally interviewed by someone from the Public Integrity Division. He told me to take my time coming in, wrap my head around it. Next thing I know, I get to the Eighth and learn from Susan that it's all going down."

"Wait, PID didn't question you?" He shook his head, and she laughed—a short, humorless bark. "PID always consults the partner first."

"What are you saying?"

"Susan told me you were in early, then left again. That wasn't Major Nichols who came to see you. It was the chameleon."

"And then, knowing I was 'wrapping my head around' the situation, the chameleon visits Nichols at the Eighth, posing as me. I confirm to Nichols you're losing it, which furthers her agenda."

"To alienate me from everyone and everything I care about. Brilliant," she muttered. "She out-played me at every move."

"More than you even know."

Micki drew her eyebrows together, not liking the sound of that. "What do you mean?"

"You might need some ice cream to help this go down easy."

"Fuck that. What did she do?"

"You tried to seduce me."

"Excuse me?"

"You came to my apartment for, well . . . you came for sex, Mick."

She made a choked sound and he went on, "You were pretty insistent. In fact, you wouldn't take no for an answer."

"What does *that* mean?"

"Use your imagination."

Her face went hot. "You should have known that wasn't me."

"I don't know how. Looked like you, sounded like you." He paused a moment for effect. "Kissed like you."

He was the picture of boyish innocence. She wanted to smack him. "You sick bastard! You're enjoying this."

"Not as much as I enjoyed that."

"It wasn't me," she said. "So whatever happened—"

"Nothing happened. I turned you down."

"You turned me down?" Her voice hit a squeaky note.

He turned serious. "I turned you down because it wasn't you."

"But you said—"

He laced his fingers with hers. "Looked like you, sounded like you . . . and so on, but wasn't *you*. I knew that and wasn't about to take advantage of whatever breakdown you were having. Even when you threatened it was 'now or never.'"

She swallowed hard, imagining saying that to him, but wishing she couldn't.

"When you confronted me after being suspended, it was an extension of that bizarre scene the night before."

It explained a lot. Natalie King had a lot to answer for.

"I do want you, Mick. I haven't made a secret out of it. But not like that."

Desire for him curled inside her, a hot, fierce flame. She extricated her hand from his. "We're partners. We can't do this."

"That's the Mick I know and care about." He sat back in his chair. "Now it's my turn. Did you hear about Major Nichols?"

CHAPTER FORTY-FOUR

4:00 A.M.

"WAKE UP, BABE. IT'S TIME."

Angel opened her eyes. They filled with Seth, kneeling beside her bed, the chill of the outdoors clinging to him, the tender smile that always made her heart skip a beat curving his beautiful, chiseled mouth. Was he real? she wondered. Or part of her dream?

"Babe, we've got to go."

She searched his dark gaze. "Is it really you?"

His eyes crinkled at the corners. "Who else?"

Angel reached up and stroked his cheek. "I was dreaming of you."

He bent and kissed her. "What were you dreaming?"

She trailed her index finger over his mouth. "I don't remember. Maybe this? There's nothing in my head anymore. Only you."

"I like that." He kissed her again. "It's time."

"To go?"

"Yes, everything's ready."

Fear made it hard to breathe. Going with him meant leaving everyone behind, venturing from the known to the unknown. Unknown, except for Seth.

She knew him. He was enough.

Angel nodded and climbed out of bed. She quickly dressed in jeans and a sweater, fitted on her hiking boots, then laced them up and looked over her shoulder at Seth. He was turned toward the window. The glow of the streetlight illuminated his face, highlighting some features, leaving others in shadow.

Part of the dream she'd awakened from filled her head. *Two Seths.*

One dark. And one light. Both with a hand out, reaching for her.

That's what he was. Part light, part dark. Just like her. Both with the ability to access the powerful force of either.

Angel brought a hand to her belly. Their baby would be the same. Which put them both in serious danger.

Seth glanced her way, and for a split second his eyes seemed to glow. In the next instant, the effect was gone.

"What's wrong?"

She blinked. "Nothing. What do I need to bring?"

"Only the essentials. We'll have access to everything there."

Her hands trembled as she filled her backpack, reviewing each item. A couple changes of clothes. Toothbrush and toothpaste, a comb and brush, a few other toiletries. Her athletic shoes. Her art sack, supplies already tucked inside.

A house. With no windows and no doors.

From her dream. She had to get it down on paper. Before she lost it.

"We need to go, babe."

"There's something I have to do."

"There's no time. Sweetheart, if it gets light, we'll lose our opportunity to escape."

She nodded and turned quickly back to her closet to grab her jacket off the hook. He took her backpack, and she slung the strap of her supply satchel across her body. "Wait, how did you get in here?"

"The help of a friend. He has a way with alarm systems and locks."

"A friend? Who?"

"His name's Bran. He's one of us."

"Are you sure you can trust him?"

"Sweetheart?" He frowned. "What's wrong?"

"I'm just scared."

"I've got you." He laid a hand over her belly. "I've got *us.*"

She stilled, waiting for their baby to react, the way it had the last time he'd touched her this way.

But nothing happened.

Seth slid the window up, made a motion to his friend, then dropped her backpack over the side. He turned and reached out his hand. She took it.

Two. One light. One dark.

She glanced down at the waiting friend. He looked up and smiled. Brown hair and brown eyes, handsome in a nondescript way.

Something uncomfortable skittered over her.

"No," she said and shook her head. "Something's wrong."

Seth took her other hand. He squeezed them both tightly. "It's me. Seth. I love you. We're going to be together. You, me, and our baby. But if we're going to have that, we have to go. Now."

She wanted that more than anything. She wanted to say yes. To acquiesce. To trust.

Bran wasn't who he claimed to be.

She opened her mouth to warn Seth, but the words froze on her lips and a shudder emerged instead.

"Don't be afraid," Seth whispered. "I've got you."

But she was afraid. And cold, so very cold. The sensation curled around and up her arms, like the roots of a tree, digging in, taking hold.

Her heart slowed; her breath became shallow. The cold sucked both the strength and urgency out of her. She couldn't move her limbs, couldn't speak, let alone scream.

Her legs gave. Seth caught her, scooped her up, maneuvered her out the window and into a stranger's arms. Her vision dimmed.

The last thing she saw was Seth's satisfied smile.

CHAPTER FORTY-FIVE

6:54 A.M.

A SOFT SNORE AWAKENED ZACH. HE cracked open his eyes, realizing he'd fallen asleep on Mick's couch. They both had—he in a sprawled sitting position, propped awkwardly by the sofa's cushions and throw pillows.

He lowered his gaze. Mick lay on her side, legs bent and head resting in his lap; she still slept soundly. He shifted, careful not to awaken her while trying to roll the kink out of his neck.

She looked so relaxed. The tension around her mouth was gone. The tiny frown that often creased the space between her eyebrows, also gone.

He lightly touched the spot with his finger, then drew his hand back when she moaned. She'd been through a lot the last couple of days; a little more sleep would be good for her.

The image of her from the night before, gun turned on herself, filled his head, and he shuddered. The way she'd looked at him—like she had nothing to live for and nowhere else to turn—would haunt him forever.

What would he have done if he'd lost her?

But he hadn't. He'd mustered a power he hadn't even known he possessed, from somewhere deep inside himself. Could he access it again? At will?

He fought the questions—the feelings the questions conjured—back. He couldn't go there, not now. They had a problem to solve.

A big one.

He and Mick had talked for a long time before falling asleep. He'd told her about Major Nichols falling from his office window, and how

Sue had confessed to him that the fall had not been an accident. He'd shared how eerily similar his account of Mercedes' suicide was to Sue's description of the major's fall. Then he'd described going back to the Eighth and picking up the energy of not only the amber-eyed woman, but another entity, as well. He'd told her about the feather he'd noticed on Nichols' window ledge, reminding her of the one she'd picked up on Thomas King's balcony.

They'd brainstormed their options. Eli and Professor Truebell were MIA. Parker was neither taking calls nor returning them. Which, Zach supposed, made him MIA as well.

That left Arianna. She was the closest thing to a Full Light they had. Zach hoped to God she'd have some insight into chameleons and how to beat them.

One thing seemed certain. They had to work together.

He looked down at Mick. She was awake and looking up at him.

He smiled. "Good morning."

"Hey." The two creases formed between her eyebrows. "How long was I asleep?"

"Not quite sure, because I only woke up a couple minutes ago." He reached for his cell phone; checked the time. "It's almost seven."

"In the morning?"

He smiled again. "Yeah, in the morning."

She sat up, stretched, then looked toward her front door. They'd patched it the night before, using a piece of plywood they found in her garage.

She looked back at him. "I was hoping it was only a nightmare."

"It happened, Mick. And it was way too real."

She was quiet a moment, then nodded. "How about I make us some coffee?"

"Or we can pick some up on the way?"

"Or both."

He followed her to her feet and stretched, feeling the effects of sleeping in that cramped position—and of kicking in two doors in less than twenty-four hours.

"You okay?" she asked.

"Let me just say, you make kicking in doors look way easier than it is."

She laughed, then grew serious once more. "You're still convinced we should bring Arianna on board?"

"I don't think we have another choice."

"We could wait. For Eli and Professor Truebell to return. Or Parker, SOB that he is, to call us back."

"What if they don't?" She looked devastated at the thought. Mick, the cynic who always acknowledged the worst-case scenario. "We have to consider the possibility, Mick. Eli and Truebell may not return and Parker may never call back."

Mick didn't argue. He saw by her determined expression that she knew he was right.

"Okay," she said, sounding resigned. "Let's get this freak show on the road."

⚜ ⚜ ⚜

Thirty minutes later, they arrived at Arianna's, coffee caddy and breakfast sandwiches in tow. Zach had called from the car; she was waiting for them.

Micki entered first; Arianna stopped him with a hand to his arm. "You're sure about this?" she asked quietly.

Zach knew what she meant—could they trust Mick? Ironic—the two most important women in his life didn't trust each other.

He nodded, and she motioned them into the living room.

"Your coffee," Micki said, handing one to Arianna. "The sandwiches are all the same. Help yourself."

Arianna took the coffee, collected a sandwich, and took a seat. "Thanks."

Micki collected her own beverage and looked around. "Where's Angel?"

"Still sleeping. I thought it would be better if I let her rest."

"She's an adult," Micki said. "Maybe she should decide what's best for her."

Arianna stiffened. "Considering the circumstances—"

"You're not her mother."

"I know what she needs—I've been through this. You haven't."

Zach stepped in. "C'mon, you two, stop it. *We're* not the enemy." He moved his gaze between them, then settled it on his mother. "Mick told me Angel's pregnant."

Arianna turned to Micki, expression accusing. "I thought we agreed we weren't going to share that information with anyone?"

"I didn't agree to anything. And Zach's not 'anyone,' he's my partner and we don't keep secrets from each other."

Zach unwrapped his sandwich. "We've got bigger things to talk about right now. And not a lot of time to do it."

Arianna shook her head. "That's where you're wrong. The baby Angel's carrying could be The Chosen One. If the Dark Leader or one of his lieutenants learns of this child's existence, they'll stop at nothing to get their hands on it." She looked pointedly at Micki. "Secrecy is our first line of defense."

Micki set aside her coffee and stood. "We can't protect what we don't know about. What's so hard to understand about *that*?"

Zach stepped between them again. "First things first. We have an enemy attacking us *now*, Arianna. And I appreciate your concern for Angel and her baby, and I promise you I'll do everything in my power to protect them, but we can only put out one fire at a time. And this one's a doozie."

"Fair enough," Arianna said, and returned to her seat.

Micki took over. "Are you familiar with a dark force called a chameleon?"

Arianna looked at her. "I've heard stories about them, but haven't crossed paths with one."

"Well, you have now," Micki said. "What can you tell us about them?"

Arianna paused a moment before answering. When she did, her tone was cautious. "A little. They rank on the High Council's most wanted list, and carry bounties on their heads, some higher than others. But they're hard to capture because of their ability to change forms."

"Wait." Micki narrowed her eyes. "Why are they wanted by the High Council?"

"Because they're Lightkeepers. Perverted versions of ones, anyway."

"Hold on," Micki said. "Back way, way up. Chameleons aren't Dark Bearers?"

"No." Arianna shifted in her chair. "They've bowed to evil, but haven't made the final transformation to become a Dark Bearer. They choose not to."

Zach recalled his and Mick's first case together, how their race to save two abducted coeds had led to a Lightkeeper in the horrific throes of that final transformation. He looked at Mick; by her expression he saw she was remembering, too. It wasn't something that could be easily forgotten.

"They can make that choice? To not give up the last of their light?" Zach dragged a hand through his hair. "And the Dark One is okay with that?"

Arianna shrugged. "Why wouldn't he be? Chameleons live to create heartbreak and chaos. He doesn't have to force them to do his will. They're already doing it."

Micki spoke up. "When she was impersonating Eli, she told me that chameleons claimed allegiance to no one but themselves. That they do whatever makes them happy. What else can you tell us about them?"

Arianna took a bite of her sandwich, expression thoughtful as she chewed. "They usually travel in pairs. I don't know the specifics, other than the gift of transformation is rare and it runs in families. Not every Lightkeeper with the gift becomes a chameleon, but when one sibling does, often the other does, as well. It's actually quite tragic for the family."

"Pairs," Zach repeated, looking at Micki. "The other dark energy I picked up, at Major Nichols' office window."

Micki nodded. "By any chance, can they transform into birds?"

Arianna looked surprised. "Yes. Other animals as well. Some are basic shifters, and others are more gifted. They're the ones who can imprint their intended victim."

Zach took the last bite of his sandwich, crumpled the wrapper and dropped it in the bag. "Let's just say, there's nothing basic about the one we're dealing with."

"Show me." Arianna held out her hand. "Maybe I'll recognize her."

He clasped it. His palm tingled, then heated. He closed his eyes, visualizing the flow of memories as ribbons of light, running down his arm, through his hand and into hers. He focused on the transfer, knowing what to do and how to control it—he and Parker had done this many times before. And he knew from those times, that because of their familial, shared light, she wouldn't just "see" his memories, she would re-live them—the sights, smells, and sounds. Even his emotional reactions.

Nichols plunging from the window. The hospital, what he'd learned from Sue. Kicking in the door at Mick's. Arianna's body jerked in response to the scene that had greeted him—Mick, the gun to her head, expression devastated.

He tightened his hand around hers. All that Mick had shared with him, his every reaction, complicated feelings, ones he wouldn't want her to know.

He refocused his memories, jumping back in time. Thomas King's suicide, Mercedes King's. The amber-eyed woman, each time he had seen her. The black feather.

He broke the connection, stopping the flow abruptly. They sprang apart. Arianna took another step back, eyes wide, rubbing her hand against her thigh. She looked at Micki. "I'm so sorry. Can you forgive me?"

"For what?"

"The way I treated you. I was wrong to act that way."

"We were all played, there's nothing to forgive. Did you recognize her?"

"Unfortunately, no. By the way, they're born with blue eyes like ours, but they turn that honey color as their light force dims. Since their eyes give them away, they often wear colored contacts."

Micki checked the time. "This thing has set her sights on me, and when she finds out I'm still alive, she's going to be really pissed off."

"Which means," Zach said, "she's going to try again, this time maybe through someone close to you. To make you suffer."

"We have to stop her." Micki looked from Zach to Arianna. "I think it's time to wake Angel up, don't you?"

"Agreed." Arianna started toward the bedrooms. "I'll get her."

Zach looked at Micki. "We'll figure this out."

"Will we? Without the law to back us up?" She shook her head. "Maybe I *should* kill her? Kill her and not worry about what happens to me."

"Not even as a last resort. You hear me, Mick?"

"I do, but think about it. She's going to go on hurting people, wrecking lives. If I'd pulled the trigger, she would have moved on."

"Yes, you, Arianna and Angel would be safe, but she would have set her sights on someone else. We have to stop her. Permanently."

Arianna returned to the room alone, Angel's sketchbook in her hands. Zach's heart sank at her expression.

"Angel's gone. This was on the floor by her bed."

She held out the art tablet, opened, Zach saw, to a drawing of a couple embracing, their lower bodies depicted as roots, twined together.

The man and woman portrayed in the drawing were easily recognizable—the happy couple was Angel and Seth.

Scrawled on the bottom of the page was the message: *I'm coming for you.*

CHAPTER FORTY-SIX

8:42 A.M.

ANGEL CAME TO WITH A broken heart. Seth had betrayed her. He had betrayed their unborn child.

She opened her eyes slowly, afraid he would be beside her. Smiling down at her, pleased with himself. Celebrating her complete devastation. Instead, only darkness greeted her. Absolute and unnatural. Like a tomb.

Buried alive? she wondered, terror rippling over her. Never to see light again?

She wouldn't put it past him, not anymore. He had proved what he was. And that she had been so very wrong about him.

Angel breathed deeply, fighting the urge to cry. She wouldn't. She couldn't. Not if she wanted to survive. Not if she wanted her baby to survive.

No watch or phone, so no connection to the outside world. She couldn't even hope for help from that direction. She focused on her surroundings instead. She lay on a cot. Head on a pillow, sheet and blanket over her. She held her breath and listened. The soft whir of a fan. Air, she thought. Some sort of ventilation system.

She moved aside the blanket and sat up. As she swung her legs over the side of the cot, she hit something and knocked it over. She reached for it and discovered it was a camping lantern.

With a squeak of relief, Angel switched it on. A warm, reassuring glow surrounded her. She stood and held it up. A rectangular space, she saw. Like a box. No windows, no doors.

Her dream. The one she'd been having when Seth came for her.

There had to be a way in and out. There always was.

Her gaze landed on a small table. Under it, a box of provisions. Beside the box, three gallons of water.

Angel crossed to the table, pulled the box out and rummaged through it. Some fruit and packaged snacks. He expected her to be here for more than a day. Three days? she wondered. A gallon of water a day? Or a week? Longer?

Her stomach rumbled, and she grabbed the banana, peeled it and wolfed it down. She went for a package of peanut butter crackers, ate several of them, then went for the water—and found a bag with more supplies. In this one: paper cups, a roll of toilet paper and paper towels, and a box of Kleenex.

It was the last that hit her like a ton of bricks. Seth expected her to need the tissues, he expected her to cry. Bastard! Betrayer! She'd show him!

After downing a glass of water, she began a careful search of the space. She started at the far short wall, feeling her way, counting her steps. Every couple of feet, rapping on the wall and calling out.

Metal walls. Angel tipped her head back and held up the lantern. Ceiling material appeared also to be metal. Like a shipping container.

Imprisoned in a shipping container.

Seth had done this to her. Something dark and terrible rose up inside her, full of fury. The tattoo on her thigh throbbed. She tipped her head back and howled.

The sound bounced off the walls and shook the container. The power of it brought her to her knees, her hands to her ears. Her baby stirred, as if disturbed. Or excited.

Angel felt sick, realizing what she had done, recognizing the part of her she had awakened. That she could use it to escape.

If she did, she would be lost. Her child would be lost.

She wrapped her arms around her middle and began to rock. This baby would be a child of the light. The darkness could not have it.

Even if they both had to die.

CHAPTER FORTY-SEVEN

10:15 A.M.

MICKI PACED. WHILE SHE DID, she kept telling herself that Angel really was with Seth, that just like she'd said over and over again, he loved her and had come back for her.

Micki kept telling herself that. Problem was, she didn't believe it. She knew to her core and with every fiber of her being that it was the chameleon, masquerading as Seth, who had her.

For Seth, Angel would go anywhere. Because of that, she had been the most susceptible of them all to the chameleon's lies.

Micki checked the time. They had decided she and Arianna would wait at LAM while Zach headed to the Eighth to put his mind-bending-powers to work getting authorization for a city-wide BOLO for Angel. After that, he was going to check in with her friends and at all her favorite spots, on the unlikely chance he found her.

Non-existent chance.

Micki stopped pacing and brought her hand to Hank's medal for what seemed like the hundredth time since putting it back on before leaving her house that morning.

She curled her fingers around it. *Please, Hank, let her be okay. I don't know what I'll do if I caused her death, the way I caused yours.*

Nothing. No response. She felt ridiculously let down.

"All the pacing and worrying in the world won't change this out-come," Arianna said softly.

Micki looked at the other woman, sitting to the side, serenely watching her. "So, I should sit calmly by and do nothing?"

"Yes."

"I can't do that."

"Trust, Michaela."

Micki drew her eyebrows together in a fierce frown. "Trust in what? Not this crazy, unpredictable world. It was bad enough when I thought humans were the monsters."

"We decided Zach should go alone. Trust our decision and Zach."

"I know what we agreed, dammit."

"No need to snap at me."

The famous Lightkeeper calm, Micki thought, glaring at her.

As if reading her thoughts, Arianna shook her head. "All that anxiety is just your need for control. It's wasted energy. Control is an illusion."

"More freaking mumbo jumbo," she muttered. "Try carrying a gun. There's some control."

Arianna shook her head. "You have to let go, Micki. You have to trust that good will win out in the end."

Arianna stood and crossed to her. She caught her hands. "Darkness cannot exist in the light. We can be the good, the light, the world needs. Each one of us."

Normally she would have scoffed. Come back with a cynical retort. But looking into Arianna's endless blue gaze made her cynicism seem mean.

"You really believe that, don't you?"

"I do. If I didn't, I'd be dead."

"What do you mean?"

"I was imprisoned in a very dark place. My light force could have been extinguished, but instead I used it to help others hold on to hope."

For a moment, as she gazed into Arianna's eyes, she saw that place—and the reality of it settled over her like a shroud, heavy and suffocating. A place of unimaginable cruelty, a landscape of despair and destruction.

But because of Arianna, not hopeless.

Micki blinked, and the sensation passed. She sucked in a deep, cleansing breath. "I wish I could be like that, I really do. But I can't."

"You can. You just don't know it yet." Arianna lowered her eyes to her chest. "Your medal—may I see it?"

Micki slipped the chain over her head and handed it to Arianna. "It's St. Michael. It was a gift from a friend."

"Yes, I know." She curved her fingers around it. "Protector of the police and military, slayer of the Dragon and guardian to all Lightkeepers." Arianna closed her eyes, a soft smile curving her lips. "I know this energy."

"Excuse me?"

"He was a friend of mine, too. A long time ago." Her voice grew faraway. "I loved him very much."

The woman was officially freaking her out, and Micki held out her hand. "If you don't mind."

But Arianna didn't move toward giving it back. "A gift you said?"

"Yes."

She let out her breath in a wistful-sounding sigh, and handed it over. "It was a generous one."

Micki slipped it back on. "I don't understand. What do you mean?"

"Your friend shared his light force with you."

Micki opened her mouth to tell her that wasn't possible. That the friend who'd given the necklace to her had been, like her, just another human.

The front buzzer sounded, cutting her off. Micki checked the monitor, saw it was, indeed, Zach, then let him in.

"Anything?" she asked.

He shook his head. "Nobody's seen her. Not her friends or people at any of her regular haunts. But I do have some good news. The BOLO has been issued and given high priority."

"What do we do now?" Arianna asked.

"I know exactly what our next move should be," Micki said, glancing at her watch. "It's just after ten. My guess is she's waiting to hear the news of my death. And I bet, if we act now, we'll still have the element of surprise on our side."

"What do you propose?" Zach asked.

"I call her. And I let her know that not only am I very much alive, but that she lost, and I won. And I offer myself to her in exchange for Angel."

"No," Zach said. "Absolutely not."

"Sorry, partner, I wasn't asking your permission."

"Dammit, Mick! Think this through."

"I think she's right," Arianna offered. "It could get us Angel and her baby back."

Zach glared at his mother.

"What?" she asked. "You have a better plan?"

"Offering an exchange isn't a plan. It's an *idea*. We don't know the first thing about capturing or killing one of these things."

"She can be killed like any other Lightkeeper, because she's flesh and blood," Arianna said. "But when you kill her, she won't revert to her true self."

"So if I kill her when she's Natalie King," Micki said, "I'm the prime suspect and will most likely go to jail."

"Let's take killing her off the table for just a moment." Zach looked at Arianna. "Is there any way we can capture her and force her to transform back into her true self?"

"That's it!" Arianna snapped her fingers. "We bring her to LAM. It's a safe house, so she won't be able to transform or use dark energy in any other way."

"How do we get her there?" Micki asked, excited.

"She won't cross the threshold willingly—she'll know it's protected." Arianna looked from one to the other of them. "We make her."

"Make her?" Mick repeated. "How do you propose we do that?"

"Handcuffs?" Arianna looked at them both. "You have those, right?"

"We handcuff her and force her into LAM?" Mick groaned. "In other words, we kidnap her."

Zach stepped in. "It's not a plan, but it's a direction." He crossed to the front window, peered out at the street, then turned back to them. "So, once we have her here, nice and secure, then what? We can't keep her here forever."

They looked at each other, the suddenly Micki knew. She smiled. "Arianna, you said chameleons make up part of the High Council's Most Wanted list. And I bet ours is way up high on it."

"Yes!" Zach snapped his fingers. "We turn her in."

CHAPTER FORTY-EIGHT

11:55 A.M.

"YOU'RE SURE YOU WANT TO do this?" Zach asked. They stood in Professor Truebell's office, the midday light cascading through the stained glass window behind his desk. It created a rainbow of color on the floor. Micki found it oddly reassuring, as if she was being watched over.

"I'm sure," she said.

"She'll come after you, Mick."

"That's the point. Right?"

He lowered his voice. "I was there last night. I saw what she did to you."

"Not this time, Zach," she said, ignoring the way her heart rate accelerated. "This time I'll be ready."

He held her gaze. "And I promise, I'll be right there with you."

"I know you will. It means a lot."

Micki dug her phone out of her pocket, and after letting out a determined breath, dialed.

King answered right away. "Hello, Detective. I've been expecting your call."

"Not surprised your sick, little game didn't work? It must happen a lot."

"On the contrary, you're one of the few. However, I saw Detective Harris arrive last night and knew there was a very good chance he'd do something ridiculously heroic and save the day."

"He kicked the door in."

"Your hero. Very macho." Her acid tone dripped disdain. "I had no choice but to move on to plan 'B.'"

"Angel?"

"Of course. Your fault, Michaela. All of it."

Micki fought the guilt that rose up and threatened to choke her. That was what the chameleon wanted, and she wouldn't give her the pleasure. "I want Angel back."

"Too bad. I have other plans for young Angel and her sweet babe."

Micki tightened her grip on the phone. "I propose an exchange, me for Angel."

"No." She laughed. "Silly, Michaela, why would I do that? I hold all the cards."

King didn't pull any punches, so neither would she. "You don't have me. You make the exchange, or I'll be the one who got away—again.

King remained quiet for the count of four. When she spoke, her tone vibrated with something dark. "Back for more?" She clucked her tongue. "What a little glutton for punishment you are."

Micki smiled, knowing she had landed a blow. "It's your turn to be punished," Micki said, smiling. "And it's been a long time coming."

"I'm surprised. A soft touch like you . . . putting your friends in danger this way?" She laughed softly, sounding pleased. "No job. Friends with targets on their backs." She lowered her voice. "What do you have to live for?"

"Vengeance," she answered simply. "For Hank. And I guess, for everything else, too. But mostly Hank."

"And how're you going to do that?"

"That's for you to find out. And you will. Because I'm stronger than you. You gave me all you had, and you didn't break me."

"You were *saved*. If not for him, you'd be dead now. We both know it."

"Do we? Let's meet. You can show me."

"I'm not stupid." She paused for a breathy laugh, then went on, "No, I have a much better idea. I deliver Angel to the Dark Bearers, as planned. Take their reward and my insurance money and disappear. Just slip away. But I'll be back. Just like this time."

Micki squeezed her eyes shut. She couldn't let that happen. She would never forgive herself. Which was precisely why the chameleon was threatening her with it.

"You're a coward," Micki said tightly. "You can't bear the thought of losing again, so you're going to run away."

King went on as if she hadn't spoken, "You won't know when I'll strike. That's the beauty of it. When you get your life back together, when you've finally grabbed a small slice of happiness—a friend, a job you enjoy, a lover or a child, there I'll be. And I'll take it all from you, the same as I took Hank."

She, too, let her words sink in. "For you, life will be so much more painful than death. So, you see, I have won."

The picture she painted *was* worse than death. Micki pressed the phone tighter to her ear. This was their chance to stop her. Mick couldn't let the chameleon though their fingers again.

"Tell yourself whatever you need to, bitch. But we both know, just like I beat you last time, I've beaten you this time. And here I am, just an ordinary human."

"You *are* an ordinary human. I'd pity you, if I cared enough."

"And you're not as clever as you think you are. Meet me and I'll prove it."

She laughed. "I know what you're up to, and it's not going to work. Better luck next time, Detective."

Better luck next time. The same as before. When she lost Hank.

Her fault. Then and now.

The phone slipped from her fingers, clattered to the floor. Micki looked at Zach and Arianna and shook her head. "She didn't go for it." Her throat closed over the words; they came out choked. "We may have . . . lost Angel."

CHAPTER FORTY-NINE

1:00 P.M.

MICKI SAT ALONE IN THE dappled, multi-colored light of the professor's stained-glass window. Zach had refused to accept that they had lost Angel. He'd left the center, planning to hunt down Natalie King and bring her to LAM, handcuffed, hog-tied—whatever it took, consequences be damned.

And here she sat. She didn't want to believe it either. But she understood what they were up against, and he didn't.

First, the chameleon had taken Hank. And now, because of her, Angel and her unborn child would be in the hands of darkness.

A sob rose to her throat. She choked it back—or tried to. She wanted to undo this so badly, but she . . . couldn't. She was beaten. The chameleon had bested her at every turn.

Micki thought of the night before. Holding the gun to her head. She imagined pulling the trigger. Imagined the sound, the shattering pain, then death.

She wished she had done it. Angel would be safe. Her baby would be safe.

"Stop it."

Micki looked up. Arianna stood in the office doorway, eyebrows drawn together in concern.

"Stop what?"

"Beating yourself up."

"Easy for you to say."

"Hank would be very upset with you right now. Feeling sorry for yourself. Thinking *those* thoughts."

"How do you know about Hank and what he would think?"

"You're a fighter, not a quitter." Arianna crossed from the doorway to Micki. "We need to finish our conversation. About your St. Michael medal."

"There's nothing left to say. Leave me alone."

"Henry was a friend of mine."

Micki blinked. "Excuse me?"

Arianna turned a chair to face Micki and sat. "He preferred Hank, I know, but I first knew him as Henry."

For a moment, Micki couldn't breathe. "Wait. How did you know him?"

"He was a dear friend. At least until he got himself in some trouble with the High Council."

It felt as if the earth was shifting under her. "Hank was a Light-keeper?"

"You didn't know?"

Micki shook her head. "No one told me and . . . no," she finished lamely.

Arianna went on, "Growing up, our families were close. Our fathers were best friends. But Henry was always getting in trouble for being too generous. Always wanting to be the hero, stepping in to save some-one."

The way he'd saved her, Micki thought. She'd always wondered how anyone could be as wise and kind as he. Now she knew. Her wonderful Hank had been special, a Lightkeeper.

Micki drew her eyebrows together. "Why would wanting to save people get him in trouble?"

"That isn't a Lightkeeper's mission, Micki. We weren't sent to save the human race, but to help steer them in the right direction. But he couldn't help himself. He'd share his light, just to brighten someone's day."

Micki imagined it and smiled. It sounded so like him. Then her smiled faded. "But he was punished for that?"

"Lightkeepers can choose to share their light. But once you give it away, it's gone."

"And you're no longer a Full Light."

"Correct. And this was at the height of the Council's concern over the rapidly declining number of Lightkeepers." She paused. "Then, he ran afoul of the High Council by publicly coming out against the law."

"The one that outlawed Lightkeeper and human unions?"

"Yes." Her expression turned sad. "When I was young, I used to imagine we'd end up together, he and I. He was older, but not that much. Then I left New Orleans and never saw him again."

Micki pictured Hank and Arianna together. It would have been good, she thought. Really good. Once, when she'd asked why he'd never married, he'd confessed to having lost the love of his life. After her, no one compared.

Could Arianna have been that woman?

"Maybe you should have the medal?" Micki said. "He would have wanted me to give it to you, I think."

She started to slip it off; Arianna stopped her. "Hank wanted *you* to have it, Micki. Not me. Use it well."

Micki searched Arianna's gaze. "Use it? I don't understand what you mean."

"The medal will provide help when you need it. But you have to ask. And trust."

Trust? Easier said than done, she thought. "I have a few issues in that department, in case you haven't noticed."

Arianna knelt in front of Micki and caught her hands. "This isn't all an accident, Micki. It isn't just because. Hank found you *for a reason*. Parker chose you *for a reason*."

"What reason? Why?"

"You're meant to be a part of this, Micki. All of it, everything happening right now. To you and around you. Think of your friend Jacqui. How you took her in. Her son, Alexander. Angel, too. And her baby."

Micki shook her head. "I lose everyone I love. I'm a curse to those I love."

"No." She tightened her fingers around Micki's. "You're a blessing to them because you'll fight to the death to protect them."

"Really?" Mick blinked against tears. "How am I doing now? Should we ask Hank? Or Angel?"

"Every hero has doubts. Every hero battles demons."

"No." She shook her head. "Zach's the hero, not me."

Arianna laughed lightly. "Of course, you would say that. Listen, you and Zach, you're meant to do this together. Together, Micki. The two of you."

"What is the *this* that we're supposed to be doing?" Micki searched

Arianna's blue gaze. "Tell me, because I don't have a clue!"

"Yes, you do. Maybe not the details, but certainly the broad strokes. You fight for what's right. You fight for good. For the vulnerable and weak. You're strong and honorable to your core. Hank knew that. And I do, too."

Arianna released her hands and stood. She crossed to the door, then stopped and looked back. "Maybe *that's* why you were chosen."

CHAPTER FIFTY

2:05 P.M.

MICKI SAT, RIGHT HAND CURVED around Hank's medal, tears slipping down her cheeks, pondering the things Arianna had said to her. About Hank. This gift of his light. She thought of the timing, the letter that had accompanied it.

The day Hank wrote that note to her, he had known he was going to die. He had known what was coming for him. But instead of running, he had stayed to die. Why? Because he had believed it was meant to be. Because he knew the future and the plan that included her—and he knew that she'd need the gift.

Whatever his reason, she trusted him.

She pressed the medal to her lips. Hank's warmth seeped into her, into the places that had turned cold, the ones that brought despair. She turned slightly and the sunshine tumbling through the stained glass fell over her hand and the medal clutched in it.

Light streamed from her closed fist, growing brighter and brighter. It pierced the spaces between her fingers, rays of brilliance, as if she held the sun in her hands. But it wasn't hot, it didn't burn.

Slowly, she relaxed her fingers. The light dazzled. Bright white, as blinding as the sun. Yet it didn't hurt her eyes.

Micki stared at it, mesmerized. She felt as if the rays penetrated every part of her being. Hank had seen the big picture. He had believed in her, believed she was meant to be a part of this, whatever it was.

"I'm in, Hank. Whatever the obstacle, whatever the plan, I know you're with me."

The light dimmed, then disappeared. Funny though, the warmth didn't exit with it.

Her cell went off. She answered. "This is Dare."

"Detective Dare?"

A woman, whispering. "Yes. Who is this?"

"Tara Green."

It took her a moment to place the name. From the ad agency Keith Gerard worked for. The woman she had interviewed about her relationship with him. "Yes, Tara? How can I help you?"

"I thought you'd want to know. Another one of Keith's girlfriends committed suicide. When he lived in Nashville."

The blood rushed to Micki's head, and she jumped to her feet. "Do you have a name?"

"No. I've got to go."

"Wait, please. Is he there now?"

"It's his last day. He resigned—"

"Where's he going?"

"Moving."

"Where?"

"New Mexico, I think. I'm late, I really need to—"

"Wait! Where is he now?"

"A party. Lucy's Retired Surfer Bar. I'm hanging up now."

She did and Micki pocketed her phone, heart thundering, thoughts racing. Zach had picked up a separate, dark entity in Nichols' office. Arianna had said chameleons usually travel in pairs, that they were often related, because the gift of transformation ran in families.

Could Keith Gerard and Natalie King be related, maybe brother and sister?

It worked, Micki thought, mentally fitting the pieces in place. Sarah Stevens' inexplicable suicide. The way Gerard had made her skin crawl—the same way Natalie King—and years before—Rene Blackwood had. And Stevens' neighbor, swearing she saw a woman there that night, the very woman Stevens had been jealous of but who also had been many states away at the time.

Not Tara Green, Micki realized. A chameleon, either Keith Gerard or his traveling buddy, Natalie King.

She could be wrong, but she bet she was right.

CHAPTER FIFTY-ONE

3:04 P.M.

ANGEL'S EYES POPPED OPEN, THE dream still unfurling in her head. Her art bag—she needed her tablet and charcoal. She had to get the images on paper before they evaporated.

Angel sat up and grabbed the camping light. She'd left it on, and the circle of light in her rectangular prison reassured her. Standing, she hurried across to the small table and her art bag on the floor beside it.

She pulled down the zipper and saw that her sketchbook wasn't there. When she'd fallen asleep she'd been drawing. In her excitement and nerves, she'd left it behind.

She wanted to weep. Not now, she told herself. She didn't have time for that. She looked frantically around her for something to draw on. Paper towels were too flimsy. Maybe a box or a paper bag—

Her gaze settled on the wall directly across from her. Smooth, painted a flat gray. It would have to do.

Angel rummaged through her drawing supplies until she found what she was looking for—her brand-new box of oil pastels. Grabbing them, she darted across and started to draw.

Having so much surface was freeing, and her hand flew—long marks, bold outlines, big arcs. She went through one stick, then another. Her heart thundered, her breath came in quick gasps.

She didn't allow herself to pause or make judgment. Get the dream down. Record every detail quickly, before it evaporated.

The act of creation was beautiful, yes. But also violent. It was as if she was retching out the images. They controlled her, not the other way around.

Emptied, she stopped. Her drawing hand ached. Her fingers were cramped, numb. Wincing, she stretched them and stepped away from the wall.

As she backed up, the drawing took shape.

A man and a woman.

Her. And Seth.

Between them, a thick wall. Above them a bird of prey. Circling, casting its shadow over them—and the light.

For in her frenzy, she had grabbed the white pastel and encased the figures and the wall between them in light.

Heart breaking for what should have been, Angel sank to the floor and wept.

CHAPTER FIFTY-TWO

3:30 P.M.

ZACH STOPPED AT HOME FOR a change of clothes. From inside his apartment came the sound of classical music. Vivaldi.

Parker. He'd done this before, shown up after being out of reach for days, and letting himself into Zach's place. It pissed him off every time.

Except this one. Parker could help locate Angel. He had connections, people and equipment at his fingertips. He could assemble a team in minutes, be it Lighkeeper or human.

Zach took a deep breath and opened the door. Sure enough, Parker—or the chameleon masquerading as him—lounged on the couch, head back and eyes closed as he listened to his favorite classical composer.

"You could have called," Zach said, snapping the door shut behind him.

Parker looked at him. "Hello, nephew."

Zach dropped his keys on the entryway table and crossed to the couch. "You look like hell."

"It's been a rough few days. What's your excuse?"

"Screw you." Zach took the chair directly across from his uncle, and met his eyes, assessing. Was this Parker? "We've been dealing with some intense shit while you've been MIA. Where have you been, P?"

"Negotiating the professor and Eli's release."

Zach narrowed his eyes. "Release?"

"They're being held by the High Council. Charged with treason."

It took Zach a moment to digest that. "For training Half Lights to develop and use their abilities?"

"Yes."

"Why weren't you charged?"

"Let's put it this way. The High Council has okayed me training Half Lights to work with humans—to solve human crimes."

Zach laced his fingers, gaze not straying from Parker's. "So, if they discovered you not only informed me of my true nature but have enlisted my help battling the Dark Bearer and his army, you wouldn't be sitting here right now?"

"I'm afraid so, yes."

"How did the High Council learn the real purpose of Professor True-bell's work with wayward Half Lights?"

"There's a spy among us."

Zach eyebrows shot up. "A spy? Who?"

"Someone in our network has turned. We don't know yet who that person is."

"Son of a bitch." Zach ran a hand through his hair. "It's hard to believe."

Parker stood and crossed to him. "This is war. People do what they have to do."

Was this Parker? Zach thought yes. Everything about him rang true. But that's what this creature did. That's what made it so deadly.

"You said you were negotiating the release of Eli and Professor True-bell. Were you successful?"

"Unfortunately, no. The Council seems immovable at this point."

"What about all the people the professor helps? All the Half Lights who go to LAM for comfort, and find a place to belong? And what of Eli, all the kids he's healed?"

"You know the answer to that, Zach. They're Half Lights, not Light-keepers."

"So they don't count." He crossed to his fireplace and rapped his knuckles on the mantle. "This is bullshit."

"Yes, it is. But for the moment, I'm afraid my hands are tied."

Zach straightened and looked back at Parker. "Would they consider a trade?"

"What kind of trade?"

"Ever heard of a chameleon?"

"Of course."

Zach crossed to him and held out his hand. If this wasn't the real Parker, he would know it the moment their hands joined.

Parker looked down at his outstretched hand, then back into his eyes—and clasped his hand. If Zach had any remaining doubts as to the true identity of the being standing before him, the instant connection and exchange of energy dispelled them.

The information coursed from him to Parker, the events of the past days—from Thomas King's suicide to Angel's disappearance. Done transmitting, Zach broke the connection and took a step back.

"I know her," Parker murmured, flexing his fingers to distribute the lingering energy. "That chameleon. Her name's Isabella Bremmond. Her misdeeds are very well known."

"You think they'll make the trade?"

"I'm hopeful." He paused. "I'm going to go present it now. Whatever you do, don't let her get away."

"You're not going to help us?"

"I'll be back as soon as I can. Until then, you, Arianna, and Micki have this."

"No, I don't think we do. Maybe call in some reinforcements?"

"For the trade, it's going to be important you pull this off solo."

"That's bullshit. Angel's life—"

Parker stopped at the door, expression thoughtful. "What about Isabella's brother? A two-for-two trade sounds even better."

"She has a brother?"

"Yes, indeed. And he's quite clever, too. But he doesn't imprint."

"Then what does he do?"

"He watches and he whispers."

"What the hell does that mean? Give me some help here."

"He transforms into animals, Zach. His shift of choice is birds."

Zach pictured the feather from Nichols' office and King's balcony. He smiled grimly. "Bingo."

CHAPTER FIFTY-THREE

4:33 P.M.

LUCY'S WAS LOCATED ON TCHOUPITOULAS Street in New Orleans' trendy Warehouse District. Micki sat at one of the sidewalk tables, nursing an iced tea and watching the front entrance for Gerard to appear. She'd come prepared: handcuffs, her fake badge, and her personal piece, tucked safely into a shoulder holster.

She'd sifted through her choices, and had decided approaching him directly was her best option. She wasn't sure exactly how that was going to play out; she'd just have to go with her gut.

He finally exited, with several others from his party. It proved easy for Micki to slip out with them. She followed behind the boisterous group, playing tourist in her New Orleans ball cap and dark sunglasses. No one paid any attention to her, and one by one, the group separated to go to their various vehicles.

Gerard cut through to Fulton Street. More people here, tourists and locals, service workers, and end-of-week colleagues starting the week-end with a cocktail. Perfect, she thought, quickening her pace and sliding her hand beneath her jacket to her gun.

She sidled up to his right side, slid her arm though his and, with the other, reached across her body with the gun. Anyone walking past would see nothing but a woman glued to her man.

"Hello, Keith," she said.

"Who the hell are—" He bit the words back as realization registered on his face.

She pressed the barrel of the gun into his side. "That's right," she said. "It's a Glock and it's loaded. Don't make any sudden moves—I have an itchy trigger finger. Just keep walking."

"What do you want?"

"Just the answers to a few easy questions."

"Screw you. Last I heard, you weren't a cop anymore."

At least she didn't have to wonder where he'd gotten that information. "You think that's a deterrent? Other way around, genius."

She went on, "I know what you are. And what you can do. And how you use that power to hurt people."

"And what's that?"

She ignored his question. "You're buddies with a woman who calls herself Natalie King. She, like you, masquerades her true form."

"You're sounding crazier and crazier."

"Am I? Good." She smiled grimly. "I want to know where she is."

"Who?"

"You know who. Your travelling buddy. She and I have unfinished business."

"You're alive," he said softly. "If I were you, I'd be grateful and dis-appear."

"Two problems with that." She tightened her arm through his. "The biggest—she has a friend of mine and I want her back."

"That's not going to happen. And the second?"

"I have a score to settle with her."

"That's not going to happen either. Like I said, you'd be smart to pull your stuff together and leave town."

"*That's* what's not going to happen, Keith. You know where she is. I want you to take me to her."

"I don't know what she'll do to me. She'll be furious." A shudder rippled over him. "This wasn't part of her plan."

"You think I care about that?"

"You should." He looked away, then back. "She scares me."

"Enough with the drama. Where's your car?"

"Just ahead on the left. The blue Infiniti coupe."

They reached it. "I'll need your keys," Micki said. "Slow, no sudden moves."

He retrieved his keys from his jacket and handed a keyless fob to her. Gun still trained on him, she unlocked the driver's side door, pocketed the fob and went for her cuffs. "You're driving, get in."

"You don't want to do this," he said. "Trust me."

"You didn't know I had trust issues? Get in the damn car."

The moment he was in the bucket seat, she snapped a cuff on his left wrist, the other around the steering wheel.

"Fuck! Really?" He shook his head. "I'll take you to her. It's your funeral."

Micki went around the car and climbed in, angling in her seat to watch his every move and keep the gun trained on him. "Let's go."

"Whatever," he said, sounding tired. "You're the boss."

He pulled into traffic. "You're not the first, you know. To think you could beat her. I used to try, but I gave up."

"Painting yourself the victim. Cheesy."

"I am her victim, cheesy cliché or not. Have been since we were kids."

"Yeah, right."

He angled onto Annunciation Street, heading toward the Pontchartrain Expressway. "She always took it too far. I like screwing with people, stirring up shit. But her—that wasn't enough. For her, it's total devastation or nothing. If I wouldn't take the extra step, she did for me."

Micki didn't respond, and he continued, "Take Sarah, for example. I didn't want her to die. Messing with her head and emotions was enough for me. Not for Isabella."

"Your sister's name is Isabella?"

"You didn't know that? I call her Izzy."

"What about you? What's your name?"

"Anthony."

Micki narrowed her eyes on him. "Let's say I buy what you're selling. How does that work? Sarah Stevens is in love with you. You plant the seed of jealousy by convincing her you're screwing around with your co-worker, Tara."

He nodded, looking pleased. "That part isn't hard. I pick someone who has low self-esteem. Or has been betrayed before. They're predisposed to being suspicious. It's hard to trust when you've been hurt, you know what I'm saying?"

She did. It had made her a perfect target. *A perfect target.* Not anymore. "You victimize victims. That's lower than low. Frankly, you make me sick."

He took the Expressway on ramp. "At least I don't make them kill themselves."

"But she does?"

"Yeah." He passed a semi at a dizzying speed.

"I've got another question."

"Yeah?"

"You could have done your chameleon thing back there, but didn't even try. Why not?"

He took the Carrolton Avenue exit, heading south. "That wasn't Tara who called you earlier."

It took her a moment to realize what he was saying. "It was Isabella?"

A smile tugged at the corner of his mouth. "Yup."

"Why? I wanted to meet with her. She refused."

"She wanted it to be on her terms, not yours." He took a right turn. "She has control issues."

Gerard rolled to a stop, and Micki became aware of where they were. She took in the nineteenth century two-story, with its welcoming, wide front porch and big front windows. The drapes on those windows were drawn now, but when they were open, Micki knew, morning light tumbled in, bathing the living room in a bright glow.

"Hank's house?" she asked, voice thick. "What are we doing here?"

"She owns it now. She's waiting for you inside."

Mick brought her hand to Hank's medal, mind flooded with memories of her times here. All of them good until that last, when she'd found him dead. She recalled that day with perfect clarity: the sound of water running in the kitchen, Hank sprawled on the floor in front of the sink, gaze blank, skin cold.

And then, keening and clinging to him, the pain almost more than she could bear.

The medal warmed. He was here, she realized. With her.

She might not win this battle, but she wasn't fighting it alone.

"I told you, Detective," Gerard said, pity in his eyes. "She plays for keeps."

"So do I." Micki opened the door and stepped out. "You stay put. I'll deal with you later."

CHAPTER FIFTY-FOUR

5:18 P.M.

MICKI STARTED UP THE SHORT front walk, stopping when she reached the porch steps. She retrieved her cell phone, seeing she had missed two calls and a text from Zach. His text told her to call him—he had important information.

Too late for that now. She texted him back:

Gerard is the chameleon's brother. He's brought me to her. Hank's old house. He's handcuffed to his car out front.

She hit send and took a deep breath. She had faced this beast already, and she fully understood what it was capable of. She'd be a fool not to be afraid. And she was no fool.

But she wasn't alone this time. Hank was with her.

She climbed the three steps to the porch. Her cell pinged the arrival of a text. As she expected, from Zach.

Stay put. On my way. Need her alive.

Micki read the last twice. Alive? That complicated things. She'd try, but wasn't about to make that promise.

She turned the phone to vibrate, pocketed it and crossed the porch. She stopped at the door, memories, one after another, tripping over her. She forced them back, focused on what was coming—and just how bad it might be.

Reaching for the doorknob, she grasped it and turned. As she expected, the door was unlocked. She pushed it open with her foot, hands steady on the grip of her Glock. The TV was on. Just as it had been that day.

Swallowing hard, she stepped into the living room. It was as if she had gone back in time. The furniture, the arrangement of it, was the same. Pictures in the same spots, but the frames, she saw, were empty. She ran her hand across the back of the leather recliner, the same color and style as Hank's was. But not Hank's. Not worn and loved. An imitation, pulled straight from her own memories.

Just the way the chameleon had conjured her Uncle Beau—the way he dressed, the sound of his voice, the smell of his breath.

Then, she had been repelled. But this illusion, this conjuring, was sweet.

She shook the thought off. "I know you're here," she called out. "And you know why I'm here. Let's do this."

"What are you caterwauling about, girl? I'm right here."

Not Natalie King's voice.

Micki's breath caught. Hank's.

He appeared at the kitchen door, smiling in that way of his, wiping his hands on a dishtowel. She longed to run to him, to throw her arms around him and breath him in. If she did, she would have him back, if only for a little bit.

But he, this, was only an illusion.

It wasn't going to work, not this time. "Where's Angel?"

"You going to shoot me, girl? Put that thing away, and come get something to eat. I'll make you one of my famous ham sandwiches."

He disappeared back into the kitchen, and Micki followed. Of course the chameleon had chosen to transform into Hank for this last confrontation. Her softest spot. Her biggest regret. How could she shoot the one person who had loved her unconditionally?

The chameleon was wrong about that. Dead wrong.

Micki reached the kitchen. The window above the sink stood open to the cold evening. In the tree beyond the window a bird squawked. It sounded oddly like a laugh.

Micki turned her gaze to the chameleon, standing at the counter, back to her. Making a ham sandwich. Like she was going to fall for this bullshit again.

"Just stop." Micki firmed her grip on the gun. "It's not going to work this time. I'm going to capture you and turn you in to the High Council, or I'm going to kill you. Those are your choices."

The chameleon laughed. The sound was high, brittle and cold, like ice cracking. She turned, transforming into a woman she'd never seen before—somewhere in her forties, with inky dark hair and unremarkable features. Except for her eyes. They were amber, like a cat's. And mesmerizingly beautiful—liquid gold irises, pupils somehow blacker than black, rimmed by thick, dark lashes.

Gooseflesh raced up Micki's arms; she told herself to look away but couldn't. Those cat-like eyes were also profane. Something once sacred had been defiled. Contorted by evil into something never meant to be.

That evil pulsed from the woman; every hair on Micki's body prickled with awareness of it. And with fear.

Hank's medal warmed. She swallowed the fear. "Where's Angel?"

"Someplace secure."

"Let's make a trade. Me for her."

"What fun would that be?" She took a step forward. "Like I said on the phone, I hold all the cards."

"Do you? Because last I looked, I have the gun, and if you take another step, I'll shoot you."

The chameleon laughed again. "I'd tell you to go ahead and do it, but it's already too late for that."

Something dark swooped across her line of vision. Startled, Micki fell back a step, head swiveling to see what it was. A crow. It came at her again, snagging her hair with its claws.

Not any crow, Micki realized. Isabella's brother had shifted himself right out of her handcuffs.

Micki swung at it and missed; with a screech, it circled back, struck again, this time pecking the hand holding the gun. She lost her grip on it and in the next instant, it wasn't the bird's claws digging into her flesh, it was Isabella's.

She gripped her wrists, the way she had that day at King's apartment. And now, like then, the burning cold radiated from her fingers, curling snake-like up her arms, penetrating her skin, seeming to reach her very marrow.

The chameleon's eyes glowed. The pupils grew larger, until the irises were little more than a gold band around them. The crow circled and cawed.

Micki shuddered, thinking of Hank. Of him dying this way. Alone.

His medal warmed. His image filled her head. He was smiling at her, gently chiding.

Have you forgotten already?

She wasn't alone. Hank, his light force.

What had Arianna said? Just trust. And ask for help.

Help me, Hank. I can't do this without you.

The medal turned hot, but it didn't burn. Instead it radiated inward, joining the spark within herself. The burgeoning light swirled up and exploded out. A tsunami of light.

The chameleon and crow screeched in unison, the bird diving at her, going for her throat. The medal, Micki realized. It was going for the medal.

From a distance, she heard her name being called.

Zach. It was Zach. She could see him. Leaping out of his car, running up the steps. Parker with him. How could that be?

Micki's vision dimmed. The chameleon crowed in triumph. The cold was winning. Instead of Zach now, she saw icy tendrils stretching, reaching almost to her wildly beating heart.

Micki pictured Hank, thought of him in this same spot. He could have saved himself. But he had saved her instead.

She couldn't give up.

A howl rent the air. Of denial. And resistance. She realized it had come from her. Another sound followed, this one of glass shattering into a billion pieces. The shell of cold surrounding her splintered, then broke, the chameleon's grip with it. Isabella flew backwards, hitting the wall and going down.

The light dimmed. Micki's legs gave and she sank to the floor. Her world turned opaque. Then went black.

CHAPTER FIFTY-FIVE

5:36 P.M.

"MICK, SWEETHEART. IT'S ME, ZACH. I've got you."
Zach's voice. Zach's touch. So good, they felt so—

Then she remembered. The amber-eyed woman and the crow. Hank, coming to her rescue.

"You're going to be okay. You have to be. You hear me? Dammit, wake up!"

Angel. They had to find Angel.

Her eyes snapped open. Zach squatted beside her, expression concerned. She struggled to sit up.

"Take it easy," Zach murmured, easing her into a sitting position. "You're pretty beat up."

"I'm fine," she said, voice a croak. "The chameleon, she—"

"Parker's here. He's got her." Zach stood so she could see.

Parker did, indeed, have her. Her wrists were secured with what looked like ropes of light. The same material was looped around her neck. The light seemed to vibrate, as if charged.

Parker smiled at her. "Hello, Dare."

She frowned at him. "Neat trick, those ropes. I could have used those a few minutes ago."

"Indeed. Believe me, she's not going anywhere with these on."

Micki nodded and held a hand up to Zach. He clasped it and helped her to her feet. She wobbled slightly, then righted herself.

"You okay?" Zach asked.

Everything hurt, but she was standing. "Yeah," she said, "I'm good." Micki turned her gaze to the chameleon. "Where's Angel?"

She smiled. "Go to hell."

Parker looked at her; the ropes crackled, and her body jerked in response. "Play nice, Izzy."

She cursed him, and the crackling came again, this time louder. And brighter.

"What is that?" Micki asked. "Is it . . . electrical?"

Parker smiled. "It feels like that to her, but it's just my light force. The darkness in her is reacting to the light. It's quite uncomfortable."

"And handy. I'll never look at my boring, old handcuffs the same way."

"Come on, Isabella." He jerked her to her feet. "We're going to see your friends at the High Council."

"Oh, no you don't." Micki retrieved her gun from the floor, and crossed to stand directly in front of the chameleon. She pointed the gun at her head. "Where's Angel?"

"Whoa, Mick," Zach said, "we need her. The council agreed to trade her for the professor."

"I've got this, Zach." She steadied her aim. "Tell me where Angel is, now."

"You're too late," she spat. "My brother's on his way to get her. And once he has her and her baby—"

"What baby?" Parker said.

"—the Council will trade me for her." She smiled thinly at Micki. "So you see, I won, after all."

"I don't think so," Micki muttered, lowered her gun and pulled the trigger. "Try transforming with a bullet in your foot, bitch."

CHAPTER FIFTY-SIX

5:58 P.M.

ANGEL SAT ON THE FLOOR in front of her drawing. She'd pulled the mattress off the cot and over to the spot, then grabbed the blanket and wrapped herself in it.

She couldn't take her eyes off the drawing. She didn't want to. It gave her hope.

When the dreams came to her the way this one had, they were prophetic. Of the future, not the past.

She tilted her head. Seth was coming for her. But not the one who had come the night before. She didn't know how it could be, but that one had been an imposter.

She knew because of the light encasing them both. The way it had once before—and they had triumphed against evil. Together.

She shifted her gaze to the rendering of the circling bird. Their enemy had returned.

Tap . . . tap . . . tap . . .

She lifted her gaze to the ceiling above her. The tapping came again. "Hello?" she called.

The tapping sounded again, this time from the far end of the shipping container.

"Who's there?" She grabbed the light and headed toward the sound. "I've been locked up in here. I need help." She pressed her hands to the wall. "If you can hear me, bring help!"

"I can hear you."

A male voice. "Who are you?"

"A friend of Seth's. He's coming. He's almost here."

A cry of relief slipped passed her lips. "Thank you! I'm Angel."

"I know who you are. Seth told me. I'm Hawke."

Her blood went cold. She looked over her shoulder at the drawing, at the circling bird.

Hawke.

"Angel? What's wrong?"

She shook her head and backed away from the wall.

He knocked again. "Angel?"

"Go away! You're a liar. I know about you."

He didn't respond. The seconds ticked slowly past as she wondered where he was and what he was doing. Then, suddenly, he spoke, "She's here! She's okay! I don't know what happened. She was talking to me, then— "

"Angel!" Seth, pounding on the wall. "It's me!"

"Seth!" She ran to the far wall and pressed her hands against it. "Run! Don't trust him. He's the enemy!"

"Hawke? No, babe, he's my friend."

"Please," she sobbed, "a bird of prey, a hawk, in my dream—"

"Listen to me. He's a friend. He and a couple others have been taking turns watching over you because I couldn't. Hawke told me they'd taken you. They're coming back. Soon, Angel. I've got to get you out of there."

Her dreams had never been wrong before. She didn't know what to do, who to trust.

"Move as far away from the wall as you can, Angel. Is there anywhere you can take cover?"

"No! It's just a box. There's no place—" Her gaze landed on the cot. "A mattress," she called. "I could put it over me."

"Do it. I'm busting you out of there.

"How?" she cried.

"There's only one way, babe. I'm sorry, but I have to use it."

His dark side, the power it supplied him.

"No! Seth, it grows stronger when you use it. It's not worth it."

"*You're* worth it, Angel. Our baby's worth it."

"Not that way." She glanced over her shoulder once more, taking in her drawing, knowing that this time she had it right. "We do it together, Seth. You and me."

"Babe, I know this will work—"

"And I know this will." She placed her palms flat on the wall. "Find my hands."

He did, and she felt the connection, like a magnet meeting metal. The way it was supposed to be. "I love you," she said, closing her eyes.

"And I love you."

"Our love can tear down these walls. . . you know it's true. Picture it, Seth! Believe it!"

The connection strengthened; she couldn't have broken it if she tried. Eyes closed, she imagined them joined, the way they were in her dream. Encased in light.

"You saved me," she said.

"And you saved me."

A glow started at her hand, pressed against the wall, anchored to Seth's on the other side. A ring of light appeared, tracing their fingers, a bold and brilliant outline. The glow spread until the shipping container filled with light and the walls vibrated, then shook. The steel groaned, as if it knew it had been bested.

The light extinguished, the connection snapped. Angel stumbled backward, Seth's name on her lips, urging him to run. And then she heard him call hers, urging her to do the same.

She made it to the mattress, managed to pull it over her as a deep rumble came from someplace beyond, followed by the scream of collapsing steel.

And then, quiet. Absolute still, not even a puff of air. Moonlight spilled through the damaged walls, and Angel saw they they stood in a vast, empty warehouse.

Within moments, Seth was at her side, helping her to her feet. "Are you okay?"

"I'm fine." Her hand went to her belly. "We're fine."

"Thank God." He cupped her face in his palms. "You were right. We did it together."

A hawk swooped in through a skylight, diving toward them. As it landed beside them, it transformed into a young man with one blue eye and one brown one.

"Hawke?" she asked.

"Good to meet ya." He looked at Seth. "The chameleon's coming. Go, now. I'll hold him off."

Seth held out his hand; Angel grabbed it. "Thanks man, I owe you."

"No I.O.U. necessary, man. This is what we do for each other."

Seth and Angel headed toward a door at the back of the warehouse.

When they reached it, they looked back.

"I'll see you at Half Moon," Hawke called to them, then burst into flight.

CHAPTER FIFTY-SEVEN

7:15 P.M.

ARIANNA MET THEM AT LAM'S back door. Micki and Zach entered, followed by Parker, pushing Isabella in a wheelchair. Parker had called in one of the medics in Professor Truebell's network.

"Parker!" Arianna cried when she saw him. "You're back! What about Eli and the professor?"

He hugged her. "The High Council has agreed to release them in exchange for this prize. Isabella Bremmond, meet my sister."

"Go to hell, Lightkeeper." She all but spat the words, and her restraints crackled. "My brother's coming back for me. Wait and see."

Parker smiled. "Yes, indeed, we will wait for him. In fact, we're counting on him coming to get you. Excuse me, I'm going to get her set up in the conference room."

Arianna looked at Micki, then Zach. "Where's Angel?"

Micki could hardly meet her eyes. "We haven't found her yet."

"But we will," Zach said. "The chameleon's right. Her brother will come back for her. And he's the weak link. We'll make him talk."

Parker returned. He looked at Micki. "I didn't get the chance to say it back there, but good work. You had her without any help from me."

Parker had never said anything like that to her before, and she wasn't sure how she felt about it now. "The chameleon—how do you know her?"

"Izzy and her brother are famous for their exploits."

Micki thought of her own near death, of King and his daughter, of Sarah Stevens and the three queens who had become victims—and the ones who had become perpetrators.

And of Hank. Especially Hank.

"So that's what you call the pain and terror she's inflicted on so many lives? Exploits?"

"Forgive me," Parker said, expression genuinely remorseful. "You're right. Her acts are crimes against humanity, ones for which she's wanted by the High Council. And serious enough for them to overlook the professor's transgressions and make the exchange for him."

"Wait." Micki frowned and looked from Parker to Zach. "What about Eli?"

"For him, they want the brother."

"You won't have him!" Isabella screeched from the conference room. "That bird's hard to keep caged."

Micki had had enough of her mouth for a while. She strode across to the conference room doorway and glared at her. "Shut up. Or I'll shoot you in your other foot."

Isabella turned her malevolent, amber gaze on Micki. "What are you going to do now? You'll never work in law enforcement again. The tape will ensure that." She laughed, the sound giddy. "And Natalie King will disappear. Without a trace. Without collecting the huge life insurance payout owed her. Foul play, they'll think."

She smiled, and Micki felt cold clear to her bones. "And who do you think they'll look to? Who will be the prime suspect? Why you, of course. Poor, unhinged Michaela Dare. Your reputation is ruined. You'll live under a cloud of suspicion for the rest of your days."

She was right, and it terrified her. But Micki wasn't about to let her know just how horrifying the thought of that was to her.

Instead she returned the chameleon's smile. "And you'll live the rest of your days in a maximum-security prison, no doubt wearing a necklace exactly like you're wearing now. Have fun with that. I like my odds better."

She reached for the door handle and snapped the door shut. Then she let out a pent-up breath and looked at Parker. "What now?"

He lifted a shoulder. "We wait for Bremmond to make his move."

CHAPTER FIFTY-EIGHT

9:25 P.M.

THE WAITING WAS HELL. MICKI paced, stopping long enough to eat a couple slices of the pizza they'd ordered in. They'd tasted like cardboard in her mouth.

They had to locate Angel. And with each minute and hour that passed, she became more afraid that they would never see her again. That she and her unborn child had fallen victim to the Dark One.

She could hear Parker in back, talking on the phone. Arianna was checking in with the center's small group leaders to let them know LAM was reopening in the morning. And Zach had disappeared upstairs.

She went in search of him, and found him in Professor Truebell's office. Zach sat at the desk, shuffling the deck of cards he'd found. Micki stopped in the doorway, watching him manipulate the deck, shuffling, cutting, and fanning like an expert.

Was there anything this man couldn't do?

She tapped on the door. He looked up.

"Hey," she said. "Can we talk a minute?"

He swept the cards into a neat stack and set them aside. "Sure."

She closed the door but didn't make a move toward him. "You're pretty good with those, partner."

"Did a stint as a dealer in Vegas. It was short-lived."

"Yeah? Why's that?"

"I figured out pretty quickly that with my gifts, I was on the wrong side of the table."

Micki smiled. "The house already has the advantage, why give them another?"

"Exactly." One corner of his mouth lifted. "So I quit to work the other side. Blackjack was my game."

"I'm sure it was." She made her way to the desk, but didn't sit in one of the chairs facing it. Instead, she stood behind one of them, using it as a kind of shield. She glanced up at the stained glass, at the hovering angels. Funny how the glass seemed to still glow, even after dark.

She could use those angels now, she thought. What she was about to reveal wasn't going to be easy.

"What happened then?" she asked him.

"I couldn't bring myself to lose."

She laughed. She could see that, too. "They didn't break your legs, did they?"

"Nothing so dramatic. They politely asked me to leave. And to never come back. All of them."

"All of them?"

"Every casino on the strip."

"You don't do anything in a small way, do you, Hollywood?"

"Go big or go home."

She laughed. "You could have been one of the greats."

"True." He held her gaze. The blue of his seemed to deepen. "But then I wouldn't have met you, Mick."

She hated when he said things like that, in that way. They made her forget who he was and who she was, and caused her heart to lurch and her breath to catch—all most disconcerting for a serious girl like herself.

"But," he went on, "I suspect you didn't come in here, closing the door behind you, to discuss my thwarted career as a professional gambler."

"No, I didn't." She rested her hands on the chair back, preparing herself. "I feel like you and I have some unfinished business."

If he made a joke, she would be saved. She would be able to push aside the nagging feeling that there was somewhere the two of them were meant to go, and it couldn't happen until she shared this with him.

She held her breath, uncertain which to hope for. But he didn't make a joke. Didn't grin or wiggle his eyebrows in mock lechery. He simply . . . waited.

No place to run, no place to hide. Not anymore.

Micki swallowed hard. Flexed her fingers. "Remember when we were first partners? And you asked me about my family?"

"And you said, 'maybe you'd tell me someday.' Yeah, I remember."

"It's someday, Zach. If you're still interested?"

"There's nothing I'm more interested in, Mick."

Her heart rate zoomed; she struggled to catch her breath. Finally, she did. "So I'm just going to say it, straight out. No drama, okay?"

"Okay."

"I was seven the first time my Uncle Beau molested me."

She heard the challenge in her voice. As if she was daring him to be skeptical or worse, condescending. As if, in a strange way, she was itching for a fight.

But instead, he was neither. Instead, like a moment ago, he just waited. Allowing her to share in her own time, in her own way. With or without drama.

"Up until then, he was my friend. My only friend in our whacked-out little family unit. We'd play Hide 'n Seek and" —her throat closed over the words and she had to force them out— "make-believe. I'd be the princess and he'd be a knight come to save me from the dragon. That was my favorite game. I even had a stuffed dragon toy. We used it as a prop."

Micki looked down at her hands, realizing she had the chair back in a death grip. She tried to relax them, but couldn't. "Then one sticky summer night, he woke me up. He held out his hand and said—"

His words, the sound of his deep drawl, slurred with bourbon and anticipation, filled her head and tripped off her lips.

"Come, Michaela, let's play a little game of make-believe."

It was the first time, in all these years, that she'd said the words aloud. They sounded so different in her own voice. Less menacing, but more profane.

She peeked at Zach. He sat frozen, save for the muscle that jumped in his clenched jaw.

She looked away and began again. "I didn't ask where he was taking me. Or why he wanted to play in the middle of the night."

She closed her eyes and remembered, as if it had happened the day before, putting her small hand in his big one and trotting along beside him. Happy to play. So trusting.

"The game changed that night. He was no longer the knight." She paused. "He was the dragon."

Zach stood, came around the desk. She shook her head, letting him know not to come closer, not to touch her. If he did, she wasn't certain she could finish.

"Somewhere along the line, I realized the knight wasn't coming back, and no one was going to save me. And that I had to save myself. Finally, I found the courage. I went to his room with a knife, I held it to his throat and told him if he ever touched me again, I'd kill him. I was twelve."

A smile touched her mouth. "He must have believed me, because he never touched me again. I blamed myself for not having the guts to do that sooner."

"You were just a little kid, Mick."

"I know. But it doesn't change the way it felt back then. And now, too." She cleared her throat. "That moment changed me. It freed me in the sense that for the first time in my life, I felt as if I had power over my own life, my own outcomes.

"Not long after that, I ran away for the first time. They found me and dragged me back. So I ran away again. And again."

Her medal warmed and she thought of Hank. She brought a hand to it. "Finally, at seventeen, Mama emancipated me. And I left for good."

"Have you seen or talked to—"

"Any of them? No."

"Did you ever tell your mother what he did to you?"

"No. I thought it was too late. Maybe if I had when I was seven or eight, but by the end she would have thought I was just lashing out, trying to hurt *her*. With Mama, everything was always about her."

"Thank you, Mick," he said softly. "For sharing that with me. I won't betray your trust."

Tears flooded her eyes. She hadn't cried once while recounting the story—tears hadn't even pricked her eyes. But now, at his sweetness, she could bawl like a baby.

"I thought I'd moved on," she said, eyes stinging, "you know . . . gotten over it. Put it all behind me. I never even told Hank. He must have guessed some of it . . . but I wasn't about to let my secret go.

"Until the chameleon, I really did think I had it all together. I was totally in charge. But she knew the truth. She knew why I held that secret so tightly, she knew what that meant. She *showed* me what it meant." Micki paused, eyes brimming with tears. "I was still the dragon's captive."

Zach turned her to him, cupping her face in his hands. "Not anymore, Mick. He doesn't have you now."

She gazed into those blue eyes, and for the first time since the night she'd put her little hand in that big one, she wholly trusted another human being.

"Thank you," she whispered and lifted her face to his. He lowered his mouth to hers. The kiss was deep, tender, and full of unspoken promises. Ones of loyalty, honesty, and commitment.

This man would not let her fall.

Colored light cascaded over them, like a slowly turning kaleidoscope. It took a moment for it to register; he became aware of it at that same moment that she did.

They lifted their faces to the stained-glass window. It was as if the watchful angels had come to life, hovering outside the circle of richly tinted glass.

The color gave way to iridescent light, flowing through the window, unfolding, taking shape. Dazzling white. Almost too brilliant to contemplate.

A figure emerged from a cocoon. Wings, she realized, unfurling. The light met the floor and transformed.

Professor Truebell stood before them, grinning like a naughty little boy caught doing something he knew he shouldn't have been.

Before either of them could say a word, Parker rapped on the door, then stuck his head in. Unlike her and Zach, he didn't seem at all surprised to see Truebell.

"Hey, Professor, glad you're back. You two—" He looked at Micki, then Zach. "I have news. Downstairs. Now."

CHAPTER FIFTY-NINE

10:10 P.M.

ZACH PARKED IN FRONT OF the abandoned warehouse. Micki looked at him and nodded. They climbed out of the car, slamming their doors in unison.

Parker had gotten a call from one of his people. Anthony Bremmond, aka Keith Gerard, had been found. Unfortunately, he was dead. Parker had sent them to ID Bremmond and search the scene.

Micki didn't know what to think, let alone hope for. If Bremmond was dead, did that mean Angel had escaped? Or that he'd been double-crossed by the Dark Bearers he'd hoped to negotiate with?

Zach handed her a flashlight. She flipped it on. He did the same with his. They fell into step together, slipping through the sliver of open door. Cavernous, derelict, a fire waiting to happen. They could make out one damaged shipping container toward the back of the structure.

And a lone figure, sprawled, lifeless nearby. Without speaking, they crossed to him. Male, she saw. She bent to get a look at his face.

"Oh, shit," she muttered, stomach heaving, something that hadn't happened to her in years.

Zach followed her lead. "Crap," he said. "They plucked his eyes out."

"Or pecked them out," Micki said. "Take a look at this." She shone her light over the floor around the victim. "Feathers."

Zach squatted down to examine them closely. "Two different birds. Some of the feathers are black."

"Like a crow's?"

He nodded. "And some are two-tone." He looked up at her. "Got some gloves?"

She handed him a pair and evidence bags. "By the way," she said and stood, "it's him."

"Well, I guess he won't be back to save his big sister." He collected a couple of each and sealed the bags. "I'm going to take a few pictures for Parker."

Micki pointed toward the shipping container. "I'll take a look over here."

She crossed to it, noting that one end was badly—and oddly—damaged, as if the right corner had been violently wrenched apart at the seams. She pointed the flashlight up. Same for the container's top.

She slipped though the opening and stopped. Moving her flashlight beam over the interior, she caught her breath. A cot and a table. Food and water. A camping light and a blanket. And on the far wall, a drawing that couldn't have been done by anyone other than Angel.

"Zach!" she shouted, sticking her head out the opening. "I found something!"

Moments later, he joined her in front of the drawing. "She was here," Micki said. "We know that for sure."

"So what happened?"

Micki studied the drawing, a knot in her throat. "I think *that* happened."

"What?"

With her flashlight beam, she traced the white in the drawing, from the female figure, through the wall and around the male figure, then back. "They broke her out of here. Together. They used their light, the way I used Hank's against Isabella."

"And look," Zach said, pointing his flashlight. "In the drawing. That's no crow."

"A hawk," she murmured. "Or some other bird of prey."

"We'll know for sure by the feathers."

"Yes." Micki looked up at him, the words she was about to say already bittersweet on her tongue. "Angel always said he'd be back for her. And that he loved her. Looks like she was right."

CHAPTER SIXTY

Saturday, February 17
12:30 A.M.

BY THE TIME SHE AND Zach arrived back at LAM, Micki was dead on her feet. They'd called ahead and shared everything they'd learned; as far as she was concerned, there was nothing left to say. Angel was gone. She had left with the man she loved, and now all Micki could do was pray Angel had made the right decision.

A beer and bed, Micki decided. Her new goals in life.

"I have good news," Parker said, from the top of the stairs. "Considering the circumstances, the High Council has agreed to also release Eli. Professor Truebell and I delivered Isabella to them while you were gone."

Micki looked at Zach. He looked as confused as she. "You delivered her? To the High Council? Already?"

The professor joined Parker. "The portal works both ways. Eli's right behind me."

Micki shook her head. Portals, necklaces imbued with superpowers, and humans metamorphosing into birds or whatever the hell else they desired to be? If she wasn't so fricking tired, she'd be completely freaked out.

As if cued, Eli emerged from the professor's office. The three men started down, all smiling from ear to ear.

Micki watched, a lump in her throat. How could she have been fooled by the chameleon's versions of Eli and the professor? Sure, they'd looked the same; Eli's strong features and startlingly light blue eyes, the professor's elfin, bearded face and compact stature, but without the light that emanated from them like an invisible force field.

She'd been fooled because she had wanted to be. Exactly what the chameleon counted on.

She hugged Eli. "I'm so glad you're back."

"I'm proud of you," he whispered in her ear, then held her at arm's length. "Not too worse for wear, I see."

She laughed. "Then you better get some glasses."

Arianna came from the kitchen with a tray of sandwiches. "Who's hungry?"

They all were and followed Arianna into the conference room. The room went silent for several minutes, as everyone helped themselves to the food and drink.

Micki broke the silence first. "What's going to happen to the chameleon?"

"Now that the High Council has her in custody, they'll convince her to turn. Or she's going to spend the rest of her life incarcerated in the light. A pretty uncomfortable prospect for someone like her."

"Turn?" Micki said, taking another bite of her sandwich.

"Chameleons have a strong instinct for self-preservation. They'll do whatever is necessary to survive."

"They would actually *trust* her?" Micki arched her eyebrows in disbelief. "No way, not ever."

"I certainly understand your feeling that way," Professor Truebell said. "I assure you, it's not instantaneous. It's a long, arduous process, but in the end the Light can be surprisingly persuasive. Especially with such self-serving creatures. And now that she's been dispatched, there's something we need to discuss. Parker?"

He nodded and began, "As you both know, Professor Truebell and Eli were arrested by the High Council and charged with treason."

"You mentioned a spy within our network," Zach said.

"Yes, but not only do we know the spy's identity, we've known all along."

"It's me," Arianna said. "I was sent by High Council to observe the activities here at LAM and report back to them." She curved her hand around Zach's. "I'm sorry I kept it from you. I had to."

Micki saw that Zach was having a hard time processing the information, so she stepped in. "You're saying you're some kind of double agent?"

Arianna's lips lifted in a small smile. "I guess you could call me that.

The High Council believes my allegiance is to them. Which it is, in a way. I believe in the survival of our race and that we need a governing body. But my first allegiance is to the Light, and abundant life for all creatures that share this planet. The work we're doing here is in service to that cause."

"She told us the moment it was safe for her to do so." Parker sent an appreciative nod in his sister's direction. "We've been working together ever since."

Micki made a sound of surprise. "But you turned Eli and the professor in? I don't understand."

Professor Truebell took over. "Arianna fed the High Council damning information on LAM's activities. But it was information I asked her to feed them."

"Wait. " Micki moved her gaze between. "Were you, or weren't you, charged with treason?"

The professor looked practically gleeful. "Let me start from the beginning. The High Council had been suspicious of our activities for some time, but Eli and I had continued to convince them that our work here was simply humanitarian.

"But you and Zach changed that." He smiled at Micki. "Your . . . achievements drew their attention. Then, in a raid on a Dark Bearer compound, they rescued Arianna. They promised to drop all charges against her if she agreed to be their eyes and ears here at LAM."

"Charges against her," Zach repeated, dropping his hands to his lap, curling them into fists. "You're telling us that she endured the horror of captivity at a breeding compound for all these years, but they still would have charged her for falling in love with my father?"

"In the end, would they have?" Professor Truebell shrugged. "I don't know. But they had it to hold over her."

"And they call themselves the good guys? Bastards."

"Son," Arianna said softly, reaching over and stroking his arm, "it's done. Yes, every one of those days imprisoned there was hell, but I brought hope to a place that otherwise would have none. I was the light for souls bereft of it. Because of that, how could I wish to change any of it?"

The table went silent. It seemed to Micki that even breathing stopped. And in that instant, she realized what a truly remarkable being Zach's mother was.

Her medal warmed. She brought her hand to it and smiled to herself.

Hank was here with them, and he agreed. She looked at Arianna, then at Zach. She tilted her head. There was something about Zach's smile that reminded her of Hank. She wondered why she'd never noticed it before?

Professor Truebell returned to his story, as if a stunningly emotional moment hadn't just happened. "We knew we would be summoned and charged with treason, maybe sooner than later. We felt the time was right to sway the Council, so we orchestrated the information Arianna brought them, focusing on your feats, Zach. And on Angel's. Your courage and accomplishments, how you've used your gifts against the Dark One and his army. They can't dismiss Half Lights anymore."

Micki cleared her throat. "Hold on, Professor. Sway the council, you said. Are we working with them now?"

"I call it an uneasy collaboration. Any last questions?" Truebell looked around the table. "It's late and I, for one, am exhausted."

"Just one," Zach said, turning to Arianna. "Why didn't you tell me the truth? When all this was going down? You didn't trust me enough?"

"That's not it, not at all. With the chameleon causing havoc in our circle, I couldn't trust that she wouldn't get the information and go to the council with it. Not only would I have been arrested, but neither Professor Truebell nor Eli would be sitting here right now."

Micki could see that Zach didn't like it, but he knew she was right. All it would have taken was shaking the wrong hand, or a clap on the back from someone he thought he knew.

Zach looked at Arianna. "Isabella must have imprinted you, too. How else could she have learned you turned the professor and Eli in?"

"She must have," Arianna agreed.

"So, how come she didn't know the whole story?" Micki asked.

"I locked it."

Micki arched an eyebrow. "Locked it? Like you put in a safe?"

"That or a chest, a bank vault or jewelry box. Every Lightkeeper visualizes their own safe box. We're taught how to do it as children, and become adept at it when we come into our full powers."

Micki pursed her lips. "Sounds a little sketchy to me."

"I suppose it does." She laughed. "But when you grow up in a society that communicates telepathically, you have to learn what's private and what's not. It's acceptable to have thoughts you don't want others to know. Not all secrets are bad."

Professor Truebell stood. "I suggest we end on that for tonight.

Tomorrow will be a better day."

For them, Micki thought, standing. For her, she wasn't so hope-ful. Yes, they'd caught the chameleon. But the damage to her career had been done. Her suspension from the force would become a dis-missal, and she would never work in law enforcement again. Natalie King's disappearance would warrant an investigation of foul play—and unhinged Detective Mad Dog Dare would be the prime suspect.

Yes, she was grateful to be alive and so very thankful those she cared for were unhurt, but the chameleon could claim a partial victory over her anyway. Being a cop, that's who she was. Her identity. The NOPD was her family. The chameleon had taken that away from her.

As she was exiting, Professor Truebell stopped her. He gave her a hug, then held her at arm's length. "The High Council will take care of everything, Michaela. Tomorrow really will be a better day."

CHAPTER SIXTY-ONE

Saturday, November 18
11:50 A.M.

MICKI AWAKENED TO THE SMELL of coffee. She stretched languorously, taking a moment to enjoy the warmth of the bed and the silkiness of the sheets against her bare legs. Only then did she open her eyes.

Zach stood in her bedroom doorway, a mug of steaming coffee in his hands. His feet were bare, his T-shirt rumpled, and he sported a serious case of bedhead.

How could the man still look so damn good?

She sat up, pushing the hair away from her face. "I hope that coffee's for me."

"Of course it is." He brought it to her, then sat on the edge of the bed.

She took a sip, made a sound of appreciation, then took another sip. "How was the couch?"

"Lumpy. How was the bed?"

Lonely. She pushed the thought away. "Very comfortable, thanks."

The knowing way he smiled made her wonder if he'd read her mind. Maybe she needed one of those mental lock-boxes? Or maybe just him off the bed and standing on the other side of the room? Or even in the kitchen?

She decided on small talk. "What time is it?"

"Almost noon."

She almost choked on the coffee. "Noon?"

"You were tired. Give yourself a break."

He was being way too sweet. And he smelled good. She sipped again, irritated with herself. "How long have you been up?"

"Couple hours."

She drew her eyebrows together. "I suppose, seeing I'm unemployed, it doesn't matter how long I sleep. What's your excuse?"

"Personal day."

He reached over and tucked a tendril of her hair behind her ear. For the space of a heartbeat, she couldn't breathe.

"And about that whole unemployed thing—"

She looked at him over the rim of the cup. "Yeah?"

"You missed a news conference this morning. I figured you'd want to see it." He took the coffee cup and handed her his phone. "It's cued up and ready."

"Can I please have my coffee back? I'm a big girl. I promise I can handle a cell phone and coffee mug without spilling."

"Don't be such a grouch." He took a sip of the brew. "Besides, in this case, I'm not so sure you can."

She hesitated and he grinned. "Just hit the play button. You'll see."

She did and practically launched out of the bed—Natalie King, standing at a podium in front of 2 River Tower and Hotel's main entrance.

"How'd she do it? How'd she get away—"

"Just wait. And listen."

" . . . and after a lot of thought and prayer—"

"Prayer? Her? Not possible—"

" . . . reflecting on the loss of my dear Thomas, the love of my life—"

"I'm going to vomit, Zach. I swear to God—"

" . . . I owe the NOPD, and particularly Detective Michaela Dare, an apology."

"Wait! What?" Micki hit the pause button and looked up at Zach. He was grinning like the Cheshire cat. "Is this for real?"

"It is. And there's more." He reached over and hit play for her.

"I made false claims against her and the police department. I see now that I was acting out of grief and despair, and I deeply regret my actions. And I apologize. Detective Dare, indeed, everyone within the NOPD acted with the upmost efficiency and professionalism. New Orleans should be proud.

"As a way to make amends," she went on, "I'm donating Thomas's life insurance benefit, the entire five million dollars, to the New Orleans Police and Justice Foundation."

The press conference ended moments later, and Micki handed him his phone. "Oh, my God. Did that really just happen?"

His lips twitched. "It did."

"How the hell did the High Council get Isabella to turn so quickly?"

"They didn't. Apparently, they have their own chameleons."

"Their own . . ." She let the thought trail off. Of course. Arianna had said some Lightkeepers were born with the gift of transformation, and that not all of them went bad.

She nodded. "So one of them transformed into Natalie King—"

"And took care of everything. You're getting your job back, Mick."

"But the tape—"

"What tape?"

Either he had developed a sudden, severe memory problem, or he was messing with her. "The video from the hallway outside King's apartment, where I look like a crazy person. That one."

"It's not an issue anymore."

Her hands trembled. With burgeoning hope, she realized. That this nightmare, all of it, might be over?

"I don't understand."

"Parker called. It's been taken care of."

"Somebody lifted it?" He nodded and she had to smile. "You're telling me a *Lightkeeper* broke into the CE&P and stole a piece of evidence?"

"Or something like that, yes."

She was grateful for their efforts, but it wouldn't be enough to get her job back. "I appreciate all of this. But physical evidence or not, what was seen cannot be unseen. Major Nichols, Captain Newman, and Chief Howard, all saw the tape. I certainly can't *unsee* it, and I can't imagine how they could either. She got me, Zach."

"That's been taken care of, too."

"Wait—" Micki tried to rein in the hope swelling inside her. "Like their memories were wiped?"

"Pretty cool, huh?"

On the nightstand, her cell phone sounded. The hope took hold again, swelling and spreading. She snatched up the device. "This is Dare."

"Hold for Chief Howard."

A moment later he came on the line, tone effusive. "Detective, how are you today?"

She wished she could tell him to cut the crap and get to the point, but doubted that would the best avenue to getting her badge back. "Very well, Chief. And you?"

"On top of the world. You saw Natalie King's press briefing?"

"I did, yes, sir."

"So you are aware that she rescinded her accusations against you?"

"I am."

"Excellent. Effective immediately, you're reinstated. I need you to report to the Eighth, ASAP. Lieutenant Jackson is in charge while the Major is recovering. He has your badge and weapon."

And that was it? As if the worst of it never happened? She didn't know how Professor Truebell pulled it off, but she didn't care.

"Welcome back, Detective."

"Yes, Chief. Thank you, Chief."

She ended the call and leapt out of bed, whooping and pumping her fists. After a minute or two, she stopped, suddenly remembering Zach's presence and the fact she wore nothing but a T-shirt and panties.

She looked over her shoulder at him. He smiled, those amazing blue eyes crinkling at the corners. "Please, don't stop on account of me."

She mock-glowered at him, then bent and snatched her jeans up off the floor.

He whistled. "Quite a view, Mick."

She looked archly at him. "A gentleman would have looked away."

He folded his arms across his chest and grinned. "I wasn't aware there was a gentleman in the room."

"Nice, Hollywood." She scowled at him and yanked on her jeans. "Very nice."

"I apologize." He laughed. "I'll never look again."

It was a lie. They both knew it. And the truth was, they both knew she was glad it was.

"I'm heading in, so you might need to get out of here so I can get ready."

"I'll hang around, since you're going to need a ride."

"The Nova's here, remember? We picked it up after . . ."

Her voice trailed off. She didn't like the look in his eyes. She liked what he started to say even less.

"You've had a lot of good news this morning. Mick—"

"Don't you say what—"

"—a little bad news would hardly make a dent in your—"

"—I think you're going to say."

But he did it anyway. "Sorry, Mick. Somebody jacked the Nova. I already called it in."

ACKNOWLEDGEMENTS

THANKS TO THE ENTIRE TRIDENT Digital Media & Publishing team, particularly Scott Miller and Nicole Robson, for making this process a breeze. To Hoffman/Miller Advertising, thanks for the amazing cover. Y'all rock. To my family, friends, and writing retreat 'Girl Power' gal pals Hailey North and Robin Wells: love, hugs, and deep appreciation for your support.

ALSO BY ERICA SPINDLER

ABOUT THE AUTHOR

Erica Spindler is the *New York Times* and International Chart best-selling author of thirty-two novels and three eNovellas. Published all across the globe, she has been called "The Master of Addictive Suspense" and "Queen of the Romantic Thriller."

The Lightkeepers is Erica's first series. It was born of her deep, personal faith and her lifelong fascination with angels, demons, and the end of days.

Erica splits her writing time between her New Orleans area home, her favorite coffeeshop, and a lakeside writing retreat. She's married to her college sweetheart, has two sons and the constant companionship of Roxie, the wonder retriever.

Erica is currently at home in New Orleans, writing her next The Lightkeepers adventure.

To learn more, visit www.ericaspindler.com
Or get social with Erica on Facebook at Erica Spindler, Author

CPSIA information can be obtained
at www.ICGtesting.com
Printed in the USA
LVOW11*1615010318
568340LV00007B/43/P